Bookstore owner and ghostv  g more
than to be part of the unendi   heritage
and the medieval MacLomair   laddagh
ring appears on her finger,   nes her
future. Though sure she was brought back in time ___ her man,
the laird's cousin soon draws her eye, then her every thought.

Recently widowed by a traitorous wife, Malcolm MacLomain has
no use for love. Merciless, he swears revenge on his enemies and
embarks for war. When courageous and persevering, Cadence
becomes part of his endeavor his broken heart starts to mend.
Caught in an unexpected journey of forgiveness and discovery, two
worlds collide and heal despite the, Wrath of the Highlander.

Wrath of the Highlander
By Sky Purington
COPYRIGHT © 2014

Edited by *Cathy McElhaney*
Cover Art by *Tamra Westberry*

Published in the United States of America

Dedication

For my husband, Travis. The most honorable man I know.

Wrath of the Highlander
The MacLomain Series-Next Generation
Book Three

By

Sky Purington

Prologue

The MacLeod clan had skipped pillaging and raping and went straight to murdering.

Or so the MacLomain's assumed.

Backs against a boulder, Malcolm and his cousins remained crouched and hidden.

"They've twenty prisoners," Colin muttered under his breath.

Bradon frowned. "All lasses."

Colin and Bradon had been steadfast in wanting to join Malcolm in this small venture. Just north of the MacLomain border they'd finally closed in on a small band of miscreant MacLeod's.

"A storm brews," Colin said softly, eyes to the sky. "The ocean roars."

And that was where the prisoners were being led...straight to the edge of a cliff overlooking the raging sea.

Malcolm cursed the Fates. He hated that so many were in harm's way. Six fortnights ago, an ongoing battle began. None would remain unscathed. His wife, Nessa, had been murdered by their sworn enemy, Keir Hamilton and his cousin, Torra, had revealed a deep secret. She was part dragon. Determined to make her his, Keir swore to find Torra even as she fled north. Vowing to bring her home, Bradon had led a small group of MacLomains deep into the highlands to save her.

But she hadn't needed saving...until she did.

She'd only ever intended to reveal the truth.

Malcolm's brother still lived.

Yet Keir had trapped her.

Under Keir's careful guidance, his powerful ally, Colin MacLeod and Malcolm's brainwashed brother, Grant, would lead tens of thousands in a war against the MacLomains. Since then, these small bands of ruthless MacLeod warriors had been sent south to wreak havoc.

Malcolm turned his head slightly and listened to the group passing mere feet from them.

"Why cannae we keep at least one for this eve's pleasure?" a man muttered.

"Nay, 'tis too close to MacLomain land," another replied. "We dump them then continue."

"What we already took will hold us 'til we find whores," another said.

Bloody hell. Malcolm clenched his fists. Some of these women had been raped before he and his cousins arrived.

Wind whipped. Lightning flashed. Thunder rumbled.

He counted thirty enemy clansmen.

Malcolm gripped his ax, Bradon his sword. Colin cocked an arrow.

"'Tis time," Malcolm murmured.

His cousins nodded.

When another ear-piercing clap of thunder roared overhead, Malcolm and Bradon rushed the enemy. Colin stayed behind and unleashed arrow after arrow.

One, two, three, four, all met their marks.

That left twenty-six.

As they ran, Malcolm and Bradon whipped several daggers.

Four more fell.

Zing. Zing. Zing.

Three more arrows sailed. Three more men fell.

Nineteen left.

There was nothing quite like the element of surprise.

The enemy scrambled to draw their weapons.

Rain started to fall and lightning zig-zagged across the blackened sky.

Reveling in the sharp feel of battle lust, Malcolm drove his foot into the groin of one clansman while swiping his ax across the legs of two others. With a quick slash, he stabbed the first man in the gut. Bradon, meanwhile, spun and swiped his blade across one man's throat while simultaneously driving his palm into another's nose sending bone fragments up into his head.

Thump. Thump. Thump. Three more arrows hit.

Only eleven left standing.

Malcolm circled three.

Bradon, borderline berserker, leapt forward and thrust his blade through one while punching the other. With a quick spin, he whipped two daggers. Each hit a man in the throat and they fell.

Thump. Thump. Colin's arrows killed two more.

Malcolm made a come-hither motion with his hand and grinned at three enemy clansmen as he slowly swung the ax around and around over his head. One stepped back, unsure. The other two charged him. *Thwak. Thwak.* With a quick parry then dip he ran the edge of his blade across their throats. The third stumbled back. Wasting no time, he swung the blade over and sliced down hard.

Thump. Colin took down one more.

That left two.

And both ran.

Thwak. Thwak.

Colin's arrows took care of those cowards.

But not before Malcolm glimpsed a woman being shoved off the cliff. He quickly took tally of the prisoners. Still twenty. But he knew what he saw.

He'd seen the glow of the ring.

Hell and damnation.

He'd only seen that once before.

He knew precisely *who* had been pushed over the edge. Both angry and fearful, he tossed aside his ax, yanked off his boots and pulled off his tunic. She'd be lucky if she survived such a fall.

With a quick prayer to his gods, he ran and dove.

Chapter One

North Salem, New Hampshire
2014

"I could sink into a hot bath right now," Cadence murmured, then balled up and tossed aside another piece of paper.

"Then you should." Sheila eyed the floor. "Be sure to pick all this up first though."

Cadence sighed, set aside her notepad and tucked a pencil in her bound up hair. She'd become the ghostwriter for the changes needed in her cousin, McKayla's upcoming novel. "I keep feeling like the heroine in this isn't quite right. Or the hero for that matter. Or even the title."

Sheila lowered what she was reading and frowned. "I thought the editing department had already approved these changes, and Leslie for that matter."

"I know. Still." She shook her head. "The hero saves the heroine from the enemy but I feel like there's more to this nemesis. Something we're not seeing." Cadence narrowed her eyes. "I've added the magic and time travel. That's not the issue. I don't know. I suppose it'll come to me."

Her cousin said nothing but returned to her book.

Cadence sat back and eyed the Claddagh ring on her finger. A few days ago she'd driven down from Maine to go over edits with her sister, Leslie only to find her and their cousins, Sheila and McKayla missing. Not particularly in the mood to drive home, she'd crashed. The next morning she discovered the stone-centered ring on her finger. Soon after, McKayla arrived.

She'd never forget the shocked look on her cousin's face when she saw the ring.

Heck, she'd been pretty shocked herself.

But nothing surprised her more than when McKayla sat her down and explained what the ring meant, and then proceeded to tell her everything that had happened to all of them over the past few weeks. Time travel. She couldn't believe her ears. McKayla, Leslie and Sheila had traveled back in time to medieval Scotland.

Not only that but they'd learned magic. And even claimed to not only believe in wizards but swore they truly existed. If that wasn't enough, they'd also discovered that they were witches. Then she spoke of an unending connection between their Broun ancestry and the MacLomain clan.

Oh, the delicious thrills that had run through her.

After all, she'd researched this.

Better yet, it'd all been plunked right in her lap.

As if Sheila sensed her thoughts, she said, "I still can't believe you read about the MacLomains." She eyed her over her book. "About Malcolm's parents."

"I know." Cadence twirled the ring. "It's hard to imagine that I found the books written about them in a box on the front door of my shop."

"Why didn't you ever tell any of us about them?"

"Because the note asked me not too."

"Ah yes, a note from Adlin MacLomain of all people."

"I own a bookstore that caters not only to readers but to those of my craft," Cadence said. "It's always best to practice discretion."

"Right, Wiccan." Sheila sighed. "Doesn't that just fit in *perfectly* with all of this."

All of *this* being in regards to Malcolm she was sure.

Malcolm was cousin to the current MacLomain chieftain and quite clearly the object of Sheila's affections. Cadence couldn't much blame her. She'd met the man when he'd appeared at their house. Though he hadn't stayed long, he made an impact. There were handsome men then there were downright jaw-dropping gorgeous men.

Malcolm MacLomain was certainly the latter.

But Malcolm was *not* the man meant for Cadence.

"I still don't understand why your ring heated so much," Sheila muttered.

Neither did she. But it had!

According to what McKayla shared, the rings and tattoo marks on several MacLomain men were created on the night Torra MacLomain finally revealed she was a dragon. It was said that the rings allowed the Broun women to travel through time at will. If

9

that wasn't enough, apparently the rings heated and their stone glowed when a Broun was with their one true love.

A MacLomain.

Not only had Cadence's stone glowed but nearly burned her when Malcolm was around. She'd not mentioned the glow but she'd told her cousins it heated. If she didn't believe in magic to begin with she might have thought all of this a little too fantastical.

"We're attracted to each other," Sheila assured. "There's no doubt about it."

She referred to Malcolm of course.

He was *all* she'd referred to for the last three days.

The truth was there had been two MacLomain warriors who arrived, Malcolm and Bradon, the chieftain's brother. Though he'd declared his love for her sister, Leslie, he didn't need to. Cadence could clearly see the adoration between them.

Though Sheila seemed so gung ho about her and Malcolm, McKayla had been very clear. The ring would get uncomfortably warm when near your true love. Sheila's had warmed when she'd been near Malcolm but based on what she'd shared not nearly as warm as it should have.

Not for the first time, Cadence asked, "Did Malcolm *ever* mention seeing your ring's stone glow?"

"He wouldn't have even if it did," she said. "He was mourning his dead wife."

"Hmm hmm." Again Cadence pointed out something else Sheila mentioned when they'd had a few glasses of wine the other night. "I still don't understand why you're not paying more attention to what happened when you were with the Hamilton clan."

Sheila set aside her book, stood and stretched. "I'm going for a walk."

"Naturally."

"What do you mean by that?"

Cadence shrugged and shoved the wadded up papers into a bag. "Ever since your ordeal with Jack you've been in some sort of warped denial."

Sheila frowned. "Warped denial?"

It wasn't easy being so blunt with Sheila especially since Cadence had supported her through the ordeal with Jack and wanted to be sensitive to her feelings. But, regardless, at one point in time they'd been best friends, and she didn't want to sugar coat the truth. "You're too darn happy, Shay, and this infatuation with Malcolm proves it. You know damned well that your ring burned the moment you saw his brother, Grant, but for whatever reason you're ignoring that."

"It was an intense moment," Sheila argued, her powder blue eyes turbulent. "We'd just seen Colin MacLeod for the first time. Then we found out Malcolm's long lost brother still lived, that he'd been kidnapped by the MacLeod clan when he was only eleven years old!"

"Right," Cadence said. "So you inwardly fumed with rage at the injustice and that ring of yours nearly caught on fire because of it."

Sheila's eyes narrowed. "Did I feel bad for Grant? Sure. He's been brainwashed, mentally abused."

"Just like you were," Cadence said softly.

"Stop that," Sheila said vehemently. "Brainwashed or not, the guy's a wizard so I suspect the same rules don't apply."

"I'd think they apply all that much more."

"Enough. I'm interested in Malcolm, not Grant." She shook her head. "Besides, the man tried to murder his parents."

Before Cadence could reply, Sheila left.

With a heavy sigh, she poured a glass of wine and headed upstairs. She barely knew her cousin anymore. It tore her up that she'd had no other choice but to stand by and watch the abuse Sheila had endured over the past seven years. She knew the moment she met Jack that he was no good. He'd been dating Sheila for several months when he decided to hit on Cadence. Naturally, she'd told Sheila immediately but it was too late. The bastard had sunk his manipulating teeth into her carefree mind and convinced Sheila that Cadence had come onto him. Unfortunately, she believed him.

So the deep friendship they'd formed as teenagers was gone in an instant. She tried for years to keep in touch but Sheila would have none of it. Better yet, Jack would have none of it.

Cadence didn't bother sharing what she knew of Sheila and Jack's twisted relationship with Leslie because she was way too busy. But she did tell McKayla. So a few months ago when Sheila finally understood what was happening to her, they were there to help her through the painful process of leaving him.

Cadence turned the tap on in the bathtub, lit a few candles and undressed. After the tub filled, she crawled into the steaming hot water, leaned her head back and draped her arms over the side. Once more she twirled the ring, her thoughts on Sheila. She prayed with all her heart that her cousin's ring would lead her to a man far better than Jack. A man who would sweep her off her feet and give her everything she deserved in life. Restore her self-confidence and make her forced happiness real.

"And what of your happiness, lass?"

Cadence closed her eyes and smiled.

Adlin MacLomain.

According to what she'd read, he'd all but birthed the MacLomain clan well over a thousand years ago. An immortal, arch wizard at one time, he'd fallen in love with his one true love, a woman like herself who was of the Broun heritage. This started a slow aging process before he passed away. But it seemed his spirit lived on and now his voice was often inside her mind. He'd been whispering in her inner ear since he'd left those books on her doorstep four years ago. She didn't mind in the least. Rather she found everything he told her quite interesting.

"I'm happier than I've ever been."

And she was. Especially now that she knew what she'd read about in those books would continue. That there would be more great loves and adventures. When she awoke with this ring and learned what it meant, Cadence had been excited and curious.

"'Twill not be easy, lass."

His words didn't frighten her at all. Life wasn't easy whether in this century or any other, of that she was sure. But she'd found her way in this one. *"Don't worry about me, my friend."*

Then Adlin left her mind. Or so she assumed when he said nothing more.

Content, muscles relaxed, she allowed her thoughts to at last wander to *him*.

Not to Malcolm as she knew Sheila was so inclined to believe, but someone else altogether. That he was a MacLomain, she had no doubt. So often, too often, she dreamt of him at the MacLomain castle. Like her, he was from another time. He loved her red hair. She loved his accent, the fire in his merry blue eyes.

Her thoughts only of him, Cadence drifted.

Sinking further into the water, she twirled the ring on her finger.

Around and around it twirled.

For a moment, she thought she heard footsteps on the stairs.

Then it faded away.

The ring heated. Warm water encased her body. Twirling and twirling.

A knock came at the door. Or was that thunder?

"Cadence?"

Sheila sounded far away. The burn of her ring increased…bubbling the water.

Until it froze.

Zawoooosh.

Cadence tried to sit up but flailed. Pain seared. Burning sugar filled her nostrils. She opened her eyes, but wasn't in the bathroom anymore. What the hell? She was sailing off a cliff.

Down, down, down, she fell until…*splash*. Frigid, unrelenting, a wall of deadly water hit her. Then down, down, down she went beneath the angry waves.

Murky, dark, she could barely see.

Push, pull, push, pull, the water thrust her violently. The jagged cliff wall rushed up but she was saved by the suck of water. Tumbling, rolling, she went out with a wave until another grabbed her and rolled her forward again. *I'm going to die! Just like this. Broken boned against hard stone. If I could get a quick breath maybe.* But the water's surface was somewhere far above and the harsh sea would not let her go.

Then, as if the man she'd been dreaming of all along knew she was there, a strong arm grabbed her around the waist. Heavy water pushed against them but she held on as tightly as her weakened limbs would allow. A gush of heavy water caught them and filled her lungs. Black flecks filled her vision. *Oh, no, please no.* Her lungs seized. Darkness edged closer. *No, I need to see him…just once. Please!*

But another wave caught them and all was ripped away.

Sinking.

Sinking.

Darkness fell.

Until it didn't.

"Open your eyes, lass." The words sounded far off. "*Now.*"

Roused by the deep growl, she struggled to open her eyes. Had she lived? Was he here with her? Had to be! Gripping at hard flesh, Cadence could do nothing but whimper. She couldn't feel her body, could barely breathe.

All I have to do is *see* him. Know that he's here…that *I'm* here.

"If you cannae function, 'twill be our end."

Well, he would think like that. But it didn't need to be his end.

"Go," she croaked.

That she'd made a sound was promising. He repositioned her body. "Open your eyes. See where you are."

Cadence nodded. She could do this. Anything to finally see him. Blinking, determined, she again worked to peer beyond the blackness of the deep sea. Slowly but surely colors became more crisp, a cave, ocean, thunderous sea and…golden eyes.

She blinked a few more times and shook her head.

A warm hand cupped her cheek, a familiar face looked down.

Just not the face she was hoping for.

"I'm all right," she whispered. "Thanks…Malcolm."

Raven black hair plastered against his head, his concerned gaze lingered on her face. But he must've seen in her eyes what he needed to because he soon looked away. "I cannae use magic here. The enemy is all around and I am weakened."

"Of course," she managed.

Why was he here and not the other? This made no sense. But she supposed if she was where she thought she was everything was about to get a whole lot stranger.

Please let me be where I think I am.

I'll find *him* later.

Cadence sat up slowly and looked around. As far as she could tell they were trapped in a cliff-side cave just beyond the seething water and raging storm. Malcolm MacLomain, of all people, sat next to her.

That couldn't be good.

But at least she wore clothes. If that's what you wanted to call the plaid swath wrapped around just enough of her to cover what shouldn't be seen. Had he done this? Obviously, based on what was clearly missing from his tartan. Which meant he'd seen her naked. *Ugh. Super.*

Weak, discombobulated, she wrapped her arms around her knees, shaking. "Where are we?"

"In a verra bad position," Malcolm grumbled as he crouched on a nearby rock.

Without doubt they were.

Sodden, confused, Cadence had no idea what to make of any of this. Save one thing. "I'm in medieval Scotland, aren't I?"

Malcolm frowned in her direction.

Obviously. Stupid question.

But the next wasn't. "Why are *you* here to save me?"

"I dinnae think I am," he said.

"Excuse me?"

"'Tis likely we will die."

"Tell me how you really feel," she muttered to herself.

"I did, lass." Malcolm frowned at her. "Are your ears full of water?"

Cadence rolled her eyes. "No, sorry, it's an expression."

His brows lowered.

"A bit of sarcasm. Again, sorry." She nodded toward the ocean. "I'm thankful you saved me from that. I just didn't expect it to be you."

Malcolm shifted uncomfortably, his restless eyes flickering to her ring. She knew he wanted to ask her if it heated but wouldn't. She remembered what he told Sheila before he'd returned to medieval Scotland. There existed no room in his heart for a lass, only for wrath and vengeance on his enemies.

Which worked out fine for Cadence.

But damn if the ring wasn't on fire right now.

If only some of that warmth would spread through the rest of her. Teeth chattering, she rocked back and forth.

Though it seemed about the last thing he wanted to do, Malcolm sat next to her and pulled her into his arms. "Let me warm you, lass."

Desperately cold, she gave no argument but cuddled closer to his large body.

Cadence couldn't help but whisper, "I'm frightened."

He held her a fraction tighter but said nothing. It was impossible not to be aware of the man. She'd been careful to keep her eyes averted from his wide shoulders and chiseled torso. But when his muscular arms wrapped around her and she was pressed against his hard flesh, Cadence became alarmingly aware of him. From the heavy thud of his heart to the musky, masculine scent of him, this highlander's aura was very much in tune with hers.

Which *wasn't* good.

For two reasons.

Her mystery man and Sheila.

The last thing she wanted was for her cousin to think something existed between her and Malcolm. She'd likely never forgive her. Eyes squeezed shut, she tried to push away the ever increasing sensations she was feeling. "How did you know that I'd arrived here?"

He hesitated just long enough that she knew he wasn't about to tell her everything.

"We'd just battled some MacLeod's who were set to throw those they'd taken prisoner over the cliff. All were saved but I swore I saw someone pushed over regardless."

Though she'd warmed some, she shivered at the sound of his deep voice. He'd said he couldn't use magic now so she assumed he hadn't been using it then. "So you jumped over a cliff because you *thought* you saw someone?"

"I knew I had," he said gruffly.

Was he growing upset with her? Not interested in griping with someone who had just saved her life, she switched topics. "How are Leslie and McKayla?"

They'd both returned to Scotland a few days ago. McKayla had come because she was now married to the MacLomain laird and her sister, Leslie, because she'd fallen in love with his brother, Bradon.

"They are well," Malcolm said. "Leslie and Bradon are to be married."

"Really?"

"Aye."

16

"When?"

"This eve."

"Oh!" Warm enough, she pulled away. "So I've arrived just in time."

"So it seems." His troubled eyes were on the frothing ocean. "If we can manage a way out of here."

"'Twill not be via the sea, lass."

"Adlin!" she said.

Malcolm's eyes flew to hers, confused.

Oh, how to explain this?

"Tell him the truth."

Cadence cleared her throat. Malcolm *was* a wizard after all so her story shouldn't surprise him. "A few years ago some old books were dropped on my bookstore's doorstep. It turned out they were published in the early nineteenth century by somebody named Beth Luken. They told several stories, one of which was how your parents came to be together."

What an odd thing to be talking to their son now!

"'Tis strange, that," he said. "But what of Adlin?"

"Though I never saw him, there was a note saying it was he who had left the books. After that, I started hearing his voice in my head." She shrugged. "We're sort of old friends now."

Malcolm's piercing eyes studied hers. "And so he's talking to you right now?"

She nodded. "Yeah, he says we won't be getting out the way we came in."

"'Tis obvious enough," Malcolm murmured as his eyes scanned the cave wall behind them. "Though I dinnae ken why he doesnae speak to me as well."

"Because there isnae room for more than one MacLomain in this lad's head."

Cadence smirked.

"What?" Malcolm asked.

"Nothing." She stood alongside him. Lord, was he intimidating. Of the Broun girls, she was the tallest at 5'10 but he topped her by a good eight inches. "Let me help you search the cave."

"There's not much of it to search," he remarked.

Still, she started exploring.

17

"Any ideas, Adlin?" she asked.

But he'd once more fled, leaving them to their own devices.

About the size of three rooms, the cave seemed larger in some parts as its ceiling vaulted up only to abruptly stop. One particular section in the back caught her attention, more because of the sound than anything else. Where the wind howled and the ocean still roared, Cadence was convinced she heard something else.

"Malcolm." She waved him over. "I swear I hear something strange."

Once more beside her, his dark brows lowered as he concentrated. It seemed he heard the strange echo as well because he peered up and walked along the wall a bit further.

"There," he murmured and nodded.

She peered up. "What? Where?"

He pointed and listened closer. "A hole. My cousins. They call down."

Her heart quickened. She saw it. Frighteningly narrow, it almost appeared to tunnel straight up. Before she could respond he cupped his hands around his mouth and released a loud, piercing whistle.

Cadence flinched. "You could've warned me you were going to do that."

"Aye," Malcolm acknowledged but didn't apologize. "Can you climb?"

Incredulous, she looked from him to the hole. "You've got to be kidding."

"Nay." His eyes ran the length of her, assessing. "Can you then?"

She was a runner, not a climber. And she didn't like how that one sweeping appraisal set fire to her body in a way that contradicted their perilous situation. "Even if I could how do you expect me to do it without a rope or climbing equipment of some sort?"

Malcolm ran a hand over the craggy surface. "Notch by notch."

Oh hell, *really*? "No way. You're out of your mind."

"Then you choose death?" he asked, his eyes darkening.

"No." She shook her head. "But it seems you do!"

"Did Adlin not just tell you this was our only way?"

Nausea rolled through her. It seemed he had.

Malcolm touched multiple nooks and crannies on the rocky surface. "Look for hand and footholds such as these. Rain water will have provided many all the way up." His steady eyes met hers. "You will go first. I willnae let you fall."

Cadence became far too aware of how short her scrap of tartan was and tugged at the material. Life or death situation, doing it this way would give him a heck of a view. She shook her head. "I think it's best if you go first."

His observant eyes didn't miss the way she'd fingered her plaid. A small smile crawled onto his face. "I willnae be looking at anything besides my next handholds, lass."

A slow burn ignited beneath her cheeks. Malcolm was one of those men she suspected usually wore a frown and somehow it suited him. The bad guy look she supposed. So who knew even a small smile would lend such a remarkable handsomeness to his already too appealing features.

"You seem a nice enough lass, but I dinnae want to die down here with you," he continued.

Nice enough lass? Not that she wasn't. She most certainly was. But that was one thing men typically didn't say to her, mostly because they were always focused on her appearance rather than her personality. Cadence almost laughed. She'd bet her appearance was something else right now!

He nodded upward. "Well?"

The truth was she had no desire to die down here either. If this was their only option, she'd better gather her courage. Though opposed to him getting a rather personal view if he climbed after her, there was a definite sense of relief that he'd be there if she slipped. Besides, she was sure he'd already got a healthy eyeful of her when he'd dragged her from the ocean.

Reining in every ounce of courage she possessed, Cadence nodded. "Okay, let's do this."

"Verra good. Now listen carefully. 'Twill be slick with rainwater." Malcolm grasped a nook and showed her the proper hold. "You grab the edge with your fingertips flat on it and your fingers arched above the tips. But dinnae crimp too hard or 'twill damage your fingers." Then he put his foot into another nook. "Watch your foot every time you take a new foothold. You dinnae take your eyes off that foot while you move it. Only once you're secure do you look for the next foothold. Do you ken, lass? 'Tis verra important you follow these instructions."

With a heavy swallow, she nodded. Cadence put her hand in a nook. "Hold like this but never too arched." She put her foot in a nook. "Always watch my foot until it's secure."

"Aye." He nodded and lightly squeezed her shoulder in reassurance. "'Twill get verra dark. Dinnae give into fear, feel your way along and climb. You'll do fine."

Again she nodded then rolled her shoulders. *I can do this. If I don't I'll die.* Before she gave it another thought, she started climbing. Cautious, careful, she paid very close attention to each spot she placed her hands then her feet. *Wow*, did this require strength. But the pressing urge to survive overrode the weakness and adrenaline kicked in. Good thing she wasn't claustrophobic because the rock tunnel was tighter than it appeared. It was wide enough for a person to climb but not much more.

Malcolm said nothing. No doubt he was focusing as thoroughly as she. Hand, foot, hand, foot. Search for the next four nooks, repeat process. Hand, foot, hand, foot. Never once did she lose focus. When it became pitch dark, she had to move far slower as she felt her way along. Still, she never gave up. In fact, she'd swear new strength filled her. On and on she climbed. She hadn't thought to ask him how high the cliff was for good reason. No need to psyche herself out.

Eventually, a light mist fell and dampened her skin.

"Be verra careful now, lass," Malcolm said softly. "We near the top. 'Twill turn far slicker."

Cadence closed her eyes and murmured a prayer to her Goddess. Not pausing long, she continued. Bit by miniscule bit, light appeared above. Careful, she climbed higher and higher. The exit wasn't that far away now. They were going to make it! Excited, she felt for another nook. Confident she'd found a good one, she grasped and pulled up. But either she'd misjudged or the rock gave way because her hand slipped free.

"Oh no!" she gasped

Caught by the momentum of her body falling, her foot slid, then her other hand. *This is it. I'm going to die after all!* Desperate, she searched for a nook and tried to grab hold.

But it was too late.

Chapter Two

The light at the end of the tunnel had excited her. Malcolm sensed her eagerness even before she did and braced himself against the wall. When she slipped, he flung up his free hand and stopped her fall.

Unfortunately, the only way to do that was to grab her bare arse.

And such an amazingly tight little arse it was too.

"Shh, dinnae move, lass," he said through clenched teeth. She was a slender, lightweight thing but that didn't make their current position any less treacherous.

"Goddess above, I'm sorry," she whispered.

"Dinnae let fear rule," he said calmly. "Focus and find your holds again."

"Okay," she murmured, breathing harshly.

Malcolm ground his jaw and waited while she slowly but surely repositioned herself. Every little movement flexed her tight backside. It didn't matter in the least that they were perched on the edge of death; his cock was coming to attention.

Bloody hell.

He'd had the same issue earlier when trying to wrap her nude body up in what he could manage to spare from his plaid. Never before had he seen such a bonnie lass. With long fiery, red hair and dainty porcelain features, she nearly took his breath away. But that wasn't all that rallied an ill-timed erection. Nay, she had a body that would make any hot-blooded Scotsman fall to his knees in worship.

"I think I'm good," she said. "You can let go now."

Honestly, that was about the *last* thing he wanted to do. "Are you sure, lass?"

"Quite," she said.

When he removed his hand, she started to climb.

They were nearly to the top when Bradon popped his head over the exit. "There they are."

Bradon vanished and Colin peered down with a grin. "Good to see you both. You had us worried."

Malcolm sighed with relief when his cousin took Cadence's hand and pulled her out.

When Bradon offered a hand down, Malcolm took it, climbed out of the hole and rolled onto his back in exhaustion.

"Cadence, thank God!" Sheila pulled her into a tight embrace.

When had she arrived?

Hell and double damnation.

Now there was another bonnie wee lass.

Not quite ready to look at her yet, he closed his eyes and let the rain pour on his face. Not that long ago, he'd been on an adventure north with her, Bradon and Leslie, amongst several other MacLomains. She'd met his parents before they'd vanished. She'd even held his Da when death was nearly upon him.

Did he find Sheila desirable? Aye. Who wouldn't?

Did her ring's stone glow for him? Nay. Not once.

He'd asked himself several times since meeting her if he hoped it would but could never seem to answer his own question. While he assumed it was guilt over Nessa, his wife, so soon gone, he'd known better the moment he'd laid eyes on Cadence.

Her ring's stone had nearly blinded him.

Not only that, his attraction to her was profound.

Malcolm had been mortified to discover he'd not felt such when he met Nessa.

Not even close.

Yet Nessa was no longer here to worry over such things.

Sheila was.

She'd made her interest in him more than clear. When last he'd seen her in the twenty-first century, he'd urged her to stay there, that his heart was only one of war now. But that hadn't been the entire truth. He had no idea how to tell her that Cadence's ring glowed for him.

"Good to see you well, Malcolm."

He cracked open one eye and looked up at Sheila. "Aye, much thanks."

"'Tis not wise to stay here long," Colin said and winked at Bradon. "The day wears on and we've a wedding to attend."

Malcolm nodded, came to his feet and made introductions. "Cadence, this is Colin, Laird of the MacLomain clan."

Cadence smiled warmly and shook his hand. "Nice to meet you and congratulations on marrying, McKayla."

He nodded, beaming. "Nice to meet you as well and thank you."

Malcolm looked at Cadence, concerned. "You were verra brave. How are you, lass?"

His breath caught. Now that her eyes were clear of stinging sea water, they were once more a bright, jolting emerald green.

When she nodded, clearly unsteady, he took her elbow.

"My legs feel like jelly," she murmured.

Jelly? "I dinnae ken the word but ken your meaning. 'Tis not far to my horse. Can you make it?"

"Yeah, I'll be fine." Her glance flickered to Sheila. "I'll walk with my cousin."

When he looked at Sheila, his guilt grew stronger. Though she tried to hide it, he saw the sadness in her eyes while she watched them. Gods above, he did not want to hurt her.

"Let's go, then," Colin said.

Malcolm didn't miss the surprised glance, Bradon tossed between him and Cadence.

So his cousin suspected.

Soon enough they were astride their mounts. Cadence rode with him, Sheila with Colin.

Though they'd not yet seen snow, winter was upon them so he covered her shoulders and legs with a fur then wrapped one over his shoulders. Back cuddled against him, Malcolm once more tried not to become aroused. With one arm around her slender waist and the brush of her soft hair against his face, it was bloody difficult.

"I hope you don't think I'm being too forward but how are the rescued prisoners?" Cadence asked.

Clearly troubled, Colin sighed. "Some are better than others. They've been escorted back by scouts we had out this way. They'll be housed and well cared for in several cottages beyond the castle. They dinnae need to be around a celebration this eve."

Cadence tensed. "How many of them are women?"

"All," Colin said softly.

"So some were raped," she murmured.

Malcolm tightened his hold on her, convinced he felt rage ripple through her.

"Don't even think about it, Cadence," Sheila said. "Not tonight."

"Think about what?" Bradon asked.

"Cadence used to work with troubled women, mostly teens," Sheila enlightened. "She was a counselor before she went all New Age."

"Really," Colin asked, interested.

Cadence nodded. "For a while a few years back. If you want me to visit with these women tomorrow or even later tonight, I will."

Colin seemed to contemplate the offer but Malcolm spoke before his cousin could. "Nay, there is no need for that. 'Tis the thirteenth century. Times are much different."

"True," Colin conceded. "But as it turns out, Malcolm, you are not yet laird of this clan. I think 'twould be good for her to visit them on the morrow." He looked at Cadence. "If you truly dinnae mind, lass."

"Of course not," she said softly.

Malcolm narrowed his eyes at his cousin. Though they'd got on amiably enough while preparing for war, dislike for his cousin still burned strong in his blood. In his opinion, the MacLomain's had too easily welcomed him back into the clan after he'd betrayed them.

Three years prior, Colin was supposed to marry Nessa to help strengthen the tenuous tie between the MacLomain's and MacLeod's. Instead, he left her at the altar and joined with a lethal band of assassins. Malcolm, meanwhile, married the lass to soothe frayed nerves between the clans. Yet his cousin eventually returned, quick to claim lairdship and even quicker to once more draw Nessa's eyes.

Granted, Nessa had proven her faithlessness with her infatuation with Colin as well as her betrayal of the MacLomain clan. Still, it didn't make losing her or accepting his cousin as chieftain any easier. Thankfully, Bradon switched topics lest he focus too much on Colin making a point of overriding him in regards to Cadence.

"What is New Age?"

"Though the two aren't related in the least, Sheila's referring to me being Wiccan. While we embrace many aspects of ancient paganism, we more specifically believe that there exists not only a male deity but a female deity."

Sheila frowned. "It's not even a recognized religion."

Now religion was something he and Sheila hadn't agreed on before. While Cadence's belief system did not sound precisely like his, it certainly sounded far closer than Sheila's Christianity.

"A religion recognized by man doesnae—"

He stopped short when Cadence pushed back slightly and put a stern hand on his thigh. She turned her head slightly and whispered, "Please. There's no point."

She turned her attention back to Sheila. "So what happened after I left the house? I thought I heard your voice outside the bathroom door."

Malcolm frowned. There *was* a point. When last he'd spoken with Sheila about religion, she had backed down some. She could be reasonable. What was this friction between the two lasses? Without doubt it went beyond religious beliefs.

"Oh, now that was some craziness," Sheila exclaimed, her eyes once more shining as she answered Cadence. "When you didn't answer, I was worried you'd fallen asleep so I came in. The water was draining but you were gone. So I turned to leave then poof, the candles went out. As soon as that happened everything started to rattle and vibrate. I stumbled, landed in the tub and whoosh, everything went nuts time-travel-style."

Bradon chuckled. "Sounds like you're getting used to traveling back, lass."

"Sure am!" She grinned. "I swear it gets a little easier every time." Her smile faltered slightly. "I just wish I could *control* it with this ring and figure out what my particular brand of magic is."

"All in good time," Bradon assured.

Though the women didn't know it, they'd just crossed nearly all of the Cowal Peninsula in a few short hours via magic. Malcolm wondered if Cadence realized her hand had made a permanent home on his thigh. He sure as hell had. The minute they'd crossed the MacLomain border earlier he'd had to use his magic to cease his determined erection.

It'd been far too long since he'd lain with a woman.

Not since his wife.

"While we're on the topic of magic," Cadence said. "I told Malcolm but wish to be honest with you all. Adlin MacLomain has been speaking telepathically to me for several years now."

Colin's jaw dropped.

Bradon's eyes rounded.

Sheila muttered, "But of course."

"How is that possible?" Colin asked.

So Cadence explained the books. "I read about all of your parents coming together." He felt a shiver ripple through her. "Amazing tales. Very romantic."

Malcolm sighed and as always, tried to suppress the sadness and rage he felt when they were brought up. Swamped by powerful magic at the Hamilton's castle they'd vanished. Where *were* they? Had Da died?

The first few snowflakes of the season fell as they left the woodland behind and entered the wide field leading to the MacLomain castle. When Cadence issued a small gasp he smiled. Even with the day late and the sky gray with churning storm clouds, the castle was a fine sight. Frothing, temperamental, the surrounding loch ebbed and flowed in greeting.

"It's all so unbelievably beautiful," Cadence whispered.

Malcolm almost put his hand overs hers but didn't. He'd have to speak with Sheila before he made any such move. She needed to understand…

When he glanced Sheila's way, he was relieved to see she looked not at them but at the castle, and at who had just crossed the second drawbridge. McKayla and Leslie. With a slight movement of his leg, his mount broke into a trot. His cousins did the same, understanding the women were eager to reunite.

In little time, the four of them were embracing, teary eyed.

"I can't believe you're getting married!" Sheila said, holding Leslie at arm's length as she looked between her cousin and Bradon still astride his horse. "Well, that's a lie." She laughed. "I can *completely* believe it. Congratulations!"

"Aye, many thanks, lass but there will be plenty of time to catch up later." Bradon held his hand down to Leslie. "I've been away too long. 'Tis time for a moment alone with my wife."

"I'm not your wife yet, sweetheart." But Leslie allowed him to pull her up onto his horse. She nodded at Cadence then winked at Sheila. "Sorry, gotta go. Chat in a bit."

McKayla squeezed her cousin's hands. "Come, let me show you around the castle. I'm thrilled you got here when you did!"

"But first," Colin leapt down from his horse, "you and me, lass."

Malcolm didn't pay much attention when Colin pulled McKayla into his arms and kissed her long and hard. He was too busy admiring the look in Cadence's eyes while she watched. The lass didn't seem the least bit aware of how sensuality poured off of her. Aye, the outfit might not help. Despite the fur cloak, it was so short and revealing it left little to the imagination.

But he knew damned well that's not what had clansmen tripping over their own feet in passing. Statuesque, she possessed an alluring sense of self-confidence and poise. When combined with the sensuous way she watched others, Cadence had the ability to make men she hadn't even glanced at envision being the object of her affection.

Her startling beauty only enhanced the almost magical affect she had on others.

"Um...someone's standing on the cold ground in bare feet," Sheila reminded gently.

This time when Malcolm glanced at Sheila, her eyes locked on his.

Though he frowned, he didn't look away. She didn't deserve that.

"Ugh, you're right," McKayla said, her eyes still lost in Colin's. Working hard at it, she pulled them away and once more took her cousin's hands. "Let's go girls."

Cadence cast Malcolm one last glance and mouthed, "Thanks," before she walked off.

Eager to dismount and slip into a warm bath, he urged his mount forward. Regrettably, Colin soon rode alongside. "What make you of Adlin speaking within Cadence's mind?"

He honestly didn't care. Nor did he wish to speak at length with his cousin. They might battle well together but that was as far as it went. It didn't matter in the least if Colin had always been in awe of Adlin MacLomain. He could ask Bradon's opinion just as easily. "I think 'tis not our way to seek council from one another, cousin."

Once, long ago, they'd been close.

But those days were gone.

Colin straightened some. "Then let us speak of the havoc you are set to create with the Broun lasses."

Malcolm cocked a brow at him. "You think to speak to me of creating havoc with lasses? 'Tis ill that."

"This eve marks my brother's marriage," Colin said, a heavy frown on his face. "Sheila has long desired you yet we all see the way you look at the other."

He *could* tell Colin that her ring glowed for him but he shouldn't have to.

"The other being Cadence," Malcolm bit out, making sure his cousin realized she had a name. "And Sheila's long desire has been but a few short fortnights."

"This clan prepares for war. Morale must stay high," Colin returned. "I willnae have the strife."

"You willnae have the strife, aye?" Renewed rage churned. It mattered little that his parents were missing and presumed dead. It meant little that Torra, his cousin, Colin's sister, was no doubt imprisoned by the enemy. "Even as your priorities were astray when you abandoned this clan, they remain equally disoriented now that you've returned."

Before Colin could speak, Malcolm continued. "I didnae lie with Sheila nor did I embrace or even kiss her. I owe her nothing." His frustration only increased. "However, I willnae make a mockery of her affections. She is a kind creature and such actions would be that of a monster."

"I didnae mean—" Colin started.

Malcolm cut him off as they crossed beneath the second portcullis. "You dinnae say anything without meaning. But you may want to remember something before you start accusing me. 'Twas you who came back to this clan and caused nothing but strife when you brought a lass from the future and all but welcomed the advances of *my* wife."

"Never *once* did I welcome Nessa's advances," Colin said, his brows lowering sharply.

"So you say." Malcolm swung down from his horse and handed the reins to a stable boy.

"We willnae speak of this now," Colin ground out softly, coming alongside. "But we *will* speak of it again."

Swarmed by several who needed one thing or another, Colin swung down from his horse and vanished into the courtyard. Malcolm shook his head. They would not talk of it. His cousin did not have the time or the inclination.

"Oh, look at ye, Malcolm MacLomain," came a small but boisterous voice. "Yer a fine sight if I ever did see one!"

Now here was a lass who could turn a lad's day around. He shot her the best grin he could manage at the moment. "Aye, lass. Have you not seen more of a lad's leg's then?"

Hands on her bony hips, young Euphemia eyed him over. "I dinnae think I have ever seen a lad with only half a plaid."

No doubt he cast a fine sight having given half his tartan to Cadence.

"Gods willing, you never will again." He chuckled and eyed the kitchens. "How go preparations?"

Her eyes rounded. "Dinnae get me started. Since I became second in command running this place, none can keep their heads about them." She leaned close and winked. "But at least now I can whack the laddie's without them whacking back."

"And how do they like that?"

She pouted a little but her eyes shone. "They dinnae like it any more than they did before but at least *now* they have to listen."

"Oh, they listened before, lass, dinnae you doubt it for a second." He ruffled her hair. "Get on back now. 'Twill only get busier."

A wide grin split her face. "Aye!"

Before she turned away, Euphemia said, "She's a verra bonnie lass you brought back from your battling."

If any could chat endlessly, it was Euphemia. Usually, he'd spend hours listening to her banter, but right now he needed rest. So he leaned over and whispered, "Aye, she is indeed. We will talk more of her later. Do me a favor?"

Euphemia blinked her sparse brows and grinned. "Anything."

"Bring her up my special bottle of mead for when she bathes. 'Twill well reward her after such a trying day."

The kitchen lass's eyes went so wide her brows touched her hairline. "Oh, aye!"

Malcolm couldn't help but grin as he walked away.

After all, his mead wasn't normal in the least.

Nay, it was spiked with a good dose of a unique brand of magic.

Chapter Three

"This is breaking Sheila's heart."

Cadence leaned against the window's eve and stared out over the dimly lit, storm enraged loch. Sheila had already headed for her chamber. Now it was just Cadence and McKayla in the spacious chamber she'd been provided.

"She has nothing to worry about," Cadence assured again. "I'm *not* here for Malcolm but someone else entirely."

"So you say yet your ring burns when you're around Malcolm." McKayla shook her head. "Someone needs to ask him if your ring's stone glows for him."

When Cadence shot her an askance look, McKayla frowned. "Oh no, not me. I try to make a habit of steering clear of Malcolm. I'm convinced he likes me about as much as he likes my husband."

"He's not a bad guy just no doubt hurting from losing his wife." Cadence plunked down on the bed beside her cousin. "After all, he saved my life."

"Did he ever," McKayla agreed and smiled. "For that I'm grateful."

It was nice to reunite with her cousins. When she and Sheila had fallen apart, she'd all but lost touch with not only her cousins, but her sister. Then Cadence and McKayla had grown a little closer after helping Sheila through her ordeal with Jack. Even so, she still missed the certain something she and Sheila had shared. It was special and all theirs.

"I still can't believe Leslie's getting married." Cadence chuckled. "Despite all the crazy amazing things I've learned in the past few days, that still wows me the most."

"I've never seen your sister so incredibly happy," McKayla said. "Honestly, I didn't know she had it in her to crack a grin never mind walk around so bloody cheerful all the time." The corner of her lip curled up. "Funny how much she reminds me of her former nemesis, our Sheila."

"I *know*." Cadence snorted. "Reality's really been turned upside down when we're chatting about how much those two remind us of one another."

Concerned, McKayla said, "The whole 'Malcolm and you' thing aside, how do you really think Sheila is doing?"

"Troubled enough that I've stayed at your house...I mean old house, the last few days because I'm worried."

"Clearly," McKayla said. "And even though it sorta...well, *really*, sucks that her ring burned for Grant, maybe that's just what she needed in light of Jack and now..."

"So she never told you or even Leslie about the ring heating?"

"Absolutely not," McKayla said. "But I haven't seen her. Leslie went on that romp north with her to the Hamilton's castle. If she knew she would have said as much. That's big news."

"Borderline traitorous news, wouldn't you say?" Cadence said softly.

Their eyes met.

McKayla understood.

"I'll talk to Colin about it tonight. He deserves to know," McKayla said on a sigh. "He cares about her. He'd never shun her because of it, especially since his sister helped create that ring."

"He better not." Cadence shook her head. "If she goes, I go."

"If she goes, all we Broun's go." McKayla squeezed her hand. "Don't you doubt it for a second."

Several servants came in and started to set up a tub of water. Cadence nearly drooled. It was going to feel incredible after the day she'd had. Already a fire crackled on the hearth and furs were hung over the windows.

One servant brought over a bottle, her gaze flickering to McKayla briefly before she held it out to Cadence. "'Tis mead, missus. For you, from the laird's good cousin, Malcolm."

The minute she took the bottle, Cadence knew there was something a tad bit different about its contents. For a split second, she almost felt as though she was once more warming herself against his hard body in the cave.

McKayla waited until the servants left before she said, "Now *what* is that look on your face, cousin." Before Cadence could say a word, McKayla snatched the bottle, a stupefied grin on her face. "And why the heck is Malcolm sending you booze?"

Cadence knew her cheeks warmed so she walked to the fire. "I really need a hot bath, sweetie." She turned and offered her best smile. "Can we catch up more after the wedding?"

McKayla stood. "Of course. Besides, I want to hear more about this mystery man you've been dreaming about." Cadence didn't miss the wry grin on her cousin's face when she put the bottle on the bedside table. "All the soaps you'll need are by the tub and your dress is laid out. When you're finished let the guard posted outside your door know and he'll get you where you need to go."

"Okay," she said and embraced her cousin before she left.

Alone at last, she instinctually went to touch the pentacle at her neck only to realize once more that it had vanished. It must've been torn from her neck during the fall into the ocean, or during the climb or who knows. But it was truly difficult to realize that it was gone. Given to her by Adlin MacLomain, it had helped her find peace after all the hardship and grief she'd witnessed when counseling. But it was gone. She made a point of not dwelling on material things. It served no purpose. Still, she was bummed.

A small smile crept onto her face as she worked to undo the plaid Malcolm had dressed her in. The silly outfit he'd created warmed her heart when it needed it most. They might not be meant for one another but the highlander surely, however unknowing, came through when she needed him most.

Cadence eyed his bottle as she slipped into the water.

She'd pass on imbibing but would be sure to thank him.

"Och, now lassie, you might just be surprised by what is in that bottle."

Adlin! Always nice to hear him. Immersed in warm water and rose petals she leaned her head back and closed her eyes.

"Now we're back to square one. Again I soak in a tub of water. This time if I'm to travel through time, would you mind giving me a head's up?" she said in her mind. *"Especially if I'm to be thrown over a cliff."*

"The future is not mine to see." But she sensed a grin in his words. *"What think you of my castle? Of my clan?"*

"Full of happiness, drama and all that good stuff," she assured with a smile. *"Well led by Colin I'd say."*

"Aye, 'tis good news, all of it..."

His words trailed away as well as his essence. How was it that she communicated with someone deceased so well and often?

Naturally, she'd researched it. Only one thing popped up time and time again.

Necromancer.

The idea that she could commune with the dead didn't bother her in the least. But then she'd only ever communicated with Adlin. Now that she'd traveled back in time to an era ripe with wizards, warlocks, ghosts and even dragons...who or *what* else might enter her mind?

Fraction by blissful fraction her muscles unlocked as the water surrounded, stroked and gave ease to her sore body. It was still hard to believe she'd survived the day. But she had. Barely opening her eyes, she stared at Malcolm's bottle.

There was something in that liquid.

Something all his.

Cadence pressed her lips together when not her mind but her body responded to the mysterious possibilities. She shook her head and sat up. Not a possibility at all. She wasn't here for Malcolm and she needed to stop this. After scrubbing and washing off, she set to getting dressed. Sure, it might seem silly to most that she entertained the concept of a man she'd only ever dreamt of over one of flesh and blood, but she did.

The man she'd dreamt of, envisioned, had been with her nearly as long as...

Adlin MacLomain.

Surely that meant something.

With a small smile on her face, she slipped into the ancient clothing, chemise first then the emerald green dress. Though tricky as hell, she managed to do up the sashes. The front was cut low, pushing up her breasts almost obscenely. Who had provided this dress? Not one to dwell, she slid on the funky shoes then set to combing out her long hair. Like Sheila, it was the one thing she refused to part with though she was in her mid-twenties.

Thick and wavy, her hair responded to whatever was in the water and dried quickly.

When a tap came at the door, she opened it, surprised to see Colin.

"You look lovely, lass," he said. "McKayla requested that I come get you. Are you ready?"

through her veins and Cadence worked at a calming breath. When she went to take the necklace, she was mortified to discover her hand shook.

When Malcolm's eyes met hers she knew he followed her every thought.

Wonderful.

Instead of taking advantage of her vulnerable state, he murmured, "Turn, let me put it on you."

Working at a heavy swallow, she nodded and did as he asked. When she pulled her hair aside and he placed the necklace around her neck she realized her vulnerable state was still very much at risk. His warm breath fanned the delicate skin on the back of her neck while his weapon-roughened fingers brushed her collarbone. She could feel the warmth of his large body against her back.

Cadence closed her eyes.

Thud. Thud. Thud.

Her heart beat so heavily she could barely draw in air.

When the cool necklace came against her heated skin, a delicious shiver raced through her.

Aware of the affect he was having on her, his lips came close to her ear as he clasped the necklace. "What is this betwixt us, lass?"

Startled, she glanced over her shoulder.

Their eyes met.

Held.

Unmistakable desire flared in the pale pools of his gaze.

"Sheila, you look amazing," McKayla said.

Ripped from the almost dreamy, surreal place she'd drifted, Cadence tore her eyes from Malcolm and searched out her cousin. Absolutely breathtaking in an ice blue dress, Sheila had finally arrived. Hair long and curling in the torchlight, she didn't think she'd ever seen her cousin look so lovely.

Naturally, Sheila's eyes went right to Malcolm.

Instead of meeting her direct regard, he frowned slightly and received a mug from a servant.

Worried about Sheila's mental state, Cadence also frowned. This attraction between Malcolm and her wasn't good...for any of them. Even if her cousin's ring burned for Grant, she truly seemed to want Malcolm. Cadence needed to be honest with him before things went too far.

That way he'd be free to pursue her cousin.

As Sheila greeted everyone, Cadence took the opportunity to lean a little closer to Malcolm. Voice soft, she said, "You need to know I'm not here for you."

His troubled eyes went to hers.

She gave a slight nod. "It's true. I've dreamt about another often. I'm sorry but *he's* the reason I've been pulled back in time."

Malcolm's eyes flickered to her ring then back to her face. "Who is he then?"

"I'll know him when I see him," she assured.

"So you dinnae know whom you seek?"

"No." She shook her head. "I mean yes. I will the minute I see him. I'm sure of it."

Expression unreadable, he sipped from his mug. When a servant tried to hand her a cup she shook her head. Malcolm took the cup and handed it to her anyway. "You will need to toast the bride."

It seemed he didn't wish to discuss the other man any further because he soon turned his attention elsewhere. It was better that they got that out of the way now, whether or not he decided to return Sheila's affections. Yet when they turned from one another, Cadence was surprised to feel his absence almost immediately.

Really good that she'd spoken with him.

There was too much attraction too fast between them.

"'Tis time," Colin announced.

"Come here, sis. You stand beside me," Leslie said.

Honored, Cadence joined her. Colin stood beside Bradon in front of the holy man.

A supportive wall, several highlanders lined up behind them including Malcolm and Bradon's father, Iain. Cadence couldn't help but peek at Iain and his wife, Arianna. She'd read their story as well. It was so cool to actually meet them.

As the holy man spoke and wrapped Leslie and Bradon's wrists together with a swath of plaid, Cadence soaked up her surroundings. Bagpipes drifted on the salty wind driven snow. Waves crashed against the shore far below. Fire crackled. Torches spit.

All smiled as the couple said the words that would bind them together.

Once the nuptials' were completed, Bradon pulled Leslie into his arms and kissed her passionately.

All present clanged their weapons, hooting and hollering.

As if they'd been waiting, a roar rose up from not only the great hall far below but from the many wall walks around the castle. It seemed to echo into the courtyard and further out onto the field.

The MacLomain clan honored the new marriage.

When all lifted their mugs to toast, Cadence did the same. Caught up in the joyous occasion, she took a healthy swig. Searing fire burned her throat then warmed her belly. *Holy Christ!* She coughed, sputtering.

A caring hand patted her on the back. "There, there now, lass. 'Tis always best to sip highland whiskey."

Eyes watering, she nodded at Iain and worked to catch her breath. When under control at last, she managed a weak, "Thanks."

He offered a warm smile and steered her toward the wall overlooking the loch. "The air is freshest in the wind. Get your bearings and dinnae take such a long swig again, aye?"

"Definitely not," she said. "I guess I got caught up in the celebration."

"'Tis easy enough to do." Iain leaned against the wall, his white hair blowing in the wind and kind eyes assessing. "I have heard my grandfather, Adlin, speaks with you from beyond the grave."

Word travels fast. But she wasn't surprised. Adlin was very important to this clan. "Yes, he does." She smiled. "He speaks very fondly of you."

Nostalgia entered his eyes as well as something else. Concern? "I hope you dinnae take this the wrong way but how do you know with certainty 'tis Adlin?"

"I don't take it the wrong way in the least. At the beginning I asked myself the same question." She shrugged. "The truth is I don't know for sure it's him. But I stopped worrying about it. Now, I simply believe he is who he says he is. In fact, I have no doubts. Regrettably, however, I can't give you the straight answer you seek."

"So the voice has never made you feel uncomfortable or asked you to do things that make no sense?" Iain said.

"Made me uncomfortable? Goddess no." She chuckled. "Asked me to do things that make no sense? Sure. But that's just Adlin."

Iain's eyes warmed. "Certainly sounds like him."

"Tell him the Sinclair comes. 'Twill take the aide of a king to see this through."

Cadence straightened. "Adlin's here."

She delivered his message.

Iain's eyes narrowed. "Alexander Sinclair?"

When Cadence tried to confirm this there was no response. Not having read about this particular man, she shook her head. "I'm sorry. Adlin's gone," she said. "Who is Alexander Sinclair?"

"Adlin's sister, Iosbail's great love." Iain shook his head. "But he lived hundreds of years ago. 'Tis impossible."

"What's impossible?" Sheila asked as she joined them.

Deep in thought, Iain gave her a small smile but didn't answer her question.

"Iosbail MacLomain's one true love, a Sinclair king who lived hundreds of years ago. According to Adlin, he's coming," Cadence provided.

"Why is that so impossible?" she asked Iain. "When I traveled back further in time to the Stewarts, a man named Shamus Flanagon had also traveled there from another time." She bit her lower lip. "Ya know, I think he said he'd traveled there from the Sinclair clan."

"Interesting," Iain murmured.

"What's so interesting, then?" a woman asked as she joined them.

As tall as Cadence, she had short, bright red hair and a fiery personality. Or at least it seemed that way by her confident swagger and flirtatious manner with every man she passed.

Sheila smiled and introduced them. "Cadence, this is Ilisa, another MacLomain cousin."

Cadence held out her hand to Ilisa. "Nice to meet you."

Ilisa eyed the hand for a moment then grabbed and shook hard. "It always is."

She grinned. Not intimidated in the least by the woman's strong presence she said, "I could see you being Arthur's daughter."

"Ah, another Broun witch!" Ilisa declared. "'Tis good indeed."

Before she could answer, Ilisa was on her way. Cadence laughed and looked at Sheila. "So did I assume right?"

"When it comes to Ilisa you can assume pretty much anything. But yes, she's Arthur and Annie's daughter." Her cousin's eyes dropped to the pentacle around her neck. Her words along with her eyes softened. "Look at that."

Cadence was about to tell her about the necklace when Sheila touched it.

She braced her hands on the wall behind her when Sheila clasped the piece. Eyelids fluttering, she watched in horror as her cousin's eyes rolled back in her head.

Iain put his hand over Cadence's. "Dinnae move, lass. She's in a trance."

No doubt sensing something dire was happening Colin, Bradon and Malcolm were there in an instant. None said a word, only surrounded her.

What the *hell* was going on?

Suddenly, near garbled words poured from Sheila's mouth, voices that didn't sound like hers at all.

"You dinnae question me, Grant!" Her head whipped to the side as if she'd been slapped.

"Nay, m'laird," she murmured. "'Twas wrong."

"Kneel before me. Now," she said.

Sheila didn't kneel but bent her knees slightly.

"Bow your head."

She did.

"You will stay just as you are until the morrow. Then you will lead my armies south."

"Aye, m'laird."

Then, as if she'd been kicked in the gut, Sheila buckled over, her hand ripped from the pentacle. Before she could crumble to the floor, Malcolm scooped her up.

"I will see to her," he growled.

Without a backward glance, he carried her away.

Chapter Four

A good amount of time passed before Sheila finally opened her eyes.

She lay on a small cot while Malcolm sat on a window ledge.

"Where am I?" she murmured, confused as she sat up.

"Nay." He quickly sat on the edge of the cot and gently pushed her down. "Lay back, lass. Dinnae rush this."

"Rush what?" Her eyes widened. "What happened?" She looked around. "And again, where am I?"

"I brought you to Torra's old chamber. 'Tis quieter here."

Despite how violent the experience, she seemed none the worse for it.

"Something happened when you touched Cadence's necklace," he said. "Do you remember any of it?"

Her brows furrowed. "Only bits and pieces." It seemed though based on her expression all was becoming clearer. She whispered, "Grant."

"So it seems," Malcolm acknowledged. "I think 'tis clear where your magic lies."

"It is?" This time when she sat up slowly he allowed it. She held her forehead. "Care to share?"

"Aye." He squeezed her hand. "Like my Da, you are a visionary."

"A what?" she started and shook her head. "Never mind. I know what the word means." Her eyes met his. "So I can see things before they happen?"

"Or even as they happen," he said.

"Wow, that's intense." When she stood, he assisted her. She appeared to be doing quite well.

"Yet it happened when I touched that necklace," she said.

"Aye, 'tis hard to say if the bauble is necessary to your gift or merely ignited it."

"Weird," she muttered. Sheila leaned against the window and breathed in the chilled air. Her eyes cut to him as she touched her stomach gingerly. "Grant isn't being treated well at all, is he?"

Troubled, Malcolm shook his head. "Nay. It doesnae seem it."

Malcolm gently grabbed her upper arms. "Not yet but I suspect you could. If your ring glows for him it will draw him as surely as Leslie's did, Bradon."

"And Cadence's, you," Sheila said softly.

"Aye," he whispered. "'Twill be unavoidable."

"Damn scary thought," she muttered.

"'Tis indeed. One thing is for sure, you must not leave this castle. The further from Grant you are the better."

"Good luck with that. You know as well as I do that I just became a crucial piece in this upcoming war," she ground out. "I'll be needed as you travel north."

Malcolm shook his head. "Nay, not *that* crucial. Not if it risks your life."

"We're all risking our lives, Malcolm. Besides, what's one life when compared to tens of thousands?" she reminded. "Because you know the information I might impart could make or break the outcome of this war."

He squeezed her arms gently then stepped away. "We will discuss this further with the others on the morrow."

"Sure, but I bet they'll agree with me."

When he looked at her, a small grin hovered on her lips. Relief flooded. Normally, her sunny attitude got on his nerves but he was glad to see it returning. Still, he worried about all they'd discussed. "Are you truly well, lass?"

Sheila knew he referred more to what he'd said about Cadence than anything else. "You know, I think I am. God knows I wish things had worked out differently but I've always been a big believer in things happening for a reason. If the good Lord wants you to be with Cadence then I trust his will."

Malcolm nodded. She meant it. "The gods know the right lad's out there for you as well, Sheila."

"Here's hoping it's not the enemy," she joked.

"Aye," he agreed. "Are you well enough to return to the celebrations then?"

Sheila shot him a winning smile. "Yes, most especially to a mug of whiskey."

"I second that." He held out his arm.

When she slid her arm in his and they left Torra's chamber, he realized something. They might not be destined to be lovers, but

46

they were most certainly friends. And friendships were something he had few of and valued above all else. As if she sensed his thoughts, she offered him a contented smile and gave him a quick peck on his cheek before they continued. When they arrived on the landing in which Bradon and Leslie had been married, everybody was rather somber.

Everyone stopped talking when they saw them.

Her cousins rushed over.

"Are you okay?" Cadence asked. "I would've come but was told not to, that you needed space."

"You look a little pale," McKayla said. "How are you feeling?"

"Here, drink this," Leslie ordered and gave her a mug of whiskey.

Grateful, Sheila drank and Malcolm moved away to give them space.

All waited to hear if Sheila was well. After she'd taken a few long pulls she nodded and smiled. "I'm fine everyone. Please, party on!"

"Are you sure?" McKayla asked, clearly not convinced.

Sheila nodded. "Yes, please, I'm good."

When McKayla nodded at the pipers, they trilled a few notes then fired up.

Meanwhile, Malcolm received a mug and downed half the cup.

"How is she really?" Colin asked as he and Bradon joined him.

"Better," he said. "On many fronts."

"'Tis good to hear," Bradon said. "So you spoke of Cadence."

Colin's eyes narrowed but he said nothing.

"'Twas amongst several things of which we spoke," Malcolm said. "But even that and her newfound gift of foresight was not the most important thing we discussed."

Malcolm told them of the ring burning for Grant and his fear about her being more in harm's way than ever. "There is no way of knowing if my brother saw her ring glow so we can only speculate as to what will come of it."

Troubled, Colin and Bradon eyed Sheila.

"She has a strong support system," Bradon said at last. "We willnae let harm befall her."

"Nay," Colin seconded. "Not to mention she has a strong, optimistic spirit. 'Twill only aide her in what lies ahead."

Malcolm couldn't help but agree. It would. Still, he worried. Grant was a mentally broken, exceptionally well-trained warrior who lived for nothing more than the next ruthless order that came from his master's mouth. Such a man was impossible to understand, never mind predict.

"We will talk more on the morn." Colin threw an arm around Bradon's shoulders. "For now 'tis time to celebrate my brother's new marriage."

"Aye!" Malcolm toasted him.

All gathered were already in full swing, dancing and spinning by, riotous peals of laughter left in their wakes. Malcolm downed the last of his whiskey, grabbed another cup and kept to the edges of the crowd. Now when his gaze swung Cadence's way it was with far less guilt. An absolute vision in green, she already danced with one of his fellow highlanders, a wide smile on her face.

The dress was absolutely stunning on her but then he supposed anything would be. The lass had more cleavage than most and while it certainly drew the eye so too did the rest of her. A heavy wall of snow fell beyond the castle's protection, an elegant backdrop as she twirled by, luxurious red hair whipping around her shoulders.

Not once since she'd told him, had Malcolm stopped thinking about the mystery man she'd mentioned. Not threatened in the least by this seemingly fictional stranger, he again debated his next move. What he *wanted* to do was spin her right out of here and shove her into a hidden castle alcove. He'd yank up her dress and take her against the hard, unrelenting wall before she drew in her next breath.

Yet what he'd *actually* do would be far different.

When she once more spun by with yet another clansman, he reached out, grabbed her wrist and pulled her against him. Stunned, breathless, her bright eyes rose to his.

"Have you found your mystery man yet, lass?" he said, so low she would feel the rumble of his inquisition through the thin material of her silky, smooth dress.

Her lips trembled, eyes wide, but she gave no answer.

Oh, but to close his lips over hers.

Yet he wouldn't do that. Not so soon after talking with Sheila.

While they might've traveled far, he'd not put his lusting for her cousin in Sheila's face. That would be unkind.

"No," Cadence finally murmured, her eyes still locked on his. "But I *will* find him."

When she licked her lips, his eyes drifted down. Wide and full, they were created for pure sin. He could only imagine them running down his body, surrounding him where it mattered most. Damnation, but he *needed* her closer.

Though he wouldn't kiss her, he'd sure as hell dance with her.

Ignoring her assurance that she was meant for another man, Malcolm pulled her into the dancing crowd. It didn't matter if the music was merry; he wasn't in the mood for speed. Besides, he needed to hide his swelling erection. This time he'd not temper the poor thing with magic. Nay, she'd feel his need while she tried to keep focus on the man she so eagerly sought.

"Goddess above, what are you *doing* to me," she whispered, voice strangled.

Arms wrapped tight around her lower back, he brought his mouth against her ear. "'Twill be no goddess giving you answers, only me." He tightened his hold. "Do you feel me then, lass?"

"How could I not?" she gasped. Hands clamped on his upper arms, she turned her face into his chest and mumbled, "You show ill respect to a man you have not met."

"I dinnae respect a man until he earns it." Malcolm closed his eyes and breathed in the sweet scent of her hair.

As each individual note trilled from the bagpipe, she melted against him more thoroughly than the icy snowflakes speckling his heated skin. Fire and drink might warm the crowd but where they stood his breath hit the air in foggy puffs. Always a fan of the cold, but an even bigger fan of a bonnie wee lass against him, he cupped one hand around the back of her neck.

Her heart thundered against his.

Her body shuddered.

"Easy, lass," he whispered. "I willnae take what you're unwilling to give."

"Yet you hold me prisoner," she murmured.

"Nay, we but dance."

"If only."

Her words were so soft he barely heard them.

Jaw grinding, he held her securely with his arm while pressing his arousal tighter against her. Och, but to be inside of her, to see the look on her face when he made her his.

"No," she whispered. Then she pulled back, her voice stronger as her eyes met his. "*No.*"

"Aye, lass." But he loosened his hold and gave her one more word before he let her go. "Soon."

Her hand fluttered to her chest and she shook her head before she turned away and vanished into the crowd. Taller than most, he watched her the whole time. Men tried to swing her back into a dance, but instead she received a mug from a servant and drank. She flinched but took another sip.

With a small, knowing smile, he turned and peered through the driving snow down onto the restless loch. He'd not engage Cadence again tonight but let her enjoy her sister's wedding. Based on what Sheila said during her vision, he knew they'd embark for war on the morrow. This time it wouldn't be to battle in the numerous smaller skirmishes north of the border but to head off the massive movement of clans heading their way.

While he could've let them come to his doorstep to save Torra, Keir Hamilton had chosen full on war. Malcolm still wondered at that. Already, they'd been led into a position that had somehow imprisoned his cousin. Whether or not Keir actually possessed her was open to debate. Based on what Bradon told him, Keir had claimed her via magic when she possessed Leslie.

So did he have the dragon?

Nobody knew.

Rumors had not been spread. No doubt, with purpose.

It was with that very thought the next morn that he made his way to the castle's kitchens. Little Euphemia, wooden spoon in hand, was waving madly at anyone willing to listen.

"Ye dinnae leave the bannocks for a bloody second, ye bunch of blackguards!" She frowned at the blackened bread then whipped one at a boy who came too close. "Come any closer and I'll shove this right up—"

Her mouth clamped shut when Malcolm took her elbow and shook his head. "Nay, lassie, dinnae say it."

Mouth twisted, Euphemia narrowed her eyes. "The troops are rallying. You travel today! Food needs to be provisioned not burned!"

Malcolm nodded and urged her to sit next to him on the castle stairs. "'Tis true enough but when at war men would relish molded bannock. Blackened would be a treat."

"Hmph." She crossed spindly arms over a narrow chest. "My MacLomains only deserve the verra best and well you know it."

"Worry naught. We will manage," he assured.

"Manage," she spat. "The MacLomains shouldnae have to *manage*."

"Regardless," he said. "We will. So stop your fretting."

Owl eyes his way, she said, "I've asked the laird that I might travel with the lot of you."

Malcolm shook his head. "Nay, 'tis a bad idea."

"Too late." She puffed up. "He said aye!"

Colin was a bloody fool so this came as no surprise. Still, there was no point in trying to convince Euphemia otherwise. If she'd been given permission all the great kings of Scotland couldn't stop her.

"So what ails ye, my friend." Her astute, wise-beyond-her-years eyes met his. "There be trouble stirring in yer soul." She winked. "More than usual that is."

There was always trouble stirring in his soul, or at least for the past several years. But that had nothing to do with why he sought her out. No, there was another reason altogether.

"I'd like to start a rumor and I think you're just the lass to help me do that," he said.

"A rumor ye say?" Her eyes narrowed and her thin lips curled up. "Takes talent to start a good rumor, one that sticks that is. How far do you want it to travel?"

"To all four corners of Scotland and beyond to all the outer isles."

If possible, her wide eyes rounded further. She smacked her lips and contemplated. "Twould have to be a mighty rumor."

"'Twill be mighty and will draw many to fight on behalf of the MacLomains who might have hesitated otherwise."

it out later. He'd just left the armory when people started to rush by, excited.

When he gave a passing warrior a pointed look, the man stopped immediately. "What's happening?"

"'Tis a king they say," he said. Though he clearly wanted to join the crowd he didn't dare move. When Malcolm cocked a brow the lad gushed, "A Sinclair from the past. Here. Now."

Malcolm nodded that he might leave and the warrior fled.

He'd heard what Cadence had said the night before when she spoke to Iain. So it seemed she did indeed communicate with Adlin MacLomain. Malcolm tried his best not to think what that might mean for her value during this war. In his mind, it made her almost as valuable as Sheila.

Heavy frown in place, he strode through the crowd. When people thickened at the drawbridge he continued to make his way through. Only once he'd hit the first drawbridge did he stop.

It didn't matter in the least that Colin, Bradon and Iain kneeled before a man. What *did* matter was that the warrior standing alongside the Sinclair already stared at a lass with his heart in his eyes.

And that lass was Cadence.

Chapter Five

There he was…right in front of her, standing beside the king. The man of her dreams.

"Up," Alexander Sinclair said to the MacLomain men. "You need not kneel for me."

All stood. Cadence's eyes remained glued to the man across from her. Not for a second did his gaze leave her either. He knew her as surely as she knew him!

"You honor us with your presence." Colin introduced his brother and father then gestured toward the castle. "Please, come. We provision for war but there's drink a plenty."

Alexander nodded and smiled. "Aye, much thanks." He gestured at the man beside him and made introductions. "This is my first-in-command and good friend, Shamus Flanagon."

"Aye, 'tis good to see you again." Bradon smiled. "Welcome to the MacLomain clan."

Cadence was surprised when her sister added to that and even more shocked when Leslie walked right over and gave him a hug. "Good to see you, Shamus. Holy surprise!"

Shamus squeezed her hand, fondness in his eyes. "Aye, lassie. 'Tis good indeed!"

Just as it had sounded in her dreams, his Irish lilt warmed the soul. But…he was no MacLomain at all! How had she never made that connection? Somehow she'd known all along he was Irish but had been convinced he was of this clan.

Naturally, Malcolm appeared alongside her, his deep voice civil to Alexander, lukewarm with Shamus. "My king, welcome, I'm Malcolm MacLomain, cousin to Colin." His attention turned to Shamus. "Cousin by marriage to Cadence."

Cadence looked skyward. If he meant to turn Shamus off her this wasn't the way to do it, at least not by twenty-first century standards. It sounded downright incestuous. But then, it didn't seem to matter when Shamus nodded at Malcolm then focused entirely on her, voice interested and warm.

"You must be Cadence then."

55

Cadence had no idea how to handle the moment. Shake his hand? Curtsy? She opted for an equally warm smile. "Yes, nice to meet you, Shamus."

Leslie looked between her and Shamus, obviously seeing something.

When Colin urged Alexander and Shamus to join him, Bradon and Malcolm followed. Cadence sort of understood how this worked. Shamus couldn't talk with her until formalities were observed.

So she and Leslie fell back, walking behind the men.

"What was *that* between you and Shamus?" Leslie murmured.

"How do you even *know* him?" she nearly hissed.

Leslie shrugged, confused by the passion in Cadence's voice. "Last time I was here, Sheila and I traveled back in time forty more years or so to the Stewart clan. Shamus was there. He sort of had a thing for me but it didn't pan out."

"He sort of had a thing for you?" Cadence felt a headache blooming. "How so?"

Leslie waved it away. "Totally doesn't matter. Brief." She again looked at him then at Cadence. "How the hell do you know him? Because you obviously do."

Just as they were entering the courtyard, a stable boy brought out Leslie's horse.

"Ah, Soul Reader," she exclaimed, abandoning Cadence.

Incredulous, she stared after her sister. Since when did she give a damn about horses? If that wasn't strange enough, Alexander and Shamus stopped short and stared at the horse as if they'd seen a ghost.

"Is all well?" Colin asked, frowning.

Eyes narrowed, Alexander walked up to the horse. Cadence gasped when it lowered its head in submission. Meanwhile, Shamus walked around the horse and shook his head.

"Shhh, lass, she reunites with a soul mate."

"Adlin? I don't understand?" Cadence said but as always, he was gone as soon as he'd come.

Suddenly, Alexander threw back his head and laughed. Stroking the horse's mane, he urged her to raise her head. Shamus chuckled as well. When Colin continued to look confused, Alexander enlightened. "Worry naught. This horse is your friend.

Keep her close." Before he turned away, the king leaned his head against the horses and whispered something close to her ear. It might have made him look insane had he not pulled away with a flourish, headed toward the castle and said, "We have much to discuss."

Cadence joined Leslie and the horse. Haughty, the beast looked down at them.

"What was that all about?" she asked her cousin.

"No freakin' clue." Leslie patted the horse. "Things have been odd since I met Soul Reader."

"Right, your horse…that you named." Cadence shook her head. "Isn't that what McKayla and Sheila called you when we were kids?"

"Yeah. Weird right?" Leslie grinned. "This horse has followed me all over time. Adlin implied it might be a MacLomain wizard."

"Huh?" A chill raced over her. She'd read about this in the books. "Wait. Like a MacLomain wizard in a horse that could help someone survive death?"

Before Leslie could respond she cut her off. "And when on Earth did you meet, Adlin?"

"Damn, are you going to let me get a word in edgewise?" Leslie said.

Cadence shook her head then nodded. "Yeah, sorry. Just processing a lot."

"I guess so," Leslie muttered. When the stable boy handed her the reins she shook her head. "Sorry, I'll have to ride her later." She nodded toward the castle and the MacLomain men entering it. "Duty calls."

As they walked up the castle stairs, Leslie explained how she'd met her horse when she'd last traveled back in time. Based on Euphemia's recommendation and the uncanny correlation with her childhood nickname, she named her Soul Reader. After that, the horse had followed her through time and remained by her side to this day. When she'd traveled back in time to the Stewart clan, Adlin had told her about the bizarre connection between MacLomain wizards.

A means to aide one another through death back into life.

Several times in MacLomain history, a wizard had possessed a horse.

Why then, was it impossible to tear her thoughts from Malcolm?

When they entered the great hall, the men stood before the fire. A hearth unlike any other, at least twenty feet wide and fifteen feet tall, only these highlanders would still look large before its impressive dimensions. Detailed portrayals of strong, god-like faces were chiseled where a mantelpiece would normally be.

Cadence was still in awe of the castle and its innards. The main hall, with its behemoth tapestries and hundreds of torches, blew her away. As a bookstore owner, no, as a ghost writer, she knew for a fact no book depicted any of this so well. Even the rushes underfoot were freshly laid.

McKayla, already standing by Colin, waved them over. When they joined them they were handed fresh cups of ale and included in the conversation.

"Shamus and I dinnae mind in the least trekking north with you," Alexander Sinclair said. "Iosbail told me I would be needed so I am here."

Cadence almost said something but Leslie beat her to it. "Adlin's sister? Truly?"

Alexander's eyes fell on her. "Aye, lass. Where I hail from she is but a young lass."

"And she told you to come here?" Cadence asked.

"Aye," Alexander said, his eyes flickering between her and Shamus. "She said 'twould serve many purposes."

Cadence met Shamus's eyes. No doubt it would.

Then, traitorous, her gaze flickered to Malcolm.

He didn't look her way but stood with his arms crossed over his chest, staring into the fire.

"'Tis a great honor to have you with us," Iain said. "But I fear you put yourself at too much risk."

"Did Adlin not say it was to be this way?"

Cadence could hardly believe she'd voiced the words but...she had. And she didn't regret it as all eyes swung her way. Shoulders back, she shrugged. "Sorry, but he did. And I'm sure he meant it."

Alexander eyed her. While his regard wasn't unkind it certainly wasn't soft. "And what do you know of Adlin MacLomain, lass?"

Most would've buckled beneath his heavy words, never mind his piercing regard.

But she'd dealt with all sorts when counseling. While Alexander certainly wasn't the bad guy he was most definitely a man who used his power to make people sway beneath his appraisal. The best way to deal with him was to give him absolute honesty, let the cards fall where they may.

"I know that he's dead," she said, thrilled to find her voice steady. "And I know he was convinced you were necessary in aiding this war. I cannot assume with any certainty that it meant aiding the MacLomains, but since you're here, it only makes sense."

Leslie, of all people, released a small gasp.

Tension fell.

But Cadence wasn't done.

"So Iosbail sent you and that's great," she said. "But how do *you* feel about it? Is this a war you're interested in fighting on behalf of the MacLomains?"

One brow slowly crept up as Alexander crossed his arms over his chest and rocked back on his heels. "Och, you surely descend from Iosbail, aye?"

Cadence had read the books. She knew a little bit about Iosbail. With a solid nod she said, "Yes, I do."

Alexander tilted back his head and studied her a moment more before he finally said, "Aye, 'tis a war I wish to offer aide on behalf of the MacLomains and not just because Iosbail asked but..." he looked at the others then back at her. "Because this clan has a great wealth of champions who believe in her cause."

All smiled.

Another round of drinks was served.

Tension lifted.

Alexander turned to another discussion.

Leslie muttered under her breath, "And I thought Ilisa was crazy. You're two peas in a friggin' pod."

Cadence grinned and wiped the sweat from her palms into the folds of her dress. "Hey, he was coming on strong. Someone needed to set things straight."

Leslie frowned and took a swig of ale. "Glad you thought that someone needed to be you."

When her sister walked away, she sighed. Their friendship had always wobbled some. Then again, so had all who called Leslie theirs. Her sister was a hard woman...or at least more so the past few years. Cadence knew it was because of her ex-boyfriend's, Patrick's untimely death. However, now that she was with Bradon, Leslie seemed to be breaking free from the death throes she'd been living under for far too long.

"Cadence."

Chills of anticipation raced through her as she turned.

Shamus.

What an odd thing to see the man from your dreams standing in front of you. About five inches taller than her with black hair and piercing blue eyes, he was everything she could've hoped for. Incredibly handsome, spirited, he held out his hand. "'Tis nice to finally see you like this."

Charmed by his lilt, she couldn't help but smile as she took his hand. "I couldn't agree more."

"So you've dreamt of me as well then?" he asked.

She nodded. "Yes."

His enigmatic eyes were far less intense than Malcolm's, his demeanor far less overwhelming and controlling. Cadence clenched her teeth. *Stop comparing them.* But even as Shamus met her eyes she wondered why they didn't rake down her ruthlessly as if he could see all that lay beneath. *Because he hasn't seen you naked, fool!*

"We disembark this eve," Shamus said. "Might we have some time alone beforehand?"

"I'd really like that," she said.

Shamus nodded, a smile on his face before he strode away. Cadence looked after him, adrift. What was she searching for? Had she hoped he'd pull her against him and whisper determined promises in her ear? Tempt her with a heavy erection that left her shaken and weak in the knees?

Cadence inhaled sharply. *Hell.* What was the matter with her?

The minute she turned, she knew.

Malcolm was making a slow walk by. He didn't say a word...only winked.

Eyes narrowed, she shook her head. She'd thought for sure that once she'd told him there was another man, better yet when that man had actually shown up, that she wouldn't have to worry about this anymore. Perhaps she didn't. Maybe that was just a friendly wink that said, "I see you found him, my best to you both."

But she knew better.

The wink had been more of a, "You think he's the one but you couldn't be more wrong."

Sheila joined her and nodded upstairs. "Mind if we talk?"

"Sure." Cadence was surprised when numbness settled over her. Was Sheila still interested in Malcolm? If so, she could tell her cousin with assurance that he was available...even if he'd acted otherwise the night before. Now Shamus was here and all was well. Why then, this feeling of trepidation?

Sheila led her up to one of many wall walks that lined the backside of the castle. With a sweeping view of the loch, it was far more secluded than the others. Only one guard stood watch and he kept to the opposite side, giving them privacy.

Face to the wind, her cousin said nothing for several long moments before she sighed. "I'm not sure I ever thanked you properly for being there for me when I left Jack."

Cadence leaned against the wall and studied her. "No need to thank me. I'm just glad you got away from him. The guy was toxic."

Sheila continued to stare at the loch, as if suddenly drowning in suppressed memories. "I know he was." She glanced at Cadence. "And I wanted to say sorry as well."

Before Cadence could respond, Sheila continued. "Sorry that he convinced me that you hit on him so long ago." She sighed. "To this day I have no idea how he manipulated me so fast. Sure, men always flocked to you but never once had you done something like that to me. We were best friends. I should've known better."

Old wounds opened but Cadence understood they were wounds not inflicted by Sheila but by the man who had molded her mind. She'd always known that. But Lord was she angry that he'd stolen so many years from her and her cousin. "I don't want you to worry about this anymore, Shay. He was sick. Still is. You were a victim. It's important that you remember that."

"Still," she argued, her sad eyes downcast. "I allowed it to go on too long and I was such a bitch to you."

Cadence squeezed her arm. "You didn't allow anything. You couldn't see what was happening." She offered a compassionate smile. "Stop blaming yourself for what happened and focus on letting it all go. You're having a lot of conflicting feelings and hiding them behind false happiness. While it's good to be happy don't force it, let it find you."

Sheila blinked away a tear and nodded, expression grim. "I think...no I know I was forcing it with Malcolm. I saw the happiness between McKayla and Colin, and then Leslie and Bradon. I wanted that." Her lips pulled down further. "I guess I assumed Malcolm had to be the guy to give it to me."

"Easy enough to understand when considering the magic and the MacLomain/Broun true love connection," Cadence allowed. "But you can well-understand that aiming for such a conflicted man, one who had just lost his wife, was more like searching out someone *you* could comfort." Her voice softened. "And by comforting him perhaps focus less on your own pain and the comfort you so desperately needed."

Her cousin nodded ever so slightly. "I guess I have been worrying about Malcolm a lot. Like you said, it's certainly kept me from looking at my own issues too closely."

"I know," she murmured and reeled Sheila in for a hug. "It's time to stop that, okay?"

Cadence didn't dare overthink the possible connection between Sheila and Grant. While Malcolm might be dealing with a lot, his brother was no doubt far more troubled. She could only hope that if Grant was meant for her cousin then they would somehow heal together. Otherwise, Sheila might be truly doomed.

Sheila held on tight and nodded. When she pulled away, her expression appeared a fraction stronger. "Enough about me. How are you doing with all this?" Now it was her turn to study Cadence. "Is your ring still hot as hell for Malcolm?"

Guarded, Cadence said, "If so how would that make you feel?"

A thin grin slid onto Sheila's face. "Honestly? I'd be okay with it. Malcolm and I had a good talk last night." Her tone softened. "He's only interested in friendship with me, Cadence."

Her heart skipped a beat. Not good. Her heart had no say.

Sheila watched her closely. "How does that make *you* feel?"

Ah, so she thought to turn the tables. Cadence offered a safe answer. "Frankly, I'm relieved. He has a lot of his own issues and I think it's too much for you right now."

Sheila crossed her arms over her chest and narrowed her eyes. "I see as clearly as everyone else how he looks at you, cousin. Have you asked him if your stone glows for him?"

"Popular question today," she muttered. "No, and I'm not going to." She peered at Sheila. "Are you upset that he..." She shook her head and trailed off.

"Seems interested in you?" Sheila shrugged. "At first but not anymore. Like I said, we talked. Malcolm and I are in a good place." She cocked her head. "But what's this thing between you and Shamus Flanagon? I definitely saw something."

Cadence again explained how she'd dreamt of him for so long. "It's so strange finally meeting him."

"Is he everything you thought he'd be?" Sheila wondered. "God knows he's handsome and beyond kind but..."

"But what?"

Sheila shrugged. "You tell me."

Cadence frowned. "Tell you what?"

"I don't know," Sheila said. "What I see between you and Shamus isn't nearly the same as what I see between you and Malcolm."

"Malcolm saw me naked, Shay, and he's been without a woman for too long." Cadence shook her head. "Not saying my body's that great but I think this is one of those cases where he's just determined to sample the goods."

Sheila laughed a little. "You must be talking about when he saved you from drowning. I saw you were wrapped up in half his plaid." Her chuckle faded. "Besides, you're in great shape. No doubt he noticed." She cocked her head. "I'm sure you turned him on but I'm seeing more than just that between you...a lot more."

Cadence shook her head. "Whatever it is, it'll pass. I'm interested in Shamus."

Sheila rolled her eyes. "So not only will we have a massive clan war but a battle between the king's right-hand man and a ruthless, vengeful highlander. It should be one hell of a show."

"No show at all. I've told Malcolm where I stand. He knows. And I expect he'll honor my wishes."

Sheila didn't look convinced. "Good luck as far as that goes. Malcolm typically follows his own set of rules."

"He'll see soon enough," she said.

"Be careful about that," Sheila murmured.

"About what?"

"I just don't see Malcolm being the sort to give up something he wants." Sheila shook her head. "Sure, he had no choice with the clan's leadership. That was a matter of honor. *You* fall into a whole different category."

"If honor is at stake, then I'd like to think he'll respect my wishes," she reiterated.

"Maybe he will," Sheila conceded, brows rising. "But you better be damn clear about what you want. If he senses for a moment that you want *him*, he'll act on it. And right now, you're definitely sending mixed signals."

Cadence pinched the bridge of her nose and sighed. "I'm trying not to he's just so …assertive. I'll talk to him again."

Sheila's lip curled up. "Sure, keep trying to reason with him."

She heard the humor in her cousin's voice but ignored it. "We should probably get back down " Cadence met Sheila's eyes. "You sure you're doing okay?"

"Yeah, stop worrying about me." She nodded. "I'm glad we talked. I wanted to clear the air a little before we embarked on this journey. Something tells me we're going to need each other more than ever."

Cadence nodded and swallowed hard. Of course they'd be traveling with the warriors. She wasn't such a fool that it hadn't occurred to her that both she and Sheila could provide invaluable information during this war. Still, she was human and everything was about to become a whole lot more dangerous. Yet Sheila was right. It was good that they'd talked. It already felt as though they'd closed some distance between them.

"Time to go, then?"

She nodded. "I suppose it must be."

Her cousin paused and eyed her. "Everything that's happened is an awful lot to process. Me, Leslie and McKayla have the benefit of having been here before. We've been in battle and some of us have already traveled across Scotland." She sighed, a small frown on her face. "It's pretty overwhelming. I know that you read

"She sure is," Leslie said.

Cadence couldn't help but add, "A darn good one too."

"Seriously," McKayla said. "I feel like a jerk staying behind. This isn't good."

Though she'd never done it before, Cadence cheated a little when she nodded at McKayla's belly. "Adlin MacLomain wants you to stay here. It's important that the clan has something positive to focus on as everyone else travels to war."

"Really?" McKayla looked at Cadence with her heart in her eyes.

"Yes," Cadence promised. Without doubt, her deities would back her in such a fib because after all, was it not for the greater good?

Sheila and Leslie looked at her then at McKayla, reassuring smiles on their faces.

"You see," Sheila said. "Even the guy who created this clan knows it's for the best."

Leslie nodded.

Cadence smiled and nodded once more.

Encouraged, McKayla looked at them. "All right then."

All grinned, happy to see McKayla cheered up.

Cadence refused to feel guilty for her lie…because after all, it wasn't really a lie, was it? Though Adlin hadn't spoken to her *surely* he would see the right of her speaking on his behalf.

"Though I'm still new at the whole empath ability thing, I know it'll come in handy," Leslie said.

"And I guess I can see things as or before they happen," Sheila contributed. "That's pretty helpful."

"I'll tell Colin the minute Adlin MacLomain speaks to me, which I'm sure will help our men steer clear of trouble," Cadence added with a self-assured nod. Then as an afterthought murmured, "I mean *your* men."

"They're all *our* men so I'm glad to hear it." McKayla smiled as she looked at them. "Thank you."

"No need to thank us," Leslie said. "We're in this together."

"No doubt about it," Sheila said.

Cadence smiled and joined in a group hug across the table.

They *were* in it together.

No sooner had they pulled apart when a servant whispered in McKayla's ear. Though it seemed her eyes watered for a second her cousin nodded and stood. "I've made sure you all were provided with warm clothes and essentials. You'll be leaving sooner than expected."

Cadence looked at her sister then at her cousins as they stood.

All nodded and once more embraced.

Though Cadence could admit to being nervous about what lay ahead, she was also eager to discover what lay north. Because whatever it was had to do with the dreams she'd had of Shamus. Sure it was dangerous. Regardless.

Even as she walked out the front doors of the MacLomain castle, she felt pumped. Determined to chat with Shamus, she eyed the courtyard as she descended the stairs. No sign of him. She'd just reached the bottom when Malcolm appeared.

He held out his hand. "Come, lass. We leave soon and I want to show you a few things first."

She could only imagine what! Though she shook her head, he pulled her after him into the armory. Cadence took a few long, steadying breaths. Not because of the endless weapons lining the walls but because she was determined to listen to Sheila. Malcolm would *not* think she desired him because she didn't...for the most part.

"I know you're traveling with us and want you to be as prepared as possible," he said, studying a wall of daggers. His doubtful eyes went to hers. "Have you ever used a weapon then?"

Cadence couldn't help but chuckle as she shook her head. "That's a negative. Not a real big need for them in my social circles. But I do know a little because of my writing...and reading."

"Well, 'tis time you learn more, the basics. Though 'tis my intention to protect you anything can happen and I dinnae think a lass should be without a blade."

She couldn't argue with that. No doubt he referred to the harsh fate that could befall a woman in this day and age without a means to defend herself. As if he read her mind he said, "I heard that you visited with yesterday's victims this morn." Though his eyes stayed on the daggers, she sensed his concern. "How are they?"

She sighed. "I spent a few hours with them but it's going to take time."

"They will be well-cared for and now have a home here," he said. "As long as they stay with the MacLomains, such harm will never again befall them."

Cadence was touched by the emotion, the vehemence, in his assurance. What had happened to them truly bothered him. How awful it must have been to come upon them after the damage was already done.

His voice grew soft. "'Tis a heavy weight you carry speaking with them about such. Are you well, lass?"

She nodded, again warmed by his concern. "Far better than them to be sure...I've learned to separate myself enough to be helpful without letting it overly affect my emotions."

"Overly," he murmured. "But some, aye?"

"Yes, some," she whispered.

Malcolm didn't question further. Instead, he removed a small dagger from the wall. "I will try to work with you more as we travel but for now I can teach you some basics. Here, hold this, become familiar with its weight." He handed it to her hilt first then grabbed another. "How you stand is verra important."

He turned to the side. "Rest your weight evenly on the ball of each foot." Malcolm made a motion with his head. "Do as I do."

So she did.

"Front knee slightly bent, elbows at your side and hands up for protection." He touched one of her hands. "This is what you cut with." Then he touched the other. "This is how you control your enemy's weapon hand." He lowered his chin. "Chin down to protect your neck."

"You dinnae want to engage the enemy and evade only to re-engage again," he continued. "If possible, you want to eliminate the threat and dislodge the dagger from his hand."

Cadence nodded. It was hard to imagine trying to do such a thing to a trained warrior, especially one as large as Malcolm, but she'd give it her best shot.

"Use your free hand to block while coming in close and thrusting." He executed the moves with precision then set aside his blade to stand behind her. "Now you do it."

With a quick block and thrust, she did what he said.

"Nay." His foot touched the back of one of hers. "Keep on the balls of your feet." He touched one arm then the other and had her repeat the move. It took all the focus she had to ignore the feel of him behind her and do as he asked. Eventually, it seemed he was satisfied because he nodded, stepped away, and then took her wrist. "While you block with one hand you cut here on the enemy's wrist." He made a fast slice across her tendon then pointed at two other spots. "Then here and here on his arm. If you do as I say, he willnae be able to grasp his blade any longer."

Cadence again nodded. "Okay, got it." She pointed at all three spots on her arm. "Here, here and here."

He nodded. "But your fight doesnae end there, lass."

"No, I suppose at that point I'll run."

"Aye, but he'll be faster." Malcolm put his dagger just beneath his chin. "You slice your blade up through the hollow cavity here to finish the job."

"Hell," she muttered. "I don't know if I could do that."

"Do you think those women yesterday would have done it if they'd had half the chance?"

"Good point." She pursed her lips and again tested the weight of the blade. "I can only hope I don't end up in such a position."

Malcolm frowned and returned their blades to the wall. Clearly the thought didn't sit well with him. "I'll make sure several daggers are provisioned for you."

Her eyes widened when he removed a long sword from another wall. "Wow!"

With a simple black hilt, he unsheathed it from its case and eyed the blade. "'Tis well sharpened now."

"I'll take your word for it," she said. Long and lethal, the sword suited Malcolm well.

With a quick motion, he re-sheathed it then attached it to his back; his intense eyes once more on her as he moved closer...far too close. "Have you any questions about what I taught you, lass?"

She shook her head, unable to look away, her voice softer than intended. "No. Thank you."

"I dinnae want you hurt," he said, voice just as soft. "And it seems no other is teaching you, not even your Irishman."

Right, Shamus. She licked her lips, far too aware of the heat fluctuating between them. "I doubt he knows whether or not I can use a dagger."

"Has he asked then?" Malcolm's eyes lowered to her lips. "'Twould be amongst the first things I would ask if I met the lass of my dreams and she was going off to war with me."

"Ah, there you are sister," Leslie said, poking her head in. "Time to change and get packed up. It's almost time to go."

Cadence blinked and stepped away from Malcolm. "Okay...yeah, sure." Eyes still on him she said, "Again, thank you. I really appreciate this."

Malcolm only nodded as they left.

"What was that all about," Leslie asked.

"He was teaching me how to use a dagger."

"Nice." Leslie nodded. "Ilisa taught me and as it turned out I had to use one. Scary stuff but good to have some knowledge of it."

With nothing but a few satchels, they were soon dressed to travel and made their way back to the courtyard. Astride their horses, Alexander, Shamus and Malcolm approached. She would've thought Malcolm would be sticking with his cousins but apparently not.

Her gaze flittered between Shamus and Malcolm. Both were sexy as hell. The MacLomain rode the same black mount he'd been on the day before and Shamus rode a buckskin colored horse. Yet where Shamus wore a wide grin, the MacLomain's demeanor was as serious as ever. And where Shamus made a point of meeting her gaze, Malcolm's eyes took a slow stroll over her face then right down her body.

Remembering Sheila's advice about not giving him an inch, she did her best to ignore him.

It was the king who took precedence as he came alongside. "I was told you dinnae know how to ride a horse."

Cadence shook her head and eyed Shamus, assuming she'd ride with him.

Alexander held down his hand. "Extra horses will be brought. You will learn how to ride along the way. Until then, ride with me."

Seriously? It was on her tongue to say no until she saw the look on Colin's face as he came alongside Alexander. One didn't say no to a king apparently.

She nodded.

With a quick lean and grab, Alexander pulled her up. Cadence held on tight when he swung the horse fast then led the way over the drawbridge.

When she glanced back it was to hoots and hollers and McKayla waving goodbye,

Quickly and without preamble, they were on their way. Well-armored, MacLomains were everywhere. In front, in back, beside, Scotsmen with nothing but war on their faces and weapons strapped to their bodies. Carts with their peddlers rambled alongside.

"'Tis a difficult time of year for war," Alexander murmured. He wrapped a fur over her shoulders. "Cold days, even colder nights, harsh weather. So I cannae help but wonder whose tent will shelter you in the eve's."

Was the king hitting on her? Sure, he was a beautiful man but…really? She glanced over her shoulder and arched a brow.

Understanding the question in her eyes, his lips pulled down and he shook his head. "Nay, 'tis not what you think. Only one lass will ever hold my heart." His gaze fell to Malcolm and Shamus who now rode ahead. "The lads need to keep their heads about them with what is to come. Distractions such as you can mean the difference between life and death."

Cadence couldn't help but frown as she looked at them. "Actually, I intended to sleep in my own tent. I don't need a man to keep me warm."

"You dinnae truly ken a highland winter, lass. Furs alone willnae fight the frigid cold," he said. "Shamus told me that he knows of you and you of him. I expect 'tis half the reason we are here. Yet I see how you look at the other."

Look at the other? She'd been purposely trying to *not* do that. "You don't see anything," she assured. "Malcolm saved my life. I consider him a friend. That's it."

"Nay, that MacLomain doesnae make friends of lasses such as you," Alexander said. "Now that other one, *she* is a friend to him."

Cadence realized Alexander was looking at Sheila who rode alongside Leslie and Bradon.

No doubt, the king had a good eye. Regardless. "Well, I haven't known Malcolm as long as she has. I'd like to think we'll become friends."

Alexander shook his head. "Mayhap if the circumstances are right."

She again glanced over her shoulder. "Is this your way of championing Shamus? You really don't have to you know."

Steely gray eyes met hers. "So you say."

This conversation seemed almost a ghost of the one she'd had with Sheila earlier. Not intimidated in the least by Alexander, she was blunt. "Ah, so you want me in Shamus's tent so that Malcolm knows I'm off limits."

"If you and he have this connection of love, 'twould be wise, would it not?"

Probably. Cadence twirled the ring on her finger, not particularly in the mood to bring up its dynamics, especially considering Shamus wasn't a MacLomain. Yet despite the fact Alexander walked a thin line with her, she felt comfortable with him. Why, she couldn't be sure. There was something about his forthrightness that she appreciated. Like her, he was always aware of problems brewing around him and quick to tackle them.

"You'd make a good therapist," she muttered.

When his brows lowered in question she said, "You're eager to help people work through their mental issues."

He released a small chuckle. "'Tis the best way to be when a laird, never mind a king. Anything to keep the peace betwixt warring clans."

Cadence chuckled as well. "I suppose all battles start in the mind."

"You've both a bold and soft way about you, lass," Alexander said. "While I can appreciate both, 'twill be your boldness that keeps those two men from warring with one another. Lay your claim so there isnae question."

"I understand where you're coming from, I really do," she said. "But in my day and age, a girl doesn't hop into bed with a guy she's only just met, even if she's dreamt of him."

"I didnae say you need share Shamus's bed, only his tent."

Cadence sighed. Alexander was right. For that matter, so was Sheila. If she made clear she was interested in Shamus from the start, Malcolm *would* back off. That, no doubt, would eliminate a lot of confusion and tension.

"Greetings, King Alexander," Ilisa said, pulling her horse alongside. "I'm Ilisa MacLomain, cousin to our laird, Colin."

Alexander greeted her.

Weapons scattered over her body, trousers on and short red hair gleaming in the sunlight, Ilisa looked amazing. Cadence hadn't realized the night before how beautiful she actually was. Instead of saying good morning to Cadence, she leaned closer to Alexander and nodded at Shamus. "Now who be that strapping lad?"

Alexander looked from Ilisa to Shamus, eyes narrowed. "That is my first-in-command, Shamus Flanagon."

"Och, so an Irish laddie then!" she exclaimed, a predatory gleam in her interested eyes.

Before Alexander could respond, Ilisa's horse lurched forward and she fell in beside Shamus, a wide smile on her animated face.

"It seems you might have a bigger problem than you thought," Cadence said.

"Bloody hell," Alexander muttered. "Mayhap I do."

Chapter Six

Arms crossed over his chest, Malcolm leaned back against a tree, stretched out his legs and watched her make a mess of things. Euphemia crouched, handed him a flagon of whiskey and shook her head at Cadence. "You really should help the lass, aye?"

"Nay, let the Irishman if he's so inclined."

Euphemia twisted her thin lips. "If 'tis to be a battle betwixt you and Shamus, 'twould do ye no harm to assist her. Lassies like such things."

"She doesnae need to string a tent," Malcolm said. "Mine is tied off well and good. And there's room enough for two."

"I suppose I better help her then," Sheila muttered when she returned with an armful of sticks. She glanced at Malcolm. "Why aren't you?"

"Because he's stubborn." Euphemia joined Sheila. "And a bloody blackguard to boot."

Mayhap he was. Mayhap he wasn't.

Since the moment they'd dismounted, Cadence had done nothing but flirt with the Irishman. And now it seemed she had competition from Ilisa. Why should he get involved in any of that? There were bigger things to worry over than the affections of a lass whose interests lie elsewhere.

"'Twill work if you tie it here, m'lady," Euphemia said, pointing up.

"Or even here." Sheila pointed at another area.

"I'll just tie it off here," Cadence said, standing on her tip toes.

Malcolm eyed the wobbly root she'd decided to perch on and sighed. When, as he knew she would, Cadence teetered then toppled over, he was there to catch her. Overly aware of the desire fluctuating between them, he carefully set her aside.

Her bonnie green eyes met his, her cheeks aflame. "Thanks."

Malcolm said nothing but set to getting her tent strung correctly.

"Sheila's sharing it with me," she provided.

Still he said nothing. If she said it to appease him, it didn't. He wanted Cadence in *his* tent.

But bloody hell if he'd say as much.

In no time, he had it erected properly.

The sun had nearly set and a cold wind whipped. It would be a good eve for body heat. Though they were still a day's ride from the MacLomain border, he knew whores would soon meander through the traveling war party. Mayhap it'd be best to enjoy one of them so he could remain focused on what was most important.

The upcoming war.

"Thank you again, Malcolm," Cadence said to his back as he grabbed his bow and arrows. Until those whores joined them, hunting some game would help keep him preoccupied. Again, he didn't bother giving her a response as he stalked away.

All bloody day he'd watched her ride with Alexander. He knew the man didn't desire her but that she'd rode with him put a bitter taste in Malcolm's mouth. Cadence was a Broun under the MacLomain's care. She *should* have ridden with a MacLomain. To make matters worse, he knew what the king was about. He spoke for his Irishman. If not for Ilisa creating her own brand of entertainment, Malcolm knew precisely where Cadence would have been sleeping.

Once before he'd been down this path with a lass, and had no desire to make the same mistake again. Granted his wife, Nessa, had been with his cousin prior, but she'd still played the flirt and ultimately pitted the two of them against one another. Aye, he remained upset with Colin, but he was no fool.

"Might I hunt with you, cousin?"

He nodded at Bradon who fell in beside him as he continued through the forest.

"Me thinks you're less about the hunt and more about the kill, aye?" Bradon said.

"I dinnae see anything good in having so many lasses along," Malcolm muttered. "'Twill be a vicious and drawn out war. 'Tis no place for them."

"I couldnae keep Leslie from coming if I tried." Bradon's grin dropped almost as fast as it appeared. "And while I worry, remember cousin that we had two of these lasses along with us last time."

"Aye, but this beast is of a different nature and well you know it."

77

Bradon nodded. "But no doubt a beast better defeated with what the Broun cousins have to offer."

"Time will tell how much they can truly contribute especially when the battling begins."

A small movement caught his attention.

Malcolm crouched, put a finger to his lips and nodded into the forest.

A small buck stood unmoving, barely discernible despite the thinning foliage.

Bradon crouched. Both remained silent.

Careful, ever so slowly, Malcolm cocked his bow and aimed.

Suddenly, Bradon put a hand on his arm, shook his head and pointed to the sword at his side. The Celtic symbols carved into it glowed softly. The blade had been given to Bradon when they'd traveled back in time to the Stewart clan. Though given to him by Adlin MacLomain and forged beneath the blood moon, Malcolm's Ma had sensed far more ancient magic in it. Frowning, he lowered the bow and arrow.

Had the buck vanished? He'd sensed no movement. Malcolm blinked several times and peered into the dusk. Something *was* moving…but it was no buck.

"Bloody hell," Bradon whispered.

Both slowly stood as a little old woman hobbled through the trees in their direction. Whoever she was, great magic was hers. Stooped over, frail boned, she didn't stop until she was in front of them. Peering up, she studied them for several moments before her eyes went to Bradon's blade. "'Tis good ye've got it by yer side, laddie."

Irish. Her accent was thicker than most before she switched to Gaelic. "Do ye both know who I am then?"

Malcolm stood up a little straighter. It couldn't be. But he knew it was.

"Fionn Mac Cumhail," he murmured and lowered his head in respect. Bradon did the same. Sometimes seen as an old woman, sometimes a fierce warrior, he, she, was the ancient Celtic god who oversaw the making of the original three Claddagh rings. Known best, however, for being one with the animals and trees of the forest.

"Nay, look me in the eyes, lads, for ye are my equals."

This time when they looked the old woman was gone. In her place stood a golden warrior even taller than them. The god had approached them in a less intimidating form.

Before either MacLomain could speak, Fionn continued. "Ye must unseal the oak. 'Tis unnatural for her to be barred so."

The oak? Malcolm shook his head.

Bradon seemed to understand and said softly, "The baby oak on the mountain that Coira saved from the MacLeod's."

"Aye." Fionn nodded. A degu jumped on his shoulder. The critter eyed them. Ghostly warriors seemed to appear then disappear behind the god.

"I know my Ma cast a spell of protection over the area," Malcolm said. "'Twill be impossible to get through."

"And even if we managed to," Bradon said. "Would that not once more leave the tree vulnerable to the MacLeod's?"

"They cannae go near that tree without the aid of the dragon," Fionn said, resting his hand on the head of a great, black wolf that now sat by his side.

"A dragon held prisoner by our enemies," Malcolm reminded.

"They cannae force the lass to do what she doesnae want to do," Fionn said. He nodded at the wolf. Malcolm froze when the beast came and sat next to him. He'd never seen one so large or in this part of Scotland.

Before Malcolm could question why the wolf sat next to him, the god said, "You belong to one another now. Name him what you will."

What? Malcolm shifted, uncomfortable. He didn't want a wolf but wasn't about to argue with Fionn.

"Uncage the tree," Fionn said once more and turned away. White fog shifted and crawled along the ground, twirling around the Celtic deity. When next he spoke, his form had returned to that of an old woman. "One more thing, Malcolm MacLomain." Her voice grew as distant as her form but the words were clear. "You must ignite the glow of your mark to harness the power of her ring."

As quickly as he'd appeared, Fionn vanished, his white fog dissipating into the trees.

Neither he nor his cousin said anything for several long moments.

It almost felt as though they'd been under a spell

But the wolf remained.

"I cannae say I'm much in the mood to hunt anymore," Bradon finally said.

Malcolm shook his head and frowned at the animal beside him. Golden eyes much like his gazed back before the wolf turned toward their encampment and waited. "I didnae even think to ask him about Ma and Da. Surely such a god would know if my parents live."

The truth was he'd been keeping that grief well-hidden.

"'Tis no small thing that we just spoke with a deity, cousin," Bradon said. "And 'tis no fault of your own that you didnae think of Coira and William. But mayhap there is something to Fionn's request. I feel it as surely as I did my need for Leslie upon meeting her."

Malcolm started back the way they'd come, ignoring the wolf that trotted alongside. "Without doubt there is. At least part of it."

"Ah, you dinnae want anything to do with that last part, aye?" Bradon chuckled. "Or mayhap you do but your pride stands in the way."

Pride, his arse. He'd not battle it out with Shamus. If Cadence wanted the Irishman, she could have him.

Naturally, Bradon continued. "Are you sure then that 'tis not Sheila's ring that glows?"

If only. That would be so much easier. But he couldn't force a desire that wasn't there. "Nay, it doesnae."

Bradon frowned. "'Tis sad that. However, I cannae say I dislike Cadence. I thought her trouble when I met her in the twenty-first century but I was wrong." He shook his head. "Well, at least not the particular brand of trouble I thought she'd be."

"She's trouble enough," he said.

"No matter. If her ring's stone shines for you there is only one way I know of to ignite the glow between your mark and the stone as Fionn requested," Bradon said.

"Was it not the blood moon that ignited you and Leslie's?"

But Malcolm knew better and his cousin said as much.

"Nay, that blood moon plus the wizards and Fionn had to do with my blade. 'Twas the coupling that created the glow of the ring and my mark. And might I remind you, 'twas the glow of both that created the magic that saved us from Keir Hamilton and Colin MacLeod," Bradon said. "'Tis verra important to be able to harness such power."

"So I have to find a way to lay with the lass whether or not she'll have me," Malcolm grumbled.

"It doesnae need to sound or be so forced as that." Bradon shook his head. "I saw you two at the castle. 'Twill be no hardship on the lass if you take her. While you seemed so determined last eve, you've been nothing but a brooding beast all day. Worse than usual, might I add."

"Irishman," Malcolm muttered.

"Need not be an issue," Bradon said. "Unless you let him be."

When Malcolm's frown deepened, Bradon's words grew soft. "She's not Nessa, cousin. You dinnae seek a lass who desires another."

"Och, but I do."

Bradon shook his head. "Have you even kissed the lass, then?"

Malcolm ground his jaw. A thousand times in his mind since he'd met her. Little good that did him though. Honestly, why would he once more pursue a woman with eyes for another? He didn't want the heartbreak all over again.

Small fires burned brightly through the trees as they approached.

They'd just entered the first small clearing when several clansmen stood, weapons drawn. It took him a moment to realize the wolf was still by his side. He shook his head and made a motion with his hand. "Lower your swords. The beast is with me."

Not one man lowered their weapon.

The Broun lasses, Ilisa, Shamus and Alexander were equally wide-eyed.

Colin had just emerged on the opposite side of the fire, arms crossed over his chest as he eyed the animal. "Explain, cousin."

"As I live and breathe, 'twas a gift from the god, Fionn Mac Cumhail," Bradon said.

Malcolm didn't bother offering any such explanation, only narrowed his eyes at the chieftain.

Colin's gaze remained not on the wolf but Malcolm. "Is it true then?"

Sarcasm nearly slipped from his tongue but Malcolm would honor his Da's wishes that their clan not see dissention between him and Colin. "Aye, 'tis true."

The laird waited another long moment before he nodded and his men warily lowered their weapons. "It cannae remain so close to the tents. 'Tis unsettling."

Malcolm eyed the wolf. How was he to make it obey? It was unbroken, wild. Thankfully, it was as easy as nodding his head toward the forest. Though clearly not impressed with the request, it skulked into the night, blending in as though it had never been there to begin with.

All continued to stare into the forest as Malcolm and Bradon joined them around the fire. Meat roasted and Colin tossed them skins of whiskey as they sat.

"Bloody hell, cousins." Ilisa shook her head. "Ye go off for a good hunt and come back with a mighty beastie."

Bradon pulled Leslie close and nodded. "'Twas a hell of an experience."

Cadence's eyes were still round as saucers as she stared at Malcolm.

Determined to push past his reservations, he stared right back.

"I have seen more than most men but I dinnae think I've ever seen anything quite like a wolf obeying a man as that one just did you," Alexander said.

Malcolm was surprised to feel a spark of pride.

"Took to him right off." Bradon grinned and slapped Malcolm on the shoulder.

"Awesome," Leslie said.

"No doubt." Sheila shook her head and chuckled. "Smart wolf."

"Funny," Leslie said and looked at Cadence. "Reminds me of a much larger version of Apollo. Sure he was a mutt but remember our pup growing up?"

"How could I forget him," she murmured.

Malcolm wondered at the faraway look in her eyes.

"Besides offering up one hell of a watch dog, what else did Fionn Mac Cumhail say?" Colin said.

Bradon shared most of the details about their encounter with the god, leaving off the last part about Malcolm needing to sleep with Cadence. "I think 'tis a journey for few. 'Twill not detour those who go but a day or two."

Colin thought about it briefly before nodding. "I dinnae ken the reason for it but I have full faith in the god whom delivered such a message."

"I will go." Malcolm looked at Cadence. "But I wish the voice of Adlin MacLomain on this venture." Then he looked at Leslie. "And she who saw the dragon through the baby oak's leaves."

Bradon nodded. "Aye, and I will go as well."

"You are amongst my best warriors and wizards." Colin sighed but obviously agreed in that his cousin and brother had received the message.

"I would like to go along as well," Shamus said. "Of the Irish, I might be of help if the god appears again."

Malcolm narrowed his eyes.

"Aye, me as well," Ilisa said.

When Colin looked at her curiously his cousin shrugged, eyes wicked. "It would do my heart good to see the baby oak again. Besides, I'm known to be helpful when least expected."

Colin considered.

"We willnae be gone long," Malcolm said.

Shamus eyed Malcolm but not overly long. While the Irishman's gaze might've flickered to Cadence they just as easily went to Ilisa. But that didn't mean a damned thing if his Broun truly wanted the man.

"Fine then," Colin said at last and looked at the six of them. "You will travel early then meet us when finished."

All nodded save Cadence. Though she didn't look displeased neither did she appear entirely thrilled. Either way, this course of action would be taken...for the safety of his clan if nothing else.

Now either he'd cater to his pride and leave her be or he'd take what he truly wanted and have access to the magic Bradon and Leslie had found. He came to a swift decision. The risk of not finding out if they were a match was foolhardy if it could save lives.

But it couldn't hurt to test the waters.

So he stood and held out his hand to Cadence. "Come lass, I wish to show you something."

Chapter Seven

Cadence looked up at Malcolm and shook her head.

No way was she going anywhere with him when he had that particular look on his face. It was as if he'd come to some sort of decision and any hope she had of keeping him at bay had vanished. It was disconcerting to watch him arrive out of the darkness with that massive wolf by his side. The two were a ferocious team.

Now he wanted her to go back that way with him?

Yeah right.

She shook her head again when he didn't move. Clearly that didn't work for him because he stepped forward and scooped her up. *Sonofabitch.* "Put me down, Malcolm."

There's no way she'd get hysterical, no way would she raise her voice.

When she looked at her sister, Leslie only shook her head and shrugged. Apparently she saw no hope for him being dissuaded. Cadence ground her teeth. "Fine, put me down and I'll walk with you."

"You had your chance," he muttered and strode past the campfires out into the blackness.

"Don't think I won't smack you," she said.

"If you intended such you would have done so already."

Not one to hit, she certainly wasn't above shoving. So she arched her body and pushed away.

"Nay, lass," he grumbled. But he let her slide down.

Hell was he tall and hard and…way too strong.

"I should have done this sooner," he said so softly she barely heard. Before she could shove him away he wrapped one muscled arm around her lower back, yanked her against him and firmly grabbed the back of her head.

She couldn't get away if she wanted to.

When his lips closed over hers, Cadence froze. Not fazed in the least by her lack of response, he was gentle at first, as if sampling something he'd tried hard to stay away from. It almost seemed for a moment that he feared. Yet as his lips warmed against hers, something else slowly surfaced. She felt it in the shift of his body, in the way his fingers spanned the back of her head.

As the tip of his tongue swept feather-light over her closed lips, they both began to tremble.

Oh no…no, *no.*

Not this man. Not now.

But she couldn't stop her body's response if she tried. Sinking, drowning, her eyes drifted shut and her lips quivered against his. When his teeth grazed and tenderly pulled at her lower lip, the last of her breath escaped. Not one to turn from opportunity, he closed his lips more securely over hers and ever so surely, opened her mouth to his.

Now there was no turning back.

In no rush, confident, his lips didn't overwhelm but slanted, roamed, and all but tenderized. Already lost beneath his sensual exploration, everything save the push, pull and direction of his desire, vanished. Time fell away as she molded, caressed and matched the rhythm that he set.

When his tongue finally made its first sweep into her mouth, she moaned.

Not a soft, breathy moan but a deep, pleasured sound that he all but devoured.

Holding on for dear life, she wrapped her arms over his shoulders and ran her fingers over the hard contours of his neck. What started as a gentle, tentative kiss turned fiery and passionate, blazing and relentless in its consumption of the soul. And that's exactly what it felt like. A slow stroll down into the deep recesses of all she'd tucked away about who she was. He didn't define her with the way he kissed her but introduced her to a sensual creature she'd never much paid attention to.

When he lifted and walked her back against a tree, Cadence didn't fight him.

Cold wind blew through the dark night and made the burning heat of his large body all that much more delicious and profound. Wrapping, possessive, his tongue twisted with hers, searching out, seeking, and demanding she give all. She was so completely lost in what he was making her feel that even his lick on her leg didn't bother her…until it did.

How the hell did he lick her leg?

Torn from oblivion, she pulled her lips away and looked down.

"Holy crap!" she squealed.

His big black wolf sat beside them, staring up in interest.

Malcolm frowned at the wolf. "Nay, off with you, lad."

Cadence liked dogs but this was no dog and it intimidated the heck out of her. Seriously, it was as tall as a Great Dane! No average wolf at all.

"Don't you dare put me down, Malcolm," she said, truly frightened.

Heavy erection evident against her belly, she heard the humor in his voice when he said, "Oh no, lass. I'll keep you safe right here."

It was so dark that she could barely make out his face. What she wouldn't do to see his eyes right now because she knew without doubt there was a glint in them that would make her smile. But then, she was smiling anyway.

"We can't keep on this way with the wolf watching," she murmured.

Now she knew he scowled when he said, "'Tis just a beastie. It doesnae care what we do."

"Okay, let me rephrase," she said. "*I* can't keep on this way with the wolf watching."

"Can you then without the wolf watching?" he said softly.

"No, not tonight." Truth told, she was so aroused it hurt. Yet she sensed it was better to slow things down. He didn't know how fragile he really was and sleeping with her right now wasn't the right course of action. "We should get back."

He hesitated, no doubt battling internally, before he swung her into his arms.

"No, Malcolm. I need to *walk* back."

It wasn't easy stepping away when he set her down. She could all but feel the heaviness of disappointment settling over him. Yet it had to be this way.

When they returned, all were chatting and eating. Though a few nodded when they sat and rejoined the conversation, none said a word about why they'd left. Shamus winked at her but soon turned his attention back to Ilisa. There was no way to know why she'd dreamt of him but she was starting to have her reservations.

Though their faces were different there was a remarkable similarity between her and Malcolm's cousin. They were both tall with red hair. Both had the same confrontational spirit, even if Ilisa's was a tad more devious.

Still. It was odd to think of all the dreams.

But had they ever been sensual or had they simply seemed that way?

Cadence said no when Malcolm offered her a skin of whiskey. Not that it was all that terrible. She just didn't want to go there right now.

Light conversation continued. As light as it could be considering what lay ahead. When Sheila looked her way and chatted alongside the rest, there was no distress in her gaze. Whatever had happened between Sheila and Malcolm at the castle had set what had been between them at ease. And it seemed their conversation had helped as well based on the occasional smile her cousin shot her way.

Eventually, Bradon looked at Malcolm. "We leave even earlier than the rest on the morn." He pulled Leslie up as he stood, his gaze encompassing Cadence too. "Rest well, aye?"

Malcolm had said next to nothing the past hour or so, his eyes mostly on the fire. He nodded. "Aye, rest well, cousin."

Cadence looked at Sheila as she stood. "Are you okay sleeping alone?"

Not surprised by her question, her cousin nodded. "Yeah, I'm good."

She looked hard at Sheila to be sure but it appeared she meant it.

Then Cadence made a point of looking at Alexander before she nodded to the rest. "Goodnight."

All either nodded or said goodnight but she didn't stick around long.

Instead, she crawled into Malcolm's tent.

Her heart thundered as she lay down on his plaid. She closed her eyes and inhaled deeply. It smelled like him, woodsy and masculine.

Alexander, the king, had requested that she not play games. He'd requested she make her intentions clear…so she had. Just not with the man he might've hoped she made them clear *with*. Could she have still slept alone? Of course. But she didn't want another day to go by with Malcolm or Shamus wondering where her interests lie. Not only that but she knew Malcolm didn't deserve a woman toying with his emotions.

They'd kissed.

And it had been out-of-this-world incredible.

That, at the very least, was worth paying attention to.

Yet now she was in a position that meant she'd have to be stronger mentally than she'd ever been. Exploring this thing with Malcolm would take a precarious amount of balance. Though Sheila might've said he took what he wanted, Cadence knew better. After what he'd been through, she suspected he'd turn from this before he'd dive headfirst. Sure, he'd have sex with her but his body wasn't what was at stake.

Nope, it was his heart.

True, she had little if no experience when dealing with heartbroken men but she *did* with heartbroken women. Sheila might better understand a manipulated mind, but Cadence better understood an unhealed heart. While Malcolm's mind might've suffered because of what happened with Nessa, his mind was not broken. No, *that* was intact, perhaps overly so. But a man like him didn't realize that there was more to who he was than just his mind and will.

Malcolm didn't join her right away but he remained as silent around the campfire once she left as he had when she'd sat by his side. When at last all grew quiet and he entered, her heart thumped all that much harder.

It seemed he knew she was awake because his voice was low and throaty when he sat next to her and spoke into the darkness. "You make a bold statement, lass."

"We're not going to have sex, Malcolm." She'd meant the words to be soft and sure, instead they'd come out as a hoarse whisper.

A candle flickered to life but he didn't look at her. "'Twas foolhardy to come into my tent otherwise."

It was impossible to tear her gaze away when he slowly removed his plaid then pulled his tunic over his head. Long muscles rippled up his back then down his arms. Her eyes traveled over his broad shoulders, captured by the way his rich black hair swept his bronzed skin. He remained silent when his hand touched her thigh. Material might bar his touch but still she felt the all-encompassing warmth…the possession.

"Spread your legs."

She shook her head. "Like I said—"

His eyes met hers, their golden depths flaring in the candlelight when his voice cut off hers. "Spread your legs, lass."

When she made to argue again, his hand flew up and cupped between her legs. Words died on her lips when he pressed the heel of his palm deep and curled a well-aimed finger over her clitoris.

She arched. Oh *hell*!

So calm it was frightening he said, "I willnae take what you are not willing to give but I will take…"

Even as she shook her head no, he turned and ran his free hand along her leg while kneading with the hand currently holding her prisoner. All the while, he watched her face, interested in exactly what touch offered the most response.

"Blow out the candle," she gasped when he made a rather creative swirl with his finger.

He shook his head slowly and whispered. "Nay, no darkness this time."

Malcolm grabbed her hand when it curled against his side. As the candlelight flickered over the tent skin so too did his lips over the delicate, thin skin of the underside of her wrist. His hot, wet tongue laved then salved before he paused over a pulsing vein. His teeth scraped lightly before he sucked while simultaneously kneading and rolling his fingers between her legs. Cadence's jaw quivered so viciously that she clamped her gaping mouth shut.

She'd meant this to be an opportunity that they talked not…*this*.

Sensing her weakness, or perhaps even her well-laid intentions, he peppered kisses into her open palm. As if he cherished each and every finger, his lips traveled up first one then the next.

Meanwhile, his free hand snaked up her thigh, testing and measuring the flesh until he hovered, skin dusting skin, on an area that was way beyond throbbing. When he pulled her finger into his mouth, he ran the finger beneath her skirts down her center, not rough, but gentle, teasing.

She leaned against the horse and watched the others all but vanish into the mountainside. "Where are we?"

"At one of the original Defiances and where the oak is located," Malcolm said. "The Defiance is inside the cave." He looked upward. "The tree up yonder."

"We will join you, cousin." Ilisa came alongside with Shamus. "This thing needs to be looked at from all angles."

Malcolm ground his jaw and shook his head. "Nay, Cadence and I will go alone."

Able to finally stand without assistance, Cadence put her hand on his chest, not to push him away but because she was grateful for his aide. "I'm good now, thanks."

"The more eyes the better." Ilisa frowned. "We will join you."

Cadence was startled when Malcolm ground back, "Nay!"

Now Shamus frowned as he looked from Cadence to Malcolm. "What is your problem with us coming with you, friend?"

Ilisa shook her head. "Not a thing. He but wishes time alone with his lass."

Though she almost said she wasn't Malcolm's lass, Cadence bit her tongue. She'd sent a very clear message to all when she'd crawled into his tent the night before. Still. Why was he being so possessive now? There was no need.

So she shook her head at Ilisa. "Would you mind catching up with us in a bit?"

Ilisa paused a moment before she finally nodded and turned away, grabbing a few more daggers from her horse.

Shamus, however, looked at Cadence. "Are you sure, lass?"

"Aye," Malcolm said with a frown as he grabbed weapons from his horse. "You heard her."

But Shamus continued to look at her.

Though they'd never been spared a minute alone since they'd met, Shamus offered her an unexpected level of respect when he said, "Aye?"

Cadence nodded. "Yes."

What a mess all this was. Yesterday had quickly proven to her that while she and Shamus might have dreamt of one another for years...their connection was strained. How could that be? But it was. When she'd flirted with him it had been fun but not what it should have been. Not at all. Cadence thought for sure when she finally met the man of her dreams that everything would fall into place, that romance would sweep her off her feet.

She would've bet her life's wages on it.

The dreams had been that intense even if they hadn't been romantic in nature.

Or at least as far as she could tell.

Dreaming about someone was misplaced and disjointed at best. Regardless, it gave you a certain sense of the other, especially if you dreamt about him time and time again.

Malcolm interrupted her thoughts when he took her hand. "Let us make haste. The day wears on."

So they headed through the forest alongside the mountain. Dim sunlight sliced through the trees as they made their way up an incline through ever thickening trees. She could have sworn she heard the sound of a waterfall. Despite the pain in her legs, she couldn't help but be curious about their destination. Cadence was tempted to engage him in conversation but was overly aware of his increasing tension.

Finally, she couldn't help but say, "So the tree was sealed by your mother's magic?"

"Both were," he said as he helped her up a particularly rocky incline. "However the larger oak is protected from the inside entrance."

"So there's an outside entrance?"

"Aye." They rounded a corner onto a sheet of rock. He looked up. "But 'tis not an easy entrance."

Wide-eyed, she stared up and up and up. "*Amazing!*"

Against the side of the mountain grew one of the mightiest oak trees she'd ever seen. With almost a four-foot wide trunk, it appeared ancient. Its top was partially hidden inside the mountain.

"Its limbs continue up and over the ledge above where it protects the baby oak." Malcolm narrowed his eyes and continued to study the trunk. "'Tis a hard climb."

What? She looked at him, incredulous. "You can't mean to climb it, Malcolm. *Way* too dangerous."

"No more dangerous than that climb we made out of the ocean side cave."

Cadence frowned but perked up some. "I know you couldn't use magic then. What about now? I'd think that would make things a whole lot safer."

He shook his head. "Nay, 'tis not a good idea to use magic around the base of this tree. 'Tis where its roots find life. I wouldnae dare disrupt that."

Before she could respond he said, "I need to speak with you about something."

His tension only seemed to increase as he leaned against the tree and crossed his arms over his chest. Steady eyes locked with hers, Cadence knew that whatever he was about to say was the reason he had wanted to be alone with her. Wary, she nodded.

"What do you know of the glow of your sister's ring and Bradon's mark?"

"I take it you're not referring to the glow of the stone that only she and Bradon see, being each other's one true love and all?"

He shook his head. "Nay, I'm referring to the brighter glow of the ring."

"Ah, well, I know that the shine of the stone possibly matches one of the four colors of Torra when in dragon form. I also know the ring and mark glow if Torra is nearby." She contemplated. "And the ring's stone becomes a key to the mark and unleashes some pretty intense magic, hence you getting out of the Hamilton's castle alive last time you were there."

Cadence twirled the ring on her finger, more aware of its heat than ever. What was he getting at?

"Aye, that is all true." Malcolm's eyes narrowed a fraction. "But what do you know of what first ignited Leslie's ring and Bradon's mark?"

"I'm not sure what you mean." She continued to twirl her ring. "I know it first happened when they traveled back in time to the Stewart Clan and that it happened during a lunar eclipse."

"'Twas not the blood moon or the Stewarts that ignited them." He cleared his throat, uncomfortable. "But something else altogether."

"I'm not sure I was ever told the specifics about that," she said but Cadence was starting to suspect. According to Sheila that's where Leslie and Bradon had first been intimate. Equally uncomfortable but curious she said, "Forgive me if I'm way off, but was it because they slept together?"

Malcolm nodded, hesitating a moment before he answered, voice deeper than normal. "Aye, 'twas."

"Interesting," she murmured.

He was still looking at her intensely so she continued. "Not sure what you're getting at, Malcolm."

"Fionn Mac Cumhail made a request last eve that I didnae share," he said.

Her heartbeat kicked up a notch. *Uh oh.* "And what was that?"

"He told me the glow of my mark and the ring's stone must ignite before I can free the oak."

Cadence swallowed hard and leaned back against a nearby rock. "And how do you intend to make that happen?"

"There is only one way," he said, eyes brighter than normal, ignited by the sunrays cutting across his face. "I must lay with the lass whose ring's stone glows for me."

Oh, sweet Goddess.

"You haven't mentioned anyone's stone glowing for you," she murmured.

"Nor have you, lass." Malcolm nodded at her ring. "Does it glow for your eyes when you're with me?"

Cadence glanced at it then back at him. Of course it did but she hadn't wanted to tell him. Not to mention, there was Shamus. Instead of answering him she asked the same. "Better yet, does it glow for you?"

He seemed hesitant but finally answered.

"Aye." He sighed. "Since the moment we first met."

Burning warmth raced through her. "You mean in the twenty-first century?"

Malcolm nodded.

"Why didn't you tell me sooner?" She frowned. "You ended anything that might've existed with Sheila. Is this why?"

"Nay," he said without hesitation. "I dinnae desire her like that."

Shaky, she ran a hand through her hair. Though she appreciated his honesty she was surprisingly nervous. Something about this man made her unsteady, out of sync.

"You have not answered my question, Cadence," he said.

No, she hadn't but she supposed she better. "Yes, it glows for you, Malcolm."

When he crossed the small space between them and stood in front of her, Cadence wished she hadn't put the rock behind her. Far too slanted to sit on she could only lean back when he braced his hand on the surface beside her. She swore little shards of lightning zipped over her skin when he took her hand, eyed the ring and ran his thumb back and forth over the stone.

At last, he said, "You didnae tell me because of Shamus, aye?"

She shook her head slowly.

His dark brows lowered as his eyes shot to hers. "What think you now of the Irishman?"

"I think I made the answer to that question clear when I slept in your tent last night."

"Slept," he murmured. "No more."

There had *certainly* been more but not what he'd truly wanted. "You knew about Fionn's request last night. Why didn't you tell me about it...or act on it. It would have been easier than ever with me in your tent."

He cupped her cheek, his touch surprisingly tender. "Because you said no and I didnae want you to feel forced or obligated."

Breathing became a struggle. A Celtic god told him the only way to free the tree was to sleep with her and he hadn't automatically obeyed. That was something. "Yet now you tell me. What will happen if I say no?"

He grazed his thumb over her cheekbone. "I dinnae know. Besides not freeing the oak, I would imagine nothing."

"But Fionn says the oak is being smothered. That's terrible," she whispered.

Malcolm nodded once, coming so close her body started to tremble. "I willnae force you to do anything."

Yet there was something new in his hot gaze, a sweet possessiveness that seemed to wrap around her as surely as his muscular arm soon did. He put a finger under her chin and titled back her head. Heavy lidded, thick, black lashes framed eyes that pulled her far closer to him than the body now pressed against her. Stark desire flared in his eyes as they roamed over first her lips then the whole of her face before once more meeting her gaze.

"I willnae hurt you, lass," he whispered.

Now that was yet to be seen. But then she knew if he turned from her now, whether or not she'd been intimate with him, it would hurt like hell. She put her hand over his heart and murmured, "And I won't hurt this."

He seemed a little surprised by her words but said nothing.

Instead, he cupped her cheeks and closed his lips over hers.

Unlike the night before, she didn't fight the feeling. No, she dove head-first into sensation after sensation. Tongue swirling, the kiss was made of both new discoveries and heart-wrenching passion.

Even when voices drew closer she was unable to pull away.

"Och, nay, we dinnae have time for that," came Ilisa's voice when she appeared in the small clearing.

Malcolm reluctantly pulled away and frowned. "You didnae give us long, cousin."

Shamus was right behind. His eyes flickered from Malcolm to Cadence before he said, "We went around the backside. That's one hell of a waterfall."

Ilisa tossed Malcolm a skin which he handed to Cadence. "Drink some, lass. 'Twill help you replenish."

Cadence nodded and took a long swig… then coughed and shook her head. "What is this?"

Malcolm frowned. "Water, I assumed."

"Nay, 'twas from the bottle strapped to your horse," Ilisa said.

Malcolm's eyes widened slightly and he yanked the skin from Cadence. "No more of this for you."

Cadence couldn't agree more. She'd really rather have water.

Ilisa looked up at the tree then at Malcolm. "This way can get us betwixt the two barriers Coira created. The waterfall, up to where the baby oak is. When's the last time you manipulated water, cousin?"

Cadence looked at Malcolm, amazed. "You can manipulate water?"

"Aye," he said.

"Why didn't you when I first arrived?" She shook her head. "Oh right, you couldn't use magic." Cadence rubbed her arms and looked around. "Can you now? What about the MacLeod's?"

"Colin has scouts everywhere. There are no MacLeods nearby. Most have joined the bulk of warriors heading south."

"I can climb this tree and help from the inside," Shamus said, pulling off his tunic.

Well-muscled, Cadence didn't doubt he could. When she glanced at Malcolm he wasn't looking at her but up into the tree. It said a lot for his confidence that he wasn't worried in the least about Shamus. But she guessed that he never really was. No, he was letting her come to her own conclusions.

Ilisa looked at Shamus with admiration then the tree, a wide grin on her face. "Oh, I can see you climbing this tree just fine, Irishman."

Shamus winked then looked at Malcolm. "Bradon and the other lasses will be climbing up the inside cave wall to try tackling it from there."

"Daylight's limited," Ilisa said. "We should do this soon."

As if he felt the urgency, the black wolf trotted by them and continued through to the woods. Malcolm nodded and took Cadence's hand. "Time to go."

"I'll stay with Shamus," Ilisa said, already eying his backside as he began the climb.

Cadence couldn't help but smile as they continued. The attraction between the two made her feel far less guilty. Not that she owed Shamus anything. Regardless, they'd shared a connection.

The further she and Malcolm traveled the louder the waterfall became. At last they arrived at the source of the sound. Immense, cascading, crashing, a waterfall poured down not one mountain but two. Caught in the fiery red rays of a dying sun, it was incredibly beautiful as it fell into a small lake.

The wolf sat staring at them.

Swirling, twisting, the water started to shimmer a thousand colors. She blinked, thinking it must be a mirage but it only intensified. Suddenly very light on her feet, she leaned against a tree. "Wow, do I feel funny."

"Bloody hell," Malcolm muttered. "Euphemia."

"Who?" she murmured.

"The cook." He cupped her cheeks and looked deep into her eyes. "The mead Ilisa put in that skin was from the bottle of mead I had sent to your chambers at the castle."

"Oh," she whispered, confused, lost and drifting.

"Cadence, please listen carefully. We must continue through the waterfall," he said. "As we do, you will hallucinate. That mead is magically enhanced. 'Twill make you...aroused." He shook his head. "Dinnae give in to it. 'Twill not really be me."

"Aroused?" But already she understood as erotic pleasure washed over her. "I *knew* you were up to no good with that stuff."

"Nay, 'twill be *verra* good, lass," he assured.

Then, as if he'd been waiting for the perfect opportunity, Malcolm lifted then slammed her back against a tree.

Chapter Eight

Malcolm caught Cadence before she fell back against the tree.

Fully under the influence of the mead's magic, she wrapped her arms around his neck. *Damnation.* The timing of this couldn't be worse. Now he had to remain focused and get them up to that tree while keeping her from an alternate version of himself. After all, with this mead she would only fantasize about him.

To make matters worse, he was connected to the magic in it.

This meant that he would be connected to what she felt. Sure, it had seemed just the thing to do when he knew she'd be alone bathing in his castle. But now? Gods no.

He carefully unwrapped his neck from her arms. "Nay, lassie. I must move the water."

"Hmm, hmm," she murmured, her eyes traveling down the length of him. "So do you like being looked at like this?" A small grin came to her lovely lips. "Like you do to me…as if you want to eat me alive."

Actually, he didn't mind it so much at all.

Determined to remain focused, he centered his being and stemmed out his magic toward the waterfall. Meanwhile, she came close and her hand crept up his thigh.

"Nay, lass," he whispered.

Sensation bombarded him. Of the icy cold water spraying over his skin while her warm hand ran up beneath his tunic.

Her mouth made a small 'o' and her eyes fluttered shut. "I love the way you touch me."

But he wasn't touching her at all. Oh no, that'd be his phantom double busy at work. And by the look on her face he was doing a good job of it too. Thank the gods he was able to pull on just enough magic to lessen one small corner of the waterfall's stream.

Not wasting any time, he threw her over his shoulder and ran.

A black shadow, the wolf followed.

He had only ever gone this way once and it was a very long time ago.

Meantime, Cadence was groaning as if he was doing something entirely different to her. In fact, based on the tightening in his groin he'd bet his body-double had her pressed up against a cave wall now. He inhaled sharply. Curse that bloody mead.

"Of course I'll help you ignite your tattoo's glow, Malcolm," she purred.

It sounded like he was being mighty persuasive based on the womanly pants escaping her mouth. He staggered a few steps when fast, sharp need blew through him. This lass would be the death of him. But he supposed he deserved this. Only fulfillment would free her from the mead's magic.

He could only hope that came soon.

The more she groaned the more difficult it became to walk the inclining passageway cutting up into the mountain. A slice of dim sunset provided minimal light from overhead. Soon they would have to crawl the last leg and she had to do that on her own.

They'd just arrived at that point when she released a small cry and dug her nails into his back. Malcolm buckled forward in pleasure, feeling a release without actually releasing. She shook as he slowly lowered her. Lips slightly parted, cheeks flushed, her almond shaped brilliantly green eyes met his.

"Malcolm," she whispered.

Now they both breathed harshly.

"Are you back then?" he said softly.

Her eyes drifted down. "You're still dressed...just a second ago you weren't...you were in me."

Where he'd like to be right now. "Aye but nay. 'Twas the mead."

"It felt *so* real." She blinked and looked around. "Where are we?"

"Nearly to the tree." They stood at a ledge that was waist high. After that, the rock inclined. He turned her. "See, 'tis not so far at all. Just a bit of crawling."

She held up her hand and looked at her ring. "I would've sworn it'd be shining brightly after that."

Standing behind her, he softly said, "Nay, 'twould take a real coupling."

His arousal was so rampant that he couldn't help but press it against her backside. Inhaling deeply, he put his cheek against her silky hair.

Cadence turned her head ever so slightly toward his. "That was a naughty thing you did with that mead."

"Aye," he whispered and couldn't help a small grin. "'Twas. But only ever meant to relax you upon arrival. 'Tis stressful traveling back in time, is it not?"

"I would have managed," she murmured when he braced his hands on the rock and ran his lips down the side of her smooth neck.

When her head fell back, he cupped her cheek and turned her lips to his.

Slow, easy, passionate, he kissed her.

Gods, he needed her. And it seemed she was not opposed to the idea based on how she pressed back against him. All the excruciating desire he'd kept in check the eve before flared stronger than ever. When he pulled his mouth away, he brought his lips close to her ear and murmured, "Do you know what I mean to do to you then, lass?"

Cadence gave no response other than to press back against him even harder.

Malcolm would have breathed a sigh of relief if he had the breath to do it. Painfully aroused, he cupped one overly plump breast while pulling up the bottom of her dress and his plaid with his free hand. He'd truly never desired a lass more. Wedging her legs apart, he grasped her hips and pulled her back just enough.

When he pushed forward he clenched his jaw. *Holy hell*, was she tight.

Grasping the rock, she managed a small whimper. Fueled by the feel of her body, by her clenching heat, he shook with the amount of restraint it took not to drive into her. He wrapped an arm around her small waist and eased slowly, giving her time to adjust. Gods, but he'd never felt anything so bloody good.

She dug her nails into his arm.

Unable to hold back any longer, he thrust fully and seated himself.

Their hearts thundered as he held her in position.

There was nothing comparable to the feeling of being so close to her...*inside* of her.

He frowned when a drop hit his arm. A tear?

"Cadence," he managed. "Have I hurt you?"

"No," she whispered. "You just feel *so* good."

Humbled yet driven by her emotional response, he put his hand over hers on the rock and squeezed. Unable to remain still any longer, he began to move. Determined to be easy on her already sore body, he was gentle, careful with his strokes.

But it took almost more than he had.

It was never his intention to take her like this...like an animal. Yet she brought out something wild in him. Not to say he didn't like things a bit on the adventurous side. He definitely did. But this, against a stone ledge in a darkening cave, was less than she deserved.

When she started to move back against him, tiny, feminine gasps coming from her mouth, his niggling conscience vanished. His patience snapped. With a sharp thrust he drove into her.

Caged by his arms and hands, Cadence was locked into position.

In. Out. In. Out.

Over and over.

Driven by her cries of pleasure, he moved faster, deeper.

"Malcolm," she cried out, her body trembling.

A roar filled his inner ear. Lights flickered in his vision.

Hellllll.

After a sharp quiver, her body shook violently in release.

Buckling forward, he groaned as his own vicious release ripped through him. It hit him so hard, he nearly lost his footing. He ground his teeth under the pure pressure clenching then swiftly draining from him before he struggled at a long draw of breath.

Meanwhile, Cadence continued to ripple around him, her body soft, pliable and relaxed as she all but draped across the rock. After brushing her hair back from her face, he closed his eyes and kissed her temple.

"'Twas unbelievable, lass," he whispered.

Before she could respond, he turned her and wrapped his arms around her, pulling her head against his chest. Now he held her the way she was meant to be held as he stroked her hair.

Some time passed before she finally pulled back and met his eyes. "It *was* unbelievable."

He cupped her cheek and grinned. "Aye, 'twas."

She touched his lips. "Look, a smile."

Malcolm couldn't help it if he tried. "So it seems."

"I did that," she murmured, a small smile crawling onto her lips.

"Aye, lass."

Her eyes went to her ring and rounded. "Look."

"It glows. 'Tis copper colored, aye?"

"For sure." She cocked her head. "Where's your mark? Let's see if it glows."

Plaid pushed down to just above and to the right of his groin, he revealed his tattoo. Still smiling, he nodded. "Aye, it glows."

"We did it then," she said softly. A warm, knowing smile blossomed on her bonnie face.

"We did," he agreed but then grew troubled as his eyes connected with hers. "But I didnae do this for the glow of the mark, Cadence."

"I know you didn't," she whispered. "Let's just call it a perk to an amazing experience." Her interested eyes drifted back down. "Quite the spot for a tattoo."

"Aye," he said, enjoying the desire in her eyes. "'Tis."

When a low whine came from behind them, he glanced over his shoulder. The wolf sat waiting, watching the exit above.

Cadence adjusted her dress. "Ugh, you think he watched us the whole time?"

"I dinnae think he knew what he watched if he did." Malcolm nodded up the incline. "'Tis time to go, lass."

"Right." Cadence twirled her ring and winked. "And we might just be better prepared now."

Malcolm couldn't help but grin in return. She brought it out in him. He cupped his hands to create a foot brace for her.

"Thanks." She stepped up. As she started to crawl she said, "Gotta admit, this is a whole lot better than the last climb we made."

He couldn't agree more...on most counts. This time he didn't have the pleasurable view of her nude backside. Nonetheless, it looked just as tempting covered with a dress. In short time, they made it to the top. After he made sure she was all right, he looked back down. The wolf stared up.

Malcolm put his fingers to his mouth and whistled.

With a quick bound, the wolf jumped, kept on its haunches and shimmied up after them. When he reached the top, Malcolm gave him a quick ruffle on the head then turned his attention to their surroundings.

Cadence had a hand over her mouth as she looked at what stood in front of them.

Only tall enough for a bairn to stand beneath, the baby oak stood beneath the last towering leaves of her mother oak.

"'Tis amazing, aye?" he said.

"Yes it is," she said softly. "Just look at the green leaves at this time of year!"

"It doesnae matter the season. 'Tis always that way."

The sun had set and the soft glow of a low moon spread over the mountain top. Malcolm took her hand. "Come. Let us see if we cannae unseal the entrance Ma erected."

Cadence nodded and followed.

As he knew would be the case, it was sealed tight with not only rocks but with powerful magic. He looked at his lass. "So you know what Leslie did to ignite the magic at the Hamilton castle?"

"Yeah." She twirled her ring so that the stone was palm side down. "She pressed it against Bradon's mark."

"'Twas unsettling. Verra powerful magic ignited." He frowned. "I dinnae like what I cannae predict. Nor do I like the danger it puts you—"

"Stop," she cut him off. "We came all this way. The glow is ignited in my ring and in your mark. We're not backing out now."

"You are courageous but I dinnae—"

"Malcolm, a god told you this was the only way." She squeezed his hand and nodded at the wall of rocks. "We're doing this. Before we lose our nerve."

"Aye, then. Ilisa and Shamus are on the other side now." Malcolm braced his hand against one of the rocks and pulled down his plaid enough so that she had access to his mark.

Fearless, she came close and pressed her ring's stone against it.

107

A deep, ground shaking vibration started to fill him. When he looked at Cadence her eyes were starting to glaze over with white as Leslie's had done when she'd ignited this type of magic. Back then, it had been Torra possessing her.

Was his cousin doing such again?

"Malcolm," Cadence murmured. But it wasn't her voice at all.

No, it was Torra's.

His desperate heart clenched. "I'm here, cousin. We're all coming for you."

Her next words came not from Cadence's mouth but through the mind.

Read the Soul. Find him evermore.

Pain, fast and furious, rippled down his arm and blasted against the rocks. Explosive, they blew inward, fizzling into a soft yet violently twisting powder. Aware of the whipping, free magic, Malcolm swung Cadence over his shoulders and shimmied down the short drop to the cave that housed the bulk of the mother oak's limbs.

At nearly the same time, the piled rocks on the opposite side blew inward and added to the rabid funnel of a magical storm. Shamus and Ilisa already stood inside the trees limbs. Not entirely understanding the pull, everyone else ran in that direction.

"Hurry now!" Shamus yelled and pulled Sheila in when the maelstrom around them tried to pull her back. Bradon had already tossed Leslie over his shoulder and managed to join the others.

"Oh my God!" Sheila cried.

When Shamus nearly lost his hold, Malcolm swung around and grabbed Sheila's wrist. No easy task holding two at once. Screaming, wicked, the magic only grew louder, angrier. Then, *boom.*

The mountain shook and the ground fell away.

Sugary sweetness filled his nostrils.

Bloody hell.

Sheila and Cadence were ripped away.

Then, as quickly as it began, it ended and he landed with a soft thump.

Malcolm pushed past disorientation and immediately searched for Cadence and Sheila. Both were nearby, holding their heads. Bradon stumbled to Leslie and pulled her into his arms. Ilisa and

Shamus were blinking rapidly as they tried to adjust to their surroundings.

After he staggered to Cadence, Malcolm crouched and cupped her head. "Are you well." Then he looked at Sheila and squeezed her hand. "And you, lass?"

"I'm okay," Sheila said.

"Me too," Cadence managed.

Once he pulled them to their feet, he peered around at the tall standing stones surrounding them, at the low grazing fog and steep jagged peaks just beyond. "Where the hell *are* we?"

"I've been here before," Shamus said, awed. "'Tis the Hebrides."

"The isles?" Bradon pulled Leslie to her feet.

"Aye, I was here years ago with Alexander, Iosbail and Caitriona."

"Adlin's sister, Iosbail?" Ilisa said.

"Aye, 'twas on that adventure she fell in love with Alexander."

"And Caitriona Stewart?" Sheila asked.

"Aye." Shamus grinned. "But she'd not yet met her love, Alan Stewart, only dreamt of him."

Malcolm didn't miss the quick glance between Cadence and Shamus. Interesting comparison. But none of that mattered now. Cadence was his good and true. When his lass's eyes met his, he knew she felt the same.

"Why do you suppose we've ended up here?" Sheila asked, her eyes wide as she gazed around. "God, it's gorgeous...in a spooky sort of way."

"Ah, Soul Reader!" Leslie exclaimed and met the horse that trotted her way.

Bradon shook his head. "What is it with that horse? No matter where we go."

"And the wolf too so it seems," Sheila added.

Cadence smiled at Malcolm when his wolf plunked down beside him.

"You've got a good friend there, sweetie," she said.

So it seemed. He rested his hand on the wolf's head, surprisingly glad to have the beast along. Then, interestingly enough, the wolf went to Cadence and sat by her side, its ears perked and eyes to the woodland as it released a low growl.

Frozen, Cadence peered down at the wolf then at him. "Must say, I'm a little nervous."

"He willnae hurt you, lass." Malcolm narrowed his eyes in the direction in which the wolf gazed.

"Someone comes," Bradon murmured and drew his blade.

Ilisa and Shamus did the same.

Slowly, bit by bit, a form started to emerge through the fog.

Slender, curvy, confident, the figure became more and more clear.

Malcolm narrowed his eyes.

When at last the person got closer, they slowed, and then walked a little faster. He put his hand on the hilt of his blade. But had no chance to draw the weapon before a woman emerged and ran the remainder of the way straight into his arms.

Baffled, confused, Malcolm could barely process anything save one thing…

Nessa had just run into his arms.

His wife was *alive*.

Chapter Nine

Cadence had no idea what she was witnessing.

"You've got to be kidding me," Leslie muttered.

"God above," Sheila added and frowned.

"How is this possible?" Bradon murmured.

"Och, *nay!*" Ilisa said and brought the tip of her blade within inches of the strange woman's neck.

But whoever she was, she didn't seem phased in the least. Instead, she cupped Malcolm's cheeks, tears in her eyes. "I *knew* you'd come, my love."

Malcolm, slowly but surely, as if he didn't know what else to do, brought his hands to her waist, his voice near strangled when he said. "I dinnae ken. I watched you die."

Watched her die? A sickening sensation settled in Cadence's stomach.

The woman shook her head and ran her hands around the back of Malcolm's neck before she leaned her head against his chest. "'Twas all a ruse put in motion by Keir Hamilton. All of it." She closed her eyes and seemed to inhale the scent of him. "Everything he's been doing has been one master plan. We're all pawns in his game."

Malcolm hung his head, clearly caught in deep emotion before he carefully pushed her away but kept his hands on her hips. A heavy scowl on his face, he said, "You betrayed me, Nessa ...you betrayed my clan." Pain flickered in his eyes. "I cannae trust your words now."

Cadence's chest squeezed so tightly she could barely breathe. She put a hand over her mouth and shook her head. This had to be Malcolm's wife. Tall, statuesque, with a hauntingly stunning beauty about her, she could be no other.

Ilisa still held out her blade, her body shaking and lips quivering in rage. "You've the right o' it, Malcolm. Dinnae believe her for a moment. She weaved lies when with us and that hasnae changed."

Again, Nessa ignored Ilisa, her sole attention on Malcolm. "Was my body left behind? Do you have actual proof of my death then?"

Malcolm tilted his head back, eyes narrowed further. "Nay, you were choked to death then swamped in dark magic."

"*Keir's* magic," she said. "I dinnae ken why he didnae kill me then. But nay, he banished me to this isle where I might stay until he has further use of me."

"And he will have further use," Malcolm said, his voice still unsteady. "Of that I dinnae doubt."

Was Malcolm wavering? Did he believe her? Cadence worked at a deep breath. Nessa sounded so convincing.

As if she sensed a weakening in the crowd, Nessa looked to Bradon. "I know what Keir intends for your sister." Then she looked at Malcolm and took his hand. "And I ken the power he has over your brother. Grant can be saved. He's not lost to the MacLomains."

"My brother is a traitor," Malcolm ground out.

"Nay." Nessa shook her head. "He is but another victim, my love."

Ilisa's expression grew more sour and her blame more sure. "Dinnae believe her for a second, cousin. Pure poison, this one."

At last, as if she offered a boon, Nessa's eyes turned to Ilisa. "Aye, lass, I deserve as much from you." Her gaze swept over the men. "All of you." Then they once more landed on Malcolm. "But I can prove it to you if you but come with me."

Sheila shook her head, her usual upbeat disposition long gone. "I'm with Ilisa. Don't trust her for a second, Malcolm."

Leslie nodded and narrowed her eyes. "I agree. She's a cunning bitch who's most likely manipulating you…all of us, with every word that comes out of her mouth."

Eyes a smidge too reluctant, Nessa nodded in their direction then lowered her head. "I deserve this."

Cadence realized Nessa hadn't once looked at her, but there was a definite sense that she was tempted to. So when at last Malcolm's wife's eyes slowly rose in her direction, she wasn't surprised in the least.

"I'm sorry, we havenae met." Kindness plastered on her face, Nessa's eyes dropped to the wolf then went back to her. "Quite the beast you call friend."

Though tempted to respond sharply, Cadence didn't. There was something in Nessa's eyes that gave her pause. She recognized it. This was a woman who had suffered and while it might seem she'd come out ahead, Cadence knew better. Having dealt with far too many troubled women, she had no problem pinpointing one that had never truly healed but merely survived in the aftermath. A mental post-apocalypse that she knew damned well Nessa still muddled through.

Malcolm nodded and pulled himself free from Nessa.

He walked over and put his hand on the wolf's head. "This is our wolf and this is Cadence." Malcolm took her hand and looked at Nessa. "My lass."

Cadence felt the block of tension in her chest slowly melt.

Nessa trembled slightly and her fist clenched at her side but she kept her head tall when she whispered, "Of course, you thought I was dead."

"I did," Malcolm said readily then repeated far softer, "I did."

Cadence felt his pain as surely as if it was hers. He was doing right by her. If more men could be so honorable the world might be a better place. But she wouldn't do that to him. He'd just found out his wife was still alive. Who was she to keep him from that? Blinking away the water in her eyes, she pulled her hand from his and looked at Nessa. "You said you had some sort of proof about Grant. Please, we need to know more."

Nessa faltered at the unexpected gesture...because it *was* a gesture. It was respect given from one woman to another. With a slow nod, she said, "Aye, I do." She held out her hand to Malcolm. "Please. Come." She paused. "Your parents are here."

Cadence's breath again left her as it seemed was the case for most of them.

"My parents?" Malcolm said.

Nessa nodded and continued to hold out her hand. "Aye, please, come."

When Malcolm looked at her, Cadence nodded. Slow, as if still wary, he took Nessa's hand and followed. She paused a moment and twirled the ring on her finger. Nothing said this ring truly had it all figured out. It had brought her and Malcolm closer and freed the oaks. Perhaps that was all it was meant to do. Sometimes a man just needed to feel loved to see clearly a bruised love from his past. Either way...Nessa had information they needed.

So they trailed after her into the mountainous land of the Scottish Hebrides.

Her thoughts were as wild and fluctuating as the jagged mountains overhead. It was impossible not to remember what had so recently transpired between her and Malcolm. The passion, the incomparable feel of him inside of her, the tender way he'd been afterward. But what right did she have to dwell on such things when his wife was alive and well?

Cadence wasn't surprised when Leslie urged Bradon to walk ahead with Ilisa and Shamus so that she and Sheila could hang back. They were determined to be with her which probably wasn't a bad idea. Because one thing was for sure, she might be willing to let Malcolm go but she'd need to acclimate to the decision and support was always welcome.

"What the hell was that?" Leslie finally said when the others were far enough ahead.

"Agreed, total bullshit," Sheila said.

All right, maybe not support in the common sense.

But Cadence knew they'd come at her with guns blazing.

With a heavy sigh, she said, "That woman has dealt with a lot of heartache and so has Malcolm. I have no intention of getting in the middle of it."

"Heartache?" Sheila said, incredulous. "I'm sorry, I know you sway toward broken women, cuz, but when it comes to this one you're dead wrong."

"However," Leslie said, shaking her head. "As much as I think she's a shit stain on mankind, you're not alone in the way you look at her."

"I'm not?" Cadence asked.

"No." Leslie frowned. "Malcolm understands as much about her. Or so he told me on our last adventure together." Her cousin's expression grew more troubled. "And while you both might be right, that doesn't dispel the notion that there's something sinister about her. Back home you might think she's just a girl who had a rough upbringing and then spent years surrounded by total jerks, but she's not your average girl, Cadence."

Before Cadence could defend her, Leslie shook her head. "I might not get along as well as I should with Colin but I think he's got this one pegged. She's evil, honey. And evil chicks don't develop into womanhood quite like an abused woman from back home would."

"I think Les is absolutely right," Sheila added. "You had to see what she was like when we first traveled back in time. I mean, seriously, set aside all the evil slyness she's capable of, she was all over Colin despite McKayla."

"And," Leslie pointed out. "Despite her husband, Malcolm."

That last part irritated her. The idea that any woman lucky enough to be with Malcolm would want to cheat on him blew her mind.

"*That* woman put a huge rift between Colin and Malcolm," Sheila muttered. "You can say it was Colin taking off for three years then returning to become laird of the MacLomains, but I don't think that's what truly pisses off Malcolm the most. No, it was always Nessa's desire for Colin."

Leslie nodded. "I couldn't agree more."

"And Colin wanted nothing to do with her," Sheila said. "But Malcolm couldn't see past it."

"Now all that's changed," Leslie said. "Now *you're* his lass."

"Declared by him in front of Nessa no less!" Sheila said.

Leslie winked. "Pretty epic by the way."

"But, sort of pointless if you just skulk away and hand the reigns over to her," Sheila said.

"He's not a horse," Leslie said dryly.

"Acting like one…well, more of a jackass," Sheila muttered. "Holding hands with her."

Cadence shook her head. "Don't you two start, okay? I've enough on my plate."

Sheila looked at Leslie. "Were we starting?"

Leslie shrugged. "I didn't think so."

"You were close," Cadence assured.

"No matter," Sheila said. "Malcolm cares about you. Don't let that get away."

Leslie eyed Cadence, interested. "That he does. By the way, how'd you two manage to break through all of Coira's impregnable magic back at the oaks? That was pretty intense stuff."

Cadence knew it wouldn't take long for her sister to question that. "Why ask a question you already know the answer to?"

"Ha!" Leslie laughed and shook her head. "I *knew* it."

"What?" Sheila asked.

Cadence shook her head and frowned at Leslie. The *last* thing she wanted Sheila to know was that she'd slept with Malcolm.

Thankfully, Shamus joined them at that moment and the conversation ended.

"Might I have a moment alone with Cadence?" he asked the others.

"Sure," both said at the same time and walked ahead.

So now she'd finally have time alone with the Irishman. Honestly, she wasn't really up for it.

"How are you, lassie?" he asked, eyes warm.

"On guard," she said without thinking. But it was the truth.

"Because of me?"

"No." She shook her head then nodded. "Actually, yes...sorry."

Though she was on guard about Nessa too, that wasn't what this conversation needed to be about.

"Please dinnae be." He seemed to contemplate his next words. "'Tis a thing that we dreamt of one another, aye?"

"It is a thing...maybe." Cadence took a deep breath. "They were always such great dreams. You have no idea how much I wanted to meet you...find you."

"Aye," he said softly. "And I you. I think, mayhap, I saw something of you when I met your sister."

She nodded. That would be understandable.

Cadence bit her lip, unsure. "You seem really great."

"As do you," he conceded. "But mayhap there was more to these dreams than we both anticipated."

Interest piqued, she looked at him. "How do you mean?"

He paused for several long moments before he said, "Ilisa, she's..."

116

When Shamus trailed off, Cadence nodded, a small smile on her face. Relieved she said, "You're interested in her."

"Aye." He cocked a grin at her. "I really am. But..."

Cadence breathed a sigh of relief. "It's okay. Really. While I'd swear I know you from the inside out I'm not sure..."

He took her hand and squeezed. "Something will come of our dreams but not what we thought, aye?"

Cadence shook her head and squeezed back. "No, not what we thought."

Then, as if he sensed it, Malcolm appeared. When his eyes went to her and Shamus's hands, she didn't pull away. He'd either trust her or he wouldn't. She wasn't playing games. But he needed to figure that out on his own. Not because she told or showed him such.

"I want you with me if Nessa is right...if my parents live," Malcolm said.

"Of course," she said. Giving Shamus's hand one last squeeze she took Malcolm's and followed.

Malcolm said nothing as they joined Nessa and continued into a massive underground cave. With a low ceiling, it was mammoth and long.

"The clan that used to house here is long gone, moved north, but some of their cottages and their main hut still stand," Nessa said.

"Look at this," Shamus murmured. "The last time I was here there were hundreds of cottages. 'Twas a thriving community."

"Now there's only me," Nessa said and stopped at the door of the large, thatch-topped cottage. "And them."

They paused at the door.

"Malcolm?"

"Ma?" he said hoarsely. His hand slipped from Cadence's as he took three long strides and pulled a small, petite woman into his arms.

"Son," she whimpered into his chest.

Arms wrapped tight, he held her.

They stayed that way as the others entered the building. Cadence couldn't help but look at the man lying on the cot in the corner. Blue, motionless, she knew...

That had to be Malcolm's father.

Tears came to her eyes and she hung her head. "Blessed be," she murmured.

"Oh no, William," Sheila whispered and went to his side. When she knelt, she took his hand and made the symbol of the cross over her chest. Bradon was soon beside her, kneeling and making the same symbol.

Leslie, of all people, walked over to Malcolm and his mother. Though she said nothing she put a comforting hand on both of their shoulders.

A long silence passed, only broken by the crackle of a low fire.

Eventually, Malcolm's mother pulled back and cupped her son's cheeks. "It does me good to see you."

Malcolm said nothing, only stared into her eyes until his gaze slowly swung in his father's direction. Cadence tried to catch her breath but couldn't. When Nessa came alongside and took his hand he shook his head. Clearly understanding, she stepped back as he made his way to the cot.

When he fell to his knees, Sheila and Bradon moved away.

This was a moment between father and son.

Cadence wiped away a tear. Cheeks wet, Sheila took her hand and whispered, "Come."

All left the hut, including Malcolm's mother.

Shamus had lit a fire beyond, a heavy frown on his face as he urged the others to join him.

"I'll go hunt," Bradon murmured and left.

Everyone else sat on logs.

No one said a word for a long time.

Even when Bradon returned and game roasted, all remained silent.

It became harder and harder to stay where she was. At last, Cadence couldn't take it anymore and whispered, "I'm sorry. I've got to go to him."

Nobody said a word as she went into the hut.

Malcolm was still, his arm draped across his father's midriff, his head resting on his chest.

Cadence said nothing as she sat beside Malcolm and lowered her head. She closed her eyes and said Wiccan prayers in her mind.

Minutes went by, maybe hours, before Malcolm whispered, "I always tried to honor him but I could have done better. He forgave when I wouldnae."

When she looked up it was to Malcolm's bloodshot eyes on his father.

"He had more time and experience behind him to better understand forgiveness," she said softly. "You will too."

"Nay." He shook his head. "I'm not like him. I'm not like any of them."

Cadence said nothing to that. He was waging a war against his demons and was far too vulnerable.

"All he wanted to see was that I forgave Colin, that I wouldnae be bitter…but I couldnae do it."

"But you've already started to," she murmured. "Don't think for a second he doesn't know that."

Anger flared in his eyes. "Nay, he knows *nothing* now but what I gave him in life."

"William's here with me, lass."

Startled, she realized Adlin had just spoken to her.

She closed her eyes and shook her head.

Now was not the time to be a medium between the living and the dead.

"I've been a fool," Malcolm muttered.

"Does he have any message for Malcolm?" she asked Adlin.

"Aye, and his lad already has it."

Cadence felt Adlin flee her mind. Cryptic, meddlesome bastard. And she wasn't sorry for thinking it. What sort of arch wizard delivered such a message then vanished? She put a hand on Malcolm's shoulder in comfort. His eyes turned her way, distant and blank for several seconds, before he sat back and pulled her into his arms. Though shocked by the unexpected intimacy, she rested her cheek against his chest. Chin resting on top of her head, he remained silent. She knew he continued to stare at his father and that his thoughts and guilt haunted him.

Unable to stay silent any longer, she finally said, "If your goal is to forgive, Malcolm, then start by forgiving yourself. You have had every right to be angry and I'm sure your father understood as much."

"Nay, I didnae have to be so bitter." His brogue thickened with emotion. "I knew the right o' it with Nessa and Colin, that it was all her. And I knew Adlin MacLomain's wishes that Colin rule for a time." His voice softened. "He was my closest friend and while I was angry that he left for so long, that he abandoned his clan, 'twas an easy enough thing to forgive. Nay, 'twas always Nessa's desire for him at the root of my fury."

"I know," she whispered. "He knows." Cadence pulled back slightly and met his eyes. "I think Colin understands your emotions, your anger. I think he continues to love you no matter the issues you've had with him."

"I dinnae doubt it," he said softly. "But I havnae made it easy."

"You were allowed to feel as you did," she reiterated.

"Aye." He touched her cheek. "And now there are new feelings."

He'd switched to a topic she wasn't nearly ready to tackle. "Take this time, Malcolm. Mourn your father. Please don't worry about anything else, okay?"

"Worry?" He frowned. "I dinnae ken. 'Tis not worry I'm feeling in regards to you, lass."

"Good." She nodded, unsure, but glad he seemed to know she'd step aside. "Because she's your wife, Malcolm. I get that."

His frown only deepened, golden eyes never leaving hers. "Nay, Nessa was never my wife as she should have been. I never had her heart and willnae suffer for it anymore." He brushed his thumb over her cheek. "And while the gods know I loved her 'twas not like this...never like this."

Her heart flipped. "Your wife's *alive*, Malcolm. You've made a binding vow to her. I haven't known her long but I can say with confidence that she's had a rough time of it. I think if you two communicate and work through some things..."

Cadence trailed off, caught in the emotion burning in his eyes. He slowly shook his head.

"Och, nay, lass," he muttered and cupped her other cheek. "If I'm to forgive myself as you suggested then I will start now for I willnae have her back. 'Tis you I want if you'll have me."

"But you're *married*," she whispered, her chest aching. "I can't be with you while you're married to another, Malcolm."

"Then the marriage must end," he said.

Cadence had never felt so torn. Sure, everyone else seemed to despise the woman but she barely knew her. Did she hate that Nessa might've cheated on Malcolm? Heck yeah. But then now he'd had sex with her so…maybe that made them even. Even if he had thought his wife was dead when he did it.

"I dinnae much like the look on your face," Malcolm said. He pulled her head back against his chest and stroked her hair. "I will find a way to make this right."

It was impossible to know just what he had in mind. Meanwhile, she knew that she would remain conflicted. They hadn't known one another very long and Malcolm had years with his wife. Yet Cadence knew that whether it was a few days or a few years, the way she already felt about him wouldn't change.

They stayed that way for a long time, neither saying a word.

So when a quiet sigh broke the silence, Cadence jerked up, startled.

At some point, Malcolm's mother had joined them. She sat on the other side of the cot, holding William's hand but looking at them.

Though Cadence tried to remove herself from Malcolm's arms, he held tight.

"I'm sorry I didnae greet you properly before, lass," his mother said softly. "I am Coira."

Cadence shook her head. "Please don't apologize. It wasn't expected." She lowered her head. "I'm so sorry for your loss."

Coira blinked away a tear but sat nobly, back straight as she nodded. Her wise eyes flickered between Malcolm and Cadence. "'Tis good what lies betwixt you and my son. I didnae expect such a thing."

Oh, but she wished Malcolm would let her off his lap. This was not how she wanted to 'meet' his mother for the first time. But his hold was secure. So she'd have to make do with as much poise as she could muster. "Honestly, I didn't expect this either."

"Nay," Coira said gently. "You thought the Irishman was for you."

Not interested in being coy in front of such a powerful woman, let alone his mother, she nodded. "Yes, I did."

"And I thought Sheila was to be with Malcolm," she said, just as honest. "But then it seems I might have had her with the wrong son."

When Malcolm tensed, Coira's eyes swung his way. "Oh, aye, I spoke with Sheila and know the truth of things now."

"Aye," Malcolm bit out. "But I dinnae want her with that monster. He murdered Da!"

"Nay." Coira shook her head. "I did it as surely as I tried to give that blade to Grant only to have Keir Hamilton use it against William." Her voice grew whisper soft. "'Twas just my foolish heart hoping that I might bring Grant back to us."

"He cannae be brought back now," Malcolm said. "His actions have sealed his fate."

"Nay," Coira said, eyes narrowed. "If anything, *your* actions will seal his fate."

Malcolm ground his jaw. "What would you have me do? Save him from the MacLeod's? Bring him back to our castle so that you might coddle him not as the killer he is but as your long lost son?" He shook his head. "I willnae do it."

"He is not just my son but your brother." Coira stood. "I've already lost my husband, the love of my life, I willnae lose my bairn as well."

Malcolm stood swiftly, set Cadence aside and pointed at his father. "I will see Grant dead for this. Da's death *must* be avenged."

"Then kill Colin MacLeod, kill Keir Hamilton, for *they* are the cause of all of this!" Coira's eyes narrowed severely. "Your brother was taken from us, his mind since addled. Do ye not ken the right o' it then, son?"

Furious, Malcolm started to pace.

Cadence was tempted to leave but just couldn't do it. And whether or not he wanted to hear it, she said, "Your mother's right, Malcolm. Another MacLomain death won't help matters any and though you think your father would be avenged if you killed Grant, I'd bet my life that William would entirely disagree."

Malcolm shook his head. "You didnae know him, lass."

"But I did and she's right," Coira said. "And well you know it!"

Though she wasn't crazy about doing it, Cadence figured she'd better share. "Adlin and your father were here earlier, Malcolm."

When both he and his mother swung incredulous eyes her way, she couldn't help but be aware that she stood between two emotionally charged wizards. Before either could speak she said, "It was when I first came in and sat with you. I asked him if he had a message for you. It was only that William said you'd already received it, Malcolm."

His brows lowered sharply. "I dinnae ken."

"Aye, you are a necromancer." Coira turned her attention from Cadence to Malcolm, an edge of desperation in her voice. "Have you received any message recently?"

Understanding dawned in his eyes. "Aye, earlier, when we implemented the magic of the ring and my mark. 'Twas Torra's voice. She said, "Read the Soul. Find him evermore.""

Coira frowned and sat by William's side, murmuring, "What does that mean, my love?" Without looking at her son, she said, "Malcolm, call in Bradon and Leslie." When he started for the door she added, "Not Nessa. I dinnac trust her."

Add her to the growing list of those who didn't trust Malcolm's wife.

Within a minute, the other two had joined them.

Coira filled them in on what Malcolm had said before continuing. "Leslie, you were the one who finally made sense of Torra's last riddle, mark thy ring, harness thy power. What make you of this one?"

"I'm still not positive I came to the answer on my own—"

"Have confidence in yourself, lass," Coira interrupted. "And think carefully."

Leslie crossed her arms over her chest and bit the corner of her lip as she contemplated. "In the case of the other riddle, I just decided not to take the words so literally. Instead of marking the ring, I brought the ring to the mark." She shook her head and murmured the recent riddle, "Read the Soul. Find him evermore."

She shrugged, a little spark entering her eyes. "If we do it like before, move the first words around. Soul read." Leslie's eyes shot to Bradon. "A little coincidental don't you think?"

His eyes rounded as he understood. "Your horse?"

123

"Soul Reader?" Cadence said.

Coira stood and whispered, "The bloody horse."

"It cannae be." Malcolm raced from the cottage with the others right behind.

"Where's my horse?" Leslie asked Shamus, excitement in her eyes.

"Right outside the caves."

Everyone ran outside…but the horse was gone.

"Where'd she go?" Leslie asked.

Shamus shook his head. "I didnae think to tie her off. There is never a need for it."

Coira shook her head, trembling as she looked at Malcolm. "Is it possible?"

Malcolm shook his head. "I dinnae know…Da's body is still here."

"Aye, but where?" Ilisa asked, joining them.

"Where what?" Bradon said.

"You were off on a horse chase so I thought to have some time alone with William." She frowned, confused. "But he isnae there."

A slow smile crept onto Coira's face. "Nay, he isnae now, is he."

"I don't understand," Cadence said.

Leslie looked at Bradon in shock. "Is this what I think it is?"

"If your horse is what Adlin suspected, if she's a MacLomain wizard, then aye," he said. "The old Viking magic might be at work."

Cadence's mouth dropped. Seriously?

Nessa joined them, eyes wide. "I cannae believe what I witnessed."

"What?" Malcolm asked.

"In the cave…your Da." She shook her head. "Alive!"

The MacLomains flew back into the cave, eager it seemed, to find Malcolm's father resurrected by old Viking magic. Sheila and Cadence were right behind them until *wham*, searing pain ripped through her body and she fell. It appeared the same happened to Sheila because she released a small screech and fell to her knees.

Alarmed, all turned.

Malcolm, eyes narrowed and wicked, tried to run back but hit some sort of unseen wall. Pain ravaged his face as he stumbled back. Slow, murderous, his gaze swung to Nessa, the only other person besides Sheila and Cadence outside of the cave.

Cadence stumbled to her feet and helped Sheila up. Both turned shocked eyes to the dozen or so men pouring out of the forest. It was impossible not to stare at the Scotsman leading them. As tall, broad and handsome as a MacLomain, his hard, pale bluish gray eyes locked on his trapped brethren.

Enraged, Malcolm clenched his fists.

"Grant," Coira murmured. "My son."

Chapter Ten

Malcolm's voice was low and deadly when he looked at Nessa. "You traitorous bitch."

Cadence and Sheila didn't have time to move before they were seized and their weapons confiscated. Nessa, meanwhile, did a slow saunter until she nearly touched the magical wall. She licked her lips and lowered her voice. "You always were too pliable, my love." A throaty laugh erupted. "Did you truly think my brother abandoned me? Nay, 'twas he who convinced Keir to spare my life, to bring me here so that I might once more assist my Laird Hamilton."

"Besides," she said, disgusted eyes swinging Cadence's way. "You've been just as traitorous, husband. It took you no time—"

"Enough," Grant said, his deep voice stopping Nessa mid-sentence. He grabbed Sheila's arm and dragged her forward. "This entrance is the only way out of this cave. Every time you try to find a way around my magic." He touched the area above and between his eyes, his regard flickering to Sheila when he spoke to Malcolm. "This one will feel the pain here." His eyes narrowed. "And we both know she is not nearly strong enough to withstand its crippling power."

"Leave Cadence behind then," Sheila pleaded. "You don't need her."

Grant's eyes remained locked with his brother's. "Nay, but *he* does."

"Son, please dinnae do this," Coira said.

But it didn't matter. They were already being led away.

Cadence met Malcolm's eyes one last time. He didn't have to say a word. The promise was there. *I will find you.*

Grant continued ahead with Nessa while Sheila and Cadence were yanked along by his men. Adorned in yellow and black plaids, they could only be MacLeod's.

Though she knew she should be petrified, Cadence felt surprisingly calm. Even more so when Adlin's voice entered her mind. *"Well, ye've got yourself in a situation now, aye lassie?"*

"So it seems. Any words of wisdom?"

"Let Sheila speak for you both." Adlin paused. *"'Twill be her words that soften the blow."*

Soften the blow? *"What do you mean?"*

But, as usual, he was gone.

Cadence realized that they were heading back toward the stones that brought them here to begin with. So their trip to the Hebrides was merely a means to take her and Sheila prisoner? That seemed odd. And what of William and Soul Reader? Was Malcolm's father alive? Doubtful. If anything, it seemed Nessa had said that as a ruse.

Then there was Malcolm's wolf. She scanned the thin trees and cliffs. Where was he? Perhaps he was lying in wait to lunge when they least expected it. But no help came and soon enough they reached the stones. Nessa, a small, hateful smile on her face, eyed Cadence. "'Tis a slippery thing that you thought to take my husband from me, lass."

"Actually, I didn't and you damned well know it." Cadence didn't care if Adlin had urged her to remain silent. She was furious. "As it turns out, Malcolm looking my way was the best move he could've made."

Nessa slapped her face so hard, Cadence's head whipped to the side. Now that *might* have been the blow Adlin spoke of but she doubted it.

The other woman's face was soon in hers. "I will have him back. Dinnae doubt it."

"Good luck with that," Sheila muttered, eyes narrowed when Nessa turned her way.

"And you must be the one he turned away." An evil grin roped across Nessa's face. "Oh, aye, I could see it from the start the way you desired him." Her eyes slid to Cadence then back to Sheila. "All for naught."

Cadence couldn't help but notice that Sheila had turned her stone into her palm. She didn't much blame her based on Grant's formidable appearance and attitude. But it didn't seem she had to worry much over the ring because his harsh eyes never left her cousin's face.

"Actually, it wasn't for naught," Sheila replied, voice steady and eyes calm as they met Nessa's. "Malcolm is my friend. I'll bet...no I know, that's far more than you can say."

"Malcolm doesnae count lasses as friends," Nessa assured. "As far as I know, he doesnae count anyone his friend."

"Shows how much you know then." Sheila shook her head. "You gave up a treasure, Nessa. Despite what an evil piece of work you are, I can't help but feel bad for you."

When Nessa went to slap Sheila, Grant grabbed her wrist before it made contact. He shook his head sharply. "Your brother doesnae want them banged up."

Nessa's eyes narrowed a fraction. "Then why let me slap the other?"

When Grant's lips thinned, Nessa went silent. It seemed this MacLomain turned MacLeod had some power over her. In fact, it seemed he wielded quite a bit of power as he began to chant and activated the standing stones.

Cadence closed her eyes as dreadful but all-too-familiar sensations swept over her.

The smell of burning sugar.

Pain.

Flailing.

Then a soft thump.

When she opened her eyes, it wasn't to the standing stones and the Hebrides, but to the long darkening forest of somewhere entirely different. It was here, as she came to her feet, that Cadence felt the first true niggling of fear. It was hard to say why. Perhaps because now she knew there was an unnamed distance between her and Malcolm... and with it, a remarkable emptiness.

One of the men nudged her in the back and Cadence stumbled forward. She heard the ocean crashing and smelled brine and sea salt on the air. It seemed wherever she ended up in Scotland, it was near water. Grant must have transported Nessa somewhere else or left her behind because there was no sign of her.

They didn't go far before the forest fell away and they walked along a rocky, wave beaten shore. She blinked against the frigid wind, surprised to see that Grant now led Sheila. But then...just maybe there was something there. Mist and fog etched the horizon as they traveled, making it impossible to see all that far. But it didn't much matter, because they soon came to a sharp curve in the shore that led out onto a small peninsula. An oblong cottage was nestled at the end. Larger than the one in the caves, it included stables and a few smaller cottages.

The inside consisted of one overly large room. A fire crackled on the hearth and several cots and wooden chairs were scattered about. Grant nodded at one of the chairs then Sheila. "Sit." Then he looked at the man holding Cadence. "Tie her off to one of the cots."

Cadence thanked the Goddess it was one that enabled her to see Sheila's face.

Grant made swift work of tying Sheila's wrists. Far looser it seemed than her own hands had been secured. After exchanging a few words in Gaelic, the other man nodded and left. Now Malcolm's brother was alone with them.

He reminded her more of his father, William than Malcolm in appearance save the scar on his temple and the slight cleft in his chin. But his build was near identical to his brother's and just as imposing when he suddenly towered over her. Unlike his brother and father, there existed no kindness in his eyes but nor was there the inherent evil she expected to see.

Cadence pulled back slightly when he crouched in front of her. What did he intend to do? Her heart thudded heavily. In their current position, she and Sheila would be powerless to stop him if he chose to hurt them.

When his hand rose, Sheila said, "Don't you dare hurt her, Grant."

Though he paused, he didn't look at her cousin. Then, before Cadence realized his intentions, he yanked off her pentacle and stood. What did he want with that? But she soon found out. With a swipe of his hand, the chain was magically fixed and he walked around Sheila.

With a heavy frown, her cousin's eyes met hers. She knew what she was thinking.

The pentacle was very likely the reason Sheila had that vision back at the MacLomain castle. And that vision had put her inside *this* man's mind. When he put the necklace around her cousin's neck, Sheila's eyes fluttered then her eyes rolled back in her head. She was going into the same trance as before! Grant pulled another chair over and sat facing her, elbows resting casually on his knees as he watched her intently.

"What are you doing to her, you bastard," Cadence bit out.

Ignoring Cadence, he continued to stare at Sheila.

As before, garbled words came from her mouth but this time her voice remained her own. "I tied you so that you wouldnae hurt yourself, lass. Do you ken?"

What the heck was she talking about?

Grant continued to stare into Sheila's eyes. "You must learn to control the power of the pentacle for this is the only communication betwixt us that cannae be heard by listening ears."

Cadence sat up straighter. Was she hearing correctly? It sounded like Grant was talking through Sheila.

Her cousin continued speaking. "You have been in my mind before, witnessed what I witnessed, so you know the truth of it. But none of this will matter if you cannae control the visions…if you cannae handle our thoughts melding."

When Sheila started to tremble, Grant put his hand over the pentacle. "'Tis a doorway that can be opened and closed by only us. You but visualize the pentacle's center in either darkness or in light. The light opens our minds to one another, the darkness blocks all."

Why was Grant doing this? Was it yet another trick? Something told her otherwise, and she didn't dare hope. Could it be Malcolm's brother was no enemy at all?

"Now block me, lass," Sheila said.

But it definitely wasn't Sheila behind the command. No, it *had* to be Grant.

There but not there at all, Sheila clenched her fists, her face twisted in concentration. Though she shook, it wasn't long before her eyes stopped fluttering and drifted shut. Grant tucked the pentacle under the front of her dress and waited.

"Is she okay?" Cadence whispered.

Grant said nothing.

Several seconds passed before Sheila slowly blinked and opened her eyes. Gone was the turbulent influence of magic and in its place, understanding. Cadence even thought for a moment that a small smile came to her cousin's lips but when she looked closer it seemed not.

Mission apparently accomplished, Grant nodded, stood and left the cottage.

Cadence looked at Sheila and shook her head. "What on Earth just happened, sweetie?"

Sheila mouthed, "I can't tell you right now."

Yet she gave her a thumb's up.

It was impossible not to sigh with relief. So it *was* what it sounded like. Grant and Sheila could communicate telepathically without Keir Hamilton or Colin MacLeod knowing. Or at least that's what she assumed. But until she knew more, Cadence didn't dare get her hopes up too high.

Within a few minutes, Grant and several men returned. When he spoke in Gaelic, a man untied Sheila and retied her to one of the corner cots. Meanwhile, Malcolm's brother propped open the slats on a few of the windows and an icy wind blew in.

Thunder rumbled and an unnatural boom shook the floor.

Sheila and Cadence glanced at one another. This couldn't be good.

Men moved aside another cot in the far corner revealing a metal handled square in the floor. Grant opened it and held down his hand. "My Laird."

Cadence couldn't help but gawk when one big black boot was followed by one of the most overpowering men she'd ever seen. Sun-streaked hair, tall, muscled and handsome in a fiercely unholy way, he wore no fur cloak. When his silvery, dangerous eyes slid her way, she knew hands down that this was Nessa's brother, Colin MacLeod.

Her eyes dropped to the tattoo on his large bicep. Beautiful, it depicted a woman surrounded by feathers. This, her cousins had said, was thought to be Torra MacLomain. Of course it was a great mystery why the enemy would have her marked on his arm.

Not wasting much time on her and her cousin, the MacLeod turned his attention to Grant. "They are nearly here then?"

"Aye," Grant responded. "'Twas weak magic that barred them."

A chill raced over her skin. *Oh no.*

Far too many warriors poured through the hole in the floor. With a sharp barked order from Colin, they exited the cottage. Every muscle in Cadence's body locked up tight. This abduction had been done with one purpose...to lure the MacLomains.

Malcolm, no, please don't come.

But it was already too late.

Colin MacLeod peered out a window and grinned. "She's with them."

Grant nodded. "Just as planned."

"Soon she will be whole," Colin whispered.

What was he talking about?

Unnatural lightning started to streak across the sky. Crackling, it looked almost like chain lightning. Deep blue and murky, the sky grew darker and darker.

"He uses the water to draw forth the storm," Grant said.

The MacLeod's grin only widened. "'Twill make the battling all that more interesting."

It was hard to believe Malcolm was creating this weather but when she thought of his repressed rage…maybe so.

Cadence tried to move her hands but she was bound up too tight. Malcolm was coming and even with the others alongside, he'd be far outnumbered. When Colin, Grant and the last of the warriors strode from the cottage she looked at Sheila, desperate. "We need to get loose. They're about to get slaughtered!"

Sheila frowned and shook her head. "You've never seen Malcolm and Bradon fight. Trust me, nobody's slaughtering them." She yanked at her bindings. "But I agree, getting loose is a great idea."

Wind roared and the front part of the cottage caved in, missing Cadence by inches. Thankfully, the support beams held. But for how much longer? Nearly getting crushed aside, they now had a much better view of what was going on outside and it didn't look good.

Malcolm and Bradon led the way, swords drawn.

"He cut his hair," Cadence said.

"Who?"

"Malcolm."

"Christ, look at that." Sheila's eyes widened. "The Devil himself couldn't make Malcolm do such a thing."

Well, *someone* clearly had and he looked amazing.

Easily outnumbered four to one, the MacLomains didn't seem daunted in the least as they approached.

Sheila narrowed her eyes, "Oh my God, is that who I think it is?"

Cadence grinned. "Yep, it sure is!"

Battleax swinging, Malcolm's father, William was alive and well, ready to fight alongside Coira.

"The Viking magic works which means," Sheila's eyes grew wider as she stared out, "that the horse was actually a MacLomain wizard."

Cadence scanned the others and nodded. "There's a woman I've never seen before."

With long black hair, she was absolutely beautiful and vicious so it seemed as she leapt past Malcolm to be the first to clash swords with an oncoming MacLeod. She might have led the way but the others were right behind.

Cadence's jaw dropped when lightning seemed to gather over Malcolm. Ferocious, he cried out as his blade gathered the electrical power moments before it crashed into Grant's sword. His brother staggered back but shook it off fast and rushed at Malcolm.

Sheila flinched. "Brother against brother. This is bad."

When Colin MacLeod swung at Coira, Bradon met his blade. Shaking, angered, the two pressed against each other until Bradon spun away then twirled back and attacked once more.

Meanwhile, Ilisa threw dagger after dagger and Shamus sliced one warrior after another with his sword. Executing the perfect roundhouse kick, Ilisa twirled and kicked a MacLeod intent to throw a dagger at Shamus. They grinned at one another before going back to back to fight off more.

Even Leslie fought, stabbing her dagger whenever she got a chance.

Storm clouds bubbled like a witch's cauldron and rain poured down in a wide sweeping swath, all but veiling their eyes from the fighting. Cadence again tugged at her bindings, frustrated. What good did it do her knowing how to use a dagger when she was left helpless like this?

Suddenly, fire flared from within the driving rain.

Colin MacLeod.

It had to be. A wizard who manipulated fire, she could only imagine the havoc he wreaked now. Thunder roared, wind whipped and rain fell in heavy gushes. Still, fire flared and crackled in long sweeps.

Through it all were the heavy curses of a woman. Closer, closer, she ranted, until Grant and Colin MacLeod leapt into the cottage. The strange woman with black hair was thrown over Colin's back and was pounding relentlessly with her fists. "Bloody blackguards, ye'll pay for this ye will!"

Irish? Or so said her lilt.

Grant and Colin flew down the doorway in the floor. Colin paused only long enough to swing back and throw out his hand. Cadence and Sheila screamed as fire devoured the ceiling. Then the door slammed shut and he was gone.

Cadence pulled up her legs when wind-fueled flames rushed down the support beams and ravaged the floor in one hungry swoop. Stinging smoke caused tears and breathing became all but impossible.

Goddess, don't let us die like this. Not burned alive. Pleasssseeee.

It wasn't her goddess who appeared through the fire.

No, it was her highlander.

Leaping out of nowhere, he fell on the cot behind her. "Dinnae try to breathe, lass, 'twill kill you for certain."

Already weakened by lack of oxygen, she fell into his arms when he cut her free. Fire was everywhere, devastating, determined. Flung over his shoulder, she was in and out of consciousness as he moved. How would he ever get them out of here?

Heat flared on her face...then cold rain soothed.

When he laid her down, Malcolm protected her face from the elements as she struggled for air. He cupped her cheeks, his voice insistent. "Breathe now, lass. Breathe!"

With a harsh gasp, she tried to pull air into her lungs but it was difficult if not impossible.

"You dinnae get to die on me," he said angrily. "I willnae allow it." Then his voice gentled as he stroked her cheeks. "Focus on my voice and relax, 'tis the only way to pull in air."

Despite his quiet plea, she felt his tension which didn't help. Regardless, she didn't want to leave him, not now that she'd truly found him.

"Think of all the great MacLomain loves, lass. Think about how they made you feel. Dinnae leave that feeling behind."

Adlin.

Listening to both Malcolm's and Adlin's advice, she let peace spread through her. Slowly but surely, she was able to breathe in a small amount of oxygen. This soon led to coughs. Those coughs led to even more oxygen. Then, at last, she was finally able to take solid if not painful breathes.

"I'm okay," she gasped.

Malcolm had just pulled her into his arms when a fresh round of fear flooded her. Sheila! She looked around frantically but soon saw her sitting up with Bradon by her side. Apparently, Leslie had been flitting back and forth. When she saw both were all right she shook her head, voice wobbly. "Don't you two *ever* do that to me again!"

"Wasn't on purpose," Sheila managed.

Before Leslie could bite back, Bradon stood and wrapped his arms around his wife. "Your fear has turned to misplaced anger, lass. All is well now."

"Thanks to you and Malcolm," she muttered into his shoulder.

Cadence knew they'd put their lives at risk to save them. "Thank you both so much."

"You guys are awesome," Sheila added. "Thank you."

It appeared the MacLomains had defeated all but Colin and Grant based on all the bodies. And it seemed based on Coira's actions it was safe to use magic because each one she touched turned to dust.

Malcolm helped her stand. Though shaky she was glad to be back on her feet. The building was now completely engulfed in flames. "Are they?" she began but stopped, confused. "I saw them go beneath the floor."

"Nay," Malcolm said, voice bitter. "They didnae stay there long. 'Twas a portal. They are somewhere else now." He turned to the others. "We must seek shelter. This storm is not all of my making and 'twill soon be snow."

"We've stables and three small huts. 'Tis enough shelter for this eve," William said.

William! She'd nearly forgotten that he'd survived. Sheila soon flung her arms around Malcolm's father. "I can't tell you how happy I am that you're alive!"

He smiled and hugged her tight. "Good to see you as well, lassie."

"Pouring rain," Ilisa reminded with a grin. "Why don't we get a fire lit in the stables then reunite?"

All nodded but Sheila shook her head. "Gotta admit, the idea of a fire isn't appealing in the least right now."

"Aye, but necessary," Coira said. "The temperature drops rapidly and ice already falls."

True enough, sleet and snow was mixing with the rain.

Everyone set to work gathering wood. While the stables weren't nearly as spacious as the main keep it was large enough for them to set up a fire and sit comfortably.

"Shamus, care to hunt some game?" Ilisa asked.

"Aye." He grinned and followed her out into the inclement weather.

Meanwhile, Coira used magic to dry them off. It was an odd sensation feeling her clothes dry instantly on her body. Not that Cadence was complaining. As promised, it was getting far colder by the moment.

It wasn't long before Malcolm's father turned her way, an interested glint in his eyes when he took her hands. "'Tis so good to meet you, Cadence. It does my heart good to see my son happy."

Cadence couldn't help but smile. This MacLomain had a certain charm about him. "Nice to meet you as well. It does my heart good to see you alive."

William's smile widened. "'Twas a thing that, aye?"

They joined the others around the fire. A spit already waited patiently for dinner. Malcolm pulled a plaid from his satchel and wrapped it over her shoulders. Grateful, she nodded, so incredibly happy that he was well.

"So the old Viking magic worked. Two MacLomain wizards walked between Heaven and hell and were resurrected," Sheila said, eyes wide as she looked at William. "What was that like? Better yet, what wizard was in the horse?"

Leslie frowned. "None other than Adlin's sister, Iosbail MacLomain." She gave William a reluctant nod. "While I'm glad you're back I can't say I'm too happy that she's been taken by the enemy."

"Wow," Sheila murmured. "Soul Reader was Iosbail."

"She was." Leslie sighed. "I loved the horse and suspect I could love the woman as much. She's something else."

"Doesn't seem you had much time to get to know her," Sheila said.

"I didn't need to. Iosbail MacLomain makes an immediate impact, one that I happened to like," Leslie said.

"Och, questionable," Malcolm muttered and touched his hair.

Bradon chuckled. "Ilisa did a good job of chopping it off, aye?"

Sheila shook her head. "Not that it doesn't look super but I didn't think you'd ever let anyone cut your hair, Malcolm. What gives?"

Cadence touched it and smiled. He looked just as good with short hair as he did with long, perhaps a little less ferocious, but certainly just as appealing. It brought out a stark handsomeness that made her breath catch.

Malcolm arched a brow Cadence's way, obviously curious at her thoughts, while answering Sheila. "Iosbail said fire would soon engulf me. When it did my hair shouldnae be long."

"And one must listen to an arch immortal wizard like Iosbail, eh?" Sheila winked. "Hey, Bradon had to do it and now look at you both, all crazy-sexy."

Malcolm scowled, offering no response.

"I couldn't agree more," Cadence added and offered him a winning smile.

"And easier when fighting to be sure, aye cousin?" Bradon said.

Malcolm muttered something that sounded a lot like, "'Twill grow back."

"Killer haircut aside, what happened after we left?" Cadence asked, cuddling closer to Malcolm for warmth.

"Well, as implied, Iosbail and William appeared," Bradon said. "Just like the tales of the past, they simply walked out of the forest, both verra much alive."

"The magical wall Grant erected was weak," Malcolm grumbled. "His magic is not nearly as strong as it should be."

"Actually," Sheila said. "Pretty sure he did that on purpose."

"We guessed as much based on the ambush but I take it you mean something else, lass." Coira said, tucked in tight next to her husband.

Sheila nodded, voice soft. "There's been an interesting and much-welcomed development."

"Ah, but good news would be welcome indeed," William said.

Coira nodded, her fingers entwined with his. "Especially about our misplaced but much loved son."

Malcolm grunted but remained silent beneath Coira's pointed look.

Sheila was careful about pulling the pentacle out from her dress. Before she continued, she looked at Cadence. "This is yours, cousin. Say the word and you know I'll return it."

"No," Cadence said. "It was clearly never meant for me. I think it's pretty safe to say Adlin MacLomain wanted *you* to have it."

Coira quickly caught William up on what had happened back at the castle and Sheila's unique ability as a visionary.

"So we've a kindred gift." William offered a warm smile. "'Tis good."

"Truthfully, I can't say with any certainty that we do. Time will tell," Sheila acknowledged. "But as it stands now, this pentacle is a means for me to communicate with Grant without Keir Hamilton or Colin MacLeod knowing."

Startled, Malcolm's parents sat forward.

"Tell us more," Coira urged.

Sheila nodded and finally explained what had transpired earlier between her and Grant. "Like before, I was inside him...mentally, yet unlike the other time it was much more focused." She gently fingered the pentacle. "He explained that we could talk telepathically through this and taught me how to open and close the doorway between us." Sheila's voice became so soft they had to strain to hear. "His mind is not as broken as I thought it would be. He's incredibly strong."

William released a long sigh and nodded. "Aye, no doubt he is...has had to be."

"He shared very little save one important thing." Sheila's expression turned grim. "Keir Hamilton wanted Iosbail MacLomain for a specific reason. He pre-planned so much of this it's downright scary. Based on what Grant shared, only Iosbail can help him secure Torra."

"That must be what Colin meant when he said, "Soon she will be whole,"" Cadence said. "He was talking about Torra."

Bradon bristled. "I dinnae ken what this means. I was there when Keir's chants caged Torra within his castle."

"Only through my mind when Torra possessed it," Leslie reminded. "Her body was not there. We all know she still flew beyond the castle walls in dragon form."

"But there have been no rumors of a dragon for weeks," Malcolm said.

"Nay, yet we all have to agree that means nothing," Coira said. "If Torra's soul is semi-trapped by Hamilton then her body may simply lie in wait, hidden."

"That sounds awful," Cadence said. "How will Keir Hamilton having Iosbail change that? Not that it sounds as if it'd be for the better."

Coira rested her chin on a closed fist, lost in thought. It was William who responded.

"Though not as powerful as her brother, Adlin, Iosbail is inarguably one of the strongest wizards ever to have lived. She was immortal because of the Celtic gods, because of their magic coursing through her veins. Like Adlin, she found true love, slowly aged and eventually passed on but now...not only does Keir possess her reincarnate but he has her immense powers at his disposal. 'Tis obvious he wishes to possess Torra more for the dragon in her than the woman beneath. So might we ask ourselves, what does he know of dragon lore that we dinnae?"

"'Tis the right line of thinking," Adlin said. *"Yet dragons are but myth. Mayhap 'tis best to further search out the bloodline from which she hails."*

"Adlin," Cadence murmured and met William's interested eyes. "He's here."

When William nodded, a warm glint in his eyes, she continued.

"He recommends that you focus less on the lore and more on her actual bloodline."

"Aren't they sort of one and the same?" Sheila asked.

Coira's eyes narrowed slightly. "Not necessarily but as many of us know, Adlin has an interesting way with words."

Sheila nearly beamed her smile grew so wide. "I love that old wizard. We had a helluva time when I traveled back to the Stewart clan."

"Aye, I've a soft spot for her as well," Adlin says.

"He feels the same about you, cousin," Cadence said.

Sheila, of course, talked to thin air. "Good to see you, my friend. Well, see might not be the best choice of words."

Malcolm sighed but surprised everybody when a small grin crawled onto his lips.

"Look at that," Leslie mentioned. "This crazy adventure of ours must be heading in the right direction if Sheila's antics are curling Malcolm's lips up not down."

Sheila winked at Malcolm. "It was only a matter of time before you gave in to my charm, sweetie."

Cadence shrugged when he glanced at her. "Hey, I approve. A smile doesn't look half bad on your mug."

"'Tis not the choicest meat but we've got food and we've already skinned it," Ilisa announced, entering the stables.

Though she and Shamus were snow-capped, both wore wide grins. Cadence smiled. It appeared they'd truly connected and she couldn't be happier. Who knows, maybe this was why she and he had dreamt of one another for years. Not because they were meant to be together but because Shamus and Ilisa were supposed to meet through their connection.

"You're a necromancer, lass," Adlin said. *"Did it not ever occur to you that his long deceased spirit might have been trying to lead you in this verra direction so that he might find his love and your ancestor, Ilisa MacLomain?"*

Her eyes widened. *"Why would you have not told me this sooner?"*

"I dinnae meddle in such things," Adlin said, amused. *"Besides, 'tis better the Irishman held some sway while you and Malcolm found your way to one another. Sometimes a third party can help love along."*

Cadence clenched her jaw. *"You really could have told me this much sooner."*

But, as always, Adlin was gone.

Unreal. But it did sort of make sense. If one thought in circles as Adlin so clearly did.

"Now if we but had something to drink," Ilisa said as she put a rabbit on the spit.

"I'm not much good at summoning fresh game but I can manage some skins of whiskey," William assured. After a brief chant, he reached into his satchel and started pulling a few out.

"Ha! You put Santa Clause to shame," Sheila said, smiling.

Malcolm nodded at Cadence when she received one. "Drink some. 'Twill warm your belly, lass."

Without doubt, it would. But only small sips. Strong stuff.

"We lit fires in the remaining huts," Shamus informed them, sitting down next to Ilisa. "Though not overly large, they're in better shape than I would have thought. 'Twill give those who need it privacy this eve."

Cadence couldn't stop a blush if she tried. Not that she should assume one of those was for her and Malcolm considering there were two married couples here. Yet if there was one thing she was officially over, it was worrying about Nessa. Malcolm's wife had truly proved herself no good.

As if she read her thoughts, Ilisa's eyes flickered between Sheila and Cadence. "By the bloody rood, I nearly forgot to ask what happened to the traitorous MacLeod bitch."

Sheila took a swig from her skin then shook her head. "With any luck, rotting in a time-loop somewhere. The last we saw of her was at the standing stones in the Hebrides." She glanced at Malcolm. "Sorry."

"Nay," he scoffed, brows pulling down. "If I never see the lass again, 'twill be too soon."

"I hope the hell she stays gone this time," Leslie muttered. Draped halfway across Bradon's lap, her cousin appeared more content than ever.

"Here's hoping." Troubled, Sheila looked at Malcolm. "Because she made it pretty clear she still wanted you."

"I dinnae care," Malcolm said. "I want the marriage ended."

"'Tis not done, son," William said.

"We took our vows before the Christian God, not my gods. 'Tis no true pact for me."

When Sheila started to talk, Cadence shook her head. "I tend to agree."

"Naturally," Sheila continued.

"Oh no," Leslie said. "It's been a rough day. If any of you start on religious talk, I'll do my best to whip out some empathic abilities and you won't like it. It's one thing to cross words, another entirely to know exactly what the other is thinking."

Sheila looked skyward. "No offense, Les, but as far as I can tell, you barely know how to use your new powers."

"But she's right." Cadence nodded and took a small sip from her skin, flinching as the liquid burned her throat. "Now's not the time nor the place."

"And, by the way, I am getting better at understanding my abilities," Leslie said. Her eyes turned to Malcolm. "I felt him you know."

"Who?" Malcolm said.

"Your brother, when you two were fighting." Her eyes turned to the fire as she murmured, "He purposefully fought you so that you wouldn't have to go up against Colin MacLeod...and he hated every minute of it."

"I dinnae much care how he feels."

"Yeah, yeah." Leslie met his eyes. "I get the whole 'I hate my brother for trying to kill my parents' thing but it's time to get past that. They're both alive now. And believe it or not, everything he's been doing has been to *help* you not hurt you."

"I agree," Sheila said softly.

As Cadence suspected, Malcolm wouldn't stick around for a compassionate talk about Grant.

"I grow weary." He stood. "Cadence and I will take one of the huts." He looked at her. "Stay, eat then join me, aye?"

Before she had a chance to respond he was gone.

"Way to bring back moody Malcolm," Sheila said to Leslie.

"Me? Didn't you just agree with what I said?"

Cadence rested her forehead in her hand. "Please stop. I'm not in the mood."

Ilisa set aside the first rabbit to cool and added another.

"'Tis just his sore heart at work, lass," William said. "If he truly wants the marriage ended I will find a way."

Grateful, she nodded. She couldn't help but be brutally honest, regardless of what anyone thought. "I appreciate that but please understand, where I respected his marriage before I no longer do. As far as I'm concerned, he's mine."

Sheila's eyes rounded.

Leslie's rolled.

Bradon grinned.

Shamus and Ilisa chuckled.

Coira nodded. "So he is then, lass."

William pulled his wife closer, something close to pride in his eyes. "As she says."

"Right now," she muttered and stood.

Before any could respond, she left.

Chapter Eleven

Though heavy snow fell and darkness had settled, she knew where to find him.

In the hut furthest from the stables, he sat on a cot, head in his hands.

Cadence sat next to him, rested her head on his shoulder and took his hand. Neither said anything for a time until he finally did. "You didnae eat."

"No, not hungry."

"Ilisa will set some aside for us," he said. "I will get it when you're ready."

"I know," she murmured. "I'm not worried."

Malcolm was again silent for some time before he finally said, "You were almost lost to me today, lass."

She turned his face to hers. "No need for what if's. Because of you I'm alive. Again, I find myself thanking you, Malcolm."

"You dinnae need to," he said. "I do for kin…for love."

Cadence closed her eyes and whispered, "Of course you do." Before he could speak, she opened her eyes. "But can you truly love so quickly?"

Eyes softer than she'd ever seen them, he nodded. "'Tis not so quick for a heart that has been without love for so long."

Now those were some melt-down-into-the-floor words. Though she was tempted to ask about his love for Nessa, she knew better. Some things were better left unsaid. Whatever might have been there for his wife was gone, suffocated by her many betrayals to both him and his clan.

When Cadence stood in front of him and started to pull down her dress, he shook his head.

Standing, he looked into her eyes. "Allow me."

Shivers rippled over her as he slowly pulled the dress down to her waist, his hands resting there. Inhaling deeply, he seemed to cherish the moment, as if the simple act of lowering her dress halfway gave him unabashed pleasure. His eyes took their time strolling down her body. There was something exceptionally erotic about the way his gaze traveled, as if he laid claim to every inch of her. Nipples pebbled as though he touched them. Gooseflesh rose on her skin as though already brushing against his body.

One finger hooked loosely into the top of her drooping dress, he walked around her so slowly that the light scrape of his touch along her skin ignited nerve endings she didn't know existed. Behind her, he brushed aside her hair and trailed his hot lips up the side of her neck. All the while, the tips of his fingers twirled in slow, barely-touching circles up her stomach.

Surprised by the sensations rippling through her, she quivered, her legs trembling. Clearly aware of her reaction, one arm locked around her midsection while the back of his knuckles skimmed the side of her breast. Arching, she pushed back against his erection.

"Not like that...not this time," he murmured.

Swoosh. By the time he came back around the front, his tunic was gone. Her eyes fell like a train-wreck down his muscled chest and six-pack abs. He was so entirely made for a woman's eyes.

This man was used to wielding weapons and it showed.

"The sword thrusts, battle ax throws, mace swings, even the draw of those bow and arrows made all this," she whispered, running the tip of her finger down his front.

A small, knowing smile came to his face and his golden eyes flared to life. "And what of the daggers?"

"A handy little side tool that allows you to move in a way that fine-tunes an already perfect package," she said but the words didn't come out all that steady. Instead, they hovered between them, a barely audible definition that he seemed to understand.

His hand wrapped around her neck and he pulled her lips to his.

Tender, soft, searching, he kissed her in such a way that Cadence couldn't doubt for a second that he desired her, even loved her. Their lips roamed and explored, consuming everything the other had to offer.

When Malcolm pulled back, his lips were moist, his eyes predatory. "Take off the rest."

Cadence let her eyes drop. "You first."

Eyes never leaving hers, he pulled off his tartan. *"Show no fear,"* she said mentally at the sight of him in all his glory. Holy heck, she must've been in a state to take him so easily in the cave. Then again, she'd been coming down from the after-effects of

'Malcolm Mead.' Visions of what that left behind flooded her mind's eye. The way he'd taken her against the tree then carried her all the way into the cave while still in her.

Oh yes, the mead had left its mark. Taken against the cave wall, he'd pushed her to heights that had her hot and bothered even now. But he knew nothing of that, only of what had happened *after* the mead wore off. She imagined *that* would be burned in her mind just as long.

"Now you, lass," he murmured.

Sliding her thumbs beneath the dress, she centimeter by centimeter pushed the fabric down over her hipbones. His thick, black lashes shielded his eyes as he watched. His breath slowed as she lowered the fabric. When the dress got below her hips, she released it.

Eager to follow in the wake of the material, his fingers trailed after until they curved around her backside. Testing, measuring, he felt her behind before pulling her flush against him. Hands grasping his shoulders, she bit her lower lip, so aware of his arousal that her heart skipped a few beats then thundered through her veins.

He sat her on the edge of the cot and fell to his knees between her legs.

With a well-aimed, albeit gentle hand pressed against her stomach, he forced her to lay back. When his hands scooped beneath her knees and his teeth nibbled up her right thigh, she knew she was in trouble. Taking his time as he drew closer, his head moved and his tongue flicked, tasting both inner thighs as he worked his way up. Frightened almost by what his talent would invoke, she put her hands on his shoulders.

But it was too late.

Fast, furious, ever the warrior, he attacked.

Instead of grasping his shoulders, she dug her nails into the cot and arched. Well-planned, perfectly executed, he laid claim to her within seconds. She squeezed her eyes shut as he grasped tighter, moved his lips more surely.

But there would be no reprieve.

Within seconds of what she knew would be a mind-blowing orgasm, he scooped her up, lay her down and came over her. His words were hoarse when he said, "This time 'twill be as it should have been betwixt us before, *this* time I will see your eyes."

Cadence cupped his cheek but said nothing. Everything he needed to know was in her gaze, in the ready, quaking need of her body. Her mouth fell open when he pushed forward. She bit her lower lip as he moved. Hard, needy, not taking no for an answer, Malcolm pressed into her. Grabbing his arms, a small sound escaped her lips.

His hand curled around the back of her head and he stopped. "Tell me if I'm hurting you."

She nodded then shook her head, unable to speak.

Kissing her gently then with more passion, she had no choice but to respond. Caught in the feel of him, in the pleasure he was determined to invoke, relaxation washed over her. Like nothing she'd ever felt, it was made of soft touches and murmured words, of a patient man and a desire that would not be relinquished.

When he thrust forward again, there was nothing but poignant emotion.

Shuttering not with orgasm but relief that they were once again so close, she ran one hand over his shoulder and the other down his back. When he squeezed forward once more, she gasped and grabbed his ass.

Damn, he felt *amazing*.

Ignited by the feel of her, or by the touch of her, he became far more ambitious.

With a long, purposeful grind up her body, he thrust even deeper.

Her legs jerked up and her hands fell to the cot because if she clawed at him now, she'd draw blood. Undeterred, he braced up on his hands and locked eyes with her. With sure strides and merciless strength, he moved. Enthralled by the way his muscles flexed, by the way his eyes never left hers, she held on tight, her fingers curling into the mattress.

Again and again, he thrust.

Then, as if he knew what would take her over the edge, he dragged his body in such a way that she was stimulated beyond the feel of him within her but by the friction of his chest against her breasts. Blown away by the extra spark, she moaned as harsh release tore through her.

Whimpering, wave after wave of pleasure throbbed and crashed over her.

With one last thrust, he drove forward, locked up and cried out.

The shaking of his body made the euphoria swamping her all that much sweeter. Toes curling, arms numb, she all but floated away. Entranced by the feel of him exploding inside of her, the feel of her muscles blowing apart, there was nowhere to go but…away.

Body still braced off hers, she could all but feel his strain.

"Let go," she whispered.

But he wouldn't put all his weight on her. Instead he rolled to the side, maintaining the intimacy. Loose, *all* his, she kept one leg draped over him. He pulled her close, tucking one arm beneath her neck.

Malcolm said nothing, only cupped the bottom of her chin and the side of her neck with one hand as his eyes lowered. Not only desire existed in his gaze, but appreciation for what had transpired between them.

Touched by his emotion, exhausted from the love-making, she closed her eyes.

Tender, his lips brushed over hers before he pulled away only to return, his warm arms pulling her close as he wrapped a blanket over them. Minutes, maybe hours later, her eyes fluttered open. When they did, his were closed.

This gave her time to study… relish him. He was only a fractional less intense while he slept. His black brows didn't arch but slashed as if anger were his natural inclination. His lips pulled down only a bit, keeping in line with who he was. But what she found most interesting was the way the corner of his lip twitched, not in a way that made you wonder if he was right in the head but in a way that said he could be funny…was *waiting* for it. Then there were his lips.

Oh, those lips.

Wide, evenly sloped, they were by all means the muscle behind his beauty. They were his main means of expression, the way he either let people close to him or pushed them away.

"Malcolm," she whispered to herself more to taste his name on her tongue than to wake him.

When he didn't stir, she carefully pulled away. After she covered him with the blanket, she slipped back into her dress and left the hut. Everyone was asleep in the stables but as Malcolm assured, food was left for them. By the time she returned he was just sitting up, his eyes on her as she entered.

He came to his feet, wrapped his plaid around his waist and took the meat.

"I would have gotten this." He wiped the snow from her hair then nodded at the cot. "Sit, lass."

She shook her head. "Please, no. I'm good." Cadence held out the food. "You need to eat more than I do. It's been one hell of a day."

Malcolm looked at the game then at her. He again urged her to sit. "We'll eat together then, aye?"

Cadence hated that her stomach grumbled. Nodding, she sat. "Sorry I woke you."

"I never really slept." A lazy grin turned her way. "Not entirely that is."

Once he'd added more wood to the fire, he grabbed a skin of whiskey and sat next to her on the cot. Their backs to the wall, they enjoyed the meat, no matter how cold.

"'Tis strange," he said, softly. "How I feel I know you well though we've had little time to talk since meeting. Mayhap 'tis the power of the ring or even my mark. Still, I'd like to know more about you, lass."

She couldn't agree more about the inherent feeling that they knew one another well already. Though still caught within the throes of what she recognized as new love, there was a connection, an age old rightness that existed between them. Yet still, it couldn't hurt to share.

"Well, I'd like to say I'm an adventuresome, well-traveled woman, but that'd be a lie." She munched a piece of meat thoughtfully. "I've been to a few countries outside of the United States but not many. Once I started counseling then opened my bookstore, I pretty much stayed in New England."

"Aye," he muttered. "'Tis a poor name given your home. Bloody Sassenachs."

Right, the word England was in there. "It's a total mix of nationalities now." She grinned. "Including Scottish."

"I've heard much of the New World and now have been there but," he paused and shook his head, "I dinnae ken why any decent Scotsman would leave his country."

Now this was a topic to tread delicately upon. "As you saw when you visited the twenty-first century, things change drastically as the centuries go by. Technology has advanced so much. Now you can easily travel the globe in under a day. People like exploring different cultures and obviously as time has gone on, have chosen to live far from where they were born."

"Yet I saw stables at your cottage," he said. "So some still travel by horse."

A small smile curled her lips. "Though cottages still exist, I live in what's called a house. As to the stables, or barn, yes, it's still used for horses. Well, just Caitlin's. As to people traveling by horse? Not so much. Some, but not like in this time period. Nowadays, they're ridden more for pleasure, or show, or even racing."

He sighed. "'Tis sad but mayhap it puts them less in harm's way. 'Tis a hard thing to see when a horse is wounded in battle."

"I can only imagine." She took another bite. When done chewing, she said, "Speaking of animals, what happened to your wolf? It never made an appearance at the Hebrides."

"It came after you left." He took a pull of whiskey. "It doesnae seem much up for protecting if it didnae stop Grant from taking you. But still it follows...even here. Yet again, it didnae help fight."

"Strange," she murmured. "Why else would a Celtic god give you a wolf like that?"

He shook his head. "I dinnae know." Interested, his eyes met hers. "But enough of that. Tell me more about yourself. I know you do this thing called ghostwriting for McKayla's book so 'tis no surprise that you would own a store that peddles books. But why did you council suffering lasses?"

Cadence figured he'd ask more about that eventually and had debated how much she actually wanted to share. Yet now, beneath his serious and concerned appraisal, she knew he deserved nothing less than the truth.

"Let's just say that when I was younger I had a similar troubling experience. Because of it, I wanted to help others who had suffered. By doing so, I was able to heal as well."

A heavy frown settled on his face and he took her hand. "You were taken against your will?"

"Yes," she whispered but didn't let the emotion take her for long. She'd long ago confronted her demons. "I don't remember much of it. There's something called a date rape drug in my time. A guy slipped it in my drink and the rest was history."

"Bloody hell," he murmured and put his arm around her shoulder. She could feel the rage trembling in his body. "Where hails this lad now? Once Keir Hamilton is defeated, I will travel with you to the twenty-first century. I am schooled not only in warfare but torture and will make his death long and painful. You may even help with your dagger. Deliver the death blow, aye? Have your revenge."

She almost smiled but didn't.

"Oh, honey, that sounds tempting." She shook her head. "But he's doing hard time in jail. It's revenge enough knowing he can't hurt any more women." She squeezed his hand and met his turbulent eyes. "Please don't worry about me. I've worked through everything and am stronger for it now. Is the pain gone forever? No. It surfaces on occasion. When it does, I seek council. It's something I'll always have to live with but I've got a solid support system. I've had relationships and intimacy since so he didn't ruin me."

"Imprisonment for him then," Malcolm muttered. "He's a lucky bastard he didnae do it here. I would have seen him castrated, disemboweled, de-skinned, drawn and—"

"I get your drift," she said, putting a finger to his lips. "And thank you for all the mental images." A wry chuckle broke from her lips. "But back home, prison's pretty brutal so take comfort in that. I certainly have."

A heavy sigh settled in his chest when she pulled her finger away.

His lips thinned and his sad eyes met hers. "I have been aggressive with you when we've lain together. I didnae know... I wouldnae have..."

"No, no." She shook her head. "Not once have you made me feel used or taken against my will, Malcolm. As to your dominant behavior... that's who you are. Somehow you manage it without a girl feeling ill used. If anything, you're pretty damn good at making me feel both beautiful and desirable."

"I will try to be less—"

"Don't even say it," she interrupted. "Feel what you want to feel when you're with me. If you don't, if you hold back, it'll only hurt us," her last few words turned to a whisper, "and I would hate that more than you know."

He gave a slow nod though he remained troubled. "Then I willnae, not ever, lass."

"Promise?"

"Aye." He stroked her cheek before he once more turned hesitant.

"What?"

"Then you have found forgiveness?" he said, concern still swamping his regard.

"Enough so," she said. "I had to. It was the only way to move on." She tapped her chest lightly. "A weight lifts from here when you let go."

Malcolm seemed to contemplate her words as he chewed.

"Aye then, 'twill be good to see my cousin, Colin again for 'tis time to forgive."

"Yes," she whispered, "it is."

Cadence reined in her courage before she continued. "There's something else you should know about me." She blinked away the moisture in her eyes, aggravated with the emotion. "Something I should have told you from the beginning."

He rested his hand on her thigh. "What is it, lass?"

"I found out something after the rape that had nothing to do with what happened." She put her hand over his, and did her best to keep her eyes on his, not turned down. "And I want you to know that I won't hold it against you if you decide to be with someone else."

Confused, frowning, he waited for her to continue.

Just push it past your lips, Cadence. Get it out. But what made it hardest was she'd never wanted to play with his emotions, keeping this information from him had done the complete opposite.

Yet he'd drawn her to him so completely that she'd turned into a coward. Well, no more. Voice only slightly wobbly, she said, "I can't have children. Or at least the chances are slim to none."

Instead of yanking away his hand or even appearing shocked, he pulled her hand into his lap and wrapped it in both of his. Eyes still on hers, he said, "I am so verra sorry. 'Tis hard that. Are you wanting bairns then?"

"I would've loved one or two. Big fan of kids." She sighed. "But I've come to terms with it. But you..."

"Och," he said, voice impassioned. "I would never take another lass because you cannae have a bairn. Yet if you want one there are ways. I dinnae ken how it is from where you hail but here there are always bairns in need of parents. Too often they are left orphaned by warfare or disease."

"Oh," she murmured, warmth spreading through her. "Back home that's called adopting or even fostering but yeah..." Emotion thickened her throat. "I'm in favor of the idea."

It occurred to her that he referred to children from this day and age which meant two things. The first, he intended that she stay here. The second and far more profound, it sounded like he wanted kids...with her. "How do you feel about children, Malcolm?"

Pain flickered across his face. "I'm fond of the wee ones." He hesitated but continued. "I had hoped I'd have a few by now."

Ah, Nessa. Clearly they had no children despite three years of marriage and she sensed not for lack of trying. She knew she'd be trying *all* the time if she had a man like Malcolm. Yet maybe the fact that he had no children was a blessing in disguise considering everything going on right now. Because something told her they'd somehow likely be used against the MacLomain's during this war.

"You will soon enough and they should be of your bloodline," she said softly.

He pulled her into his lap. "It doesnae matter, lass. Not if you mother them."

There it was. He'd made it clear. Still, she couldn't help but feel like she'd be taking something from him after so much had already been taken. He deserved his own flesh and blood child.

He ran his fingers through her long hair and his astute eyes studied her face. "Even if I couldnae read your thoughts, I'd ken what you were thinking." His fingers dropped to her ring. "I dinnae care if there are eight hundred years separating us or the scant space betwixt our bodies now, you are mine. There is great love here and I willnae see it thrown away."

His passionate words invoked yet another rush of warmth. How often did he read her thoughts? She'd nearly forgotten about the wizardly gift she'd read about in the books Adlin had given her. But she'd ask him more about it later. Right now his assertive nature was once more kicking in. Cadence knew enough to drop the subject of children because at the moment it was a no win situation. Running her fingers along the edge of his strong jawline, she gently kissed his cheek. Revved, it seemed, to take control, his ravenous lips closed over hers.

Desire burned through her.

This time there was nothing slow and sensual about undressing.

Desperate, fumbling, they tore away their clothes.

Kneeling on the cot, he hooked his arms beneath her knees, lifted and pressed her back against the wall. Shaking with anticipation, she wrapped her arms around his neck. *Thump. Thump. Thump.* His heart beat as hard and rapidly as hers. Though fiery heat flared between them she swore she felt soothing mist as well. When his eyes found hers, she shivered. They appeared to almost glow gold.

His magic had ignited.

This hadn't happened the other times. Nervous but intrigued, sharp arousal flared as she pressed her breasts against his chest. He moved against her but not within quite yet. Not to say he wasn't ready. Holy heck was he ready, his thickness winding her up and up and up. Then he growled against her neck. *Sweet sin*, she swore the vibration of his lips against her skin shot right down to her womb.

It didn't take long for her to start begging, her voice desperate. *"Please."*

He lowered until he took one pebbled nipple into his mouth. Twirling his tongue, he suckled then nipped then salved. Squirming, restless, she released a long groan that sputtered then continued as he then focused on the other breast. By the time he was finished, her belly was clenching and her groin throbbing.

When at last he gave her what she needed most, slick sweat coated their bodies.

This time he didn't take it slow but thrust deep, driving her up the wall.

"Och, lass," he breathed against her ear. "'Twill be different this time. I cannae stop the magic."

If any other man had said that she might have chuckled at such a sappy romantic statement but she knew damned well he was being literal. She could feel it in the searing heat spreading through her body, in the sizzling charge crawling over her skin and into the deepest recesses of her being.

As he held her backside with one hand, he braced the other on the wall. With enviable energy, his measured thrusts came rapidly. Unable to stop, she dug her nails into his back, small pleasured cries escaping her lips over and over.

Magic crackled between them, sharpening to a pin point all the deliciously erotic feelings. It was impossible to know where she ended and he began as throbs mixed and stirred with the ever increasing friction of their bodies.

When a sudden and sharp crescendo struck, she bucked, nearly paralyzed by the beautiful lights flickering in her vision and the rippling and releasing of so many muscles. Wave after wave of pleasure washed over her alongside a slew of unstoppable emotions. Wonderful, never-ending, freeing emotions.

He rode out her pleasure and only brought more before he pulled her away from the wall, wrapped his arms tight and thrust one last time. Magic all but burst around them, seen in a thousand shooting shards of varying shades of black, red and gold wrapped in mist. *His* colors... intense, unyielding, powerful shades that ghosted his very being.

It almost felt as though their aura's merged as she held tight.

Chin resting on her shoulder, face buried in her hair, he held her that way for a long time. So spent, near drowned in sated desire, she must have dozed at some point because the next thing she knew, he was sitting on the edge of the cot, tender eyes on her face. Dim, gray light seeped through the small cracks on either side of the door. Not self-conscious in the least that he'd been watching her sleep, she whispered, "Hey there."

A small smile warmed his face. "Good morn to you, lass."

"You're getting better and better at smiling," she murmured.

He brought the back of her hand to his lips. "'Tis impossible not to with you around."

Cadence was about to respond when her eyes spotted the wolf curled up in the corner. She sat up, surprised. "When did he join us?"

Malcolm shrugged. "Some time during the eve. 'Twas good for the beast to get out of the storm."

Smiling, she said, "You've grown pretty fond of him, eh?"

"Aye, I suppose," he said. "For all his uselessness during battle."

"Oh, I think he's just timing it out is all," she said. "You really should give him a name other than beast."

"I dinnae name animals," he muttered.

"But you *could*," she urged.

"What would you have me name him then?"

She shook her head. "Nope, not mine to name."

"But how to name a beastie," he said.

"Well, there are several ways. You could name him based on his appearance, his demeanor or even his actions."

Malcolm appeared to contemplate this as he helped her dress.

"The wolf did do one thing I took notice of." His eyes settled on the animal. "At the Hebrides, he growled when he knew Nessa was coming and he stayed by your side upon her arrival. That, to my mind, makes him wise and intelligent if nothing else." Malcolm nodded. "An old Irish Gaelic name for a gift from a Celtic god. We will call him Kynan."

In response, the wolf raised his head and perked his ears.

"I think he likes that," Cadence said, still smiling.

"Mayhap, if he proves himself, I'll give him a warrior's name in time."

"No way. Kynan's a good, strong name." She ran her fingers through her hair. "Besides, it's not cool to rename an animal. It only confuses them."

"Cool? 'Tis a wolf, lass. Made for this weather. I dinnae think the temperature—"

"It's a twenty-first century expression," she cut him off, "It means great." She chuckled. "Let's tackle this later. I'll teach you some of my words and you can teach me some Gaelic. Deal?"

He nodded before he paused and looked at her. Talk of the twenty-first century must've prompted the next question. "When you first met the wolf...Kynan, your sister spoke of a dog, Apollo."

That's right, she had. "Yes, he was our childhood dog. Let's just say, Leslie and I saw a lot more of him than our parents. Though he wasn't a wolf, Kynan really does look like a larger version of him. I guess in his own way the wolf lends a certain sense of comfort to a pretty daunting adventure."

"That is understandable." Malcolm frowned. "It seems you Brouns have not led the easiest of lives, aye?"

"Oh, it hasn't been that bad. We've managed." Yet Scotland was no doubt good for them. "But I think traveling back in time and meeting you MacLomain's have helped all of us heal in one way or another."

"Aye," he murmured. "And mayhap the same could be said about us MacLomains that you are all here."

She nodded, pleased that he felt that way.

Malcolm pulled her into his arms. "You're a rare beauty in the morn." His fingers grazed her cheek. "Your skin glows."

Cadence warmed. "Pretty sure I have you to thank for that."

Unlike the morning after the night in the tent, he wasn't fleeing. Instead, he kissed her so thoroughly her knees all but buckled.

"Good morn to ye both!" Ilisa said, her head popping in the door.

Malcolm was about to respond but his cousin shook her head sharply.

"Nay lad, no time for talk. Coira received a message from our laird, Colin. He's furious indeed. It seems rumors have spread that Adlin MacLomain is alive and well."

"What?" Cadence said.

"Aye!" Ilisa's eyes went round. "What's worse, clans have started to arrive and all are demanding to see him."

"That's not so bad," Malcolm murmured.

"Mayhap not...if one of those clans hadn't witnessed his death and are now claiming us liars and dragon-breeding heathens. It could be that war has come to us before the real war has even begun."

That didn't sound good. Why would clans be thinking such a thing?

Nine inches of snow had fallen and icy wind gusted as Malcolm, Cadence and even the wolf, Kynan, joined the others. All were bundled in fur cloaks, faces grim as they discussed their next move.

"We're in a desolate corner of Scotland," William said. "'Twould take weeks to reunite with our brethren. There is a portal much like that at the Standing Stones beneath the burnt building. 'Tis our only way to travel."

"Darn," Sheila said. "Not my favorite method of moving around."

"But our only choice," Coira said. "Winter is here and any other way would be long and treacherous."

"Grant had some sort of control over us arriving in the Hebrides," Bradon said. "Now he and Colin MacLeod used this portal in which to travel. Does it not seem likely 'tis also controlled by one of them?"

"Aye, but 'tis a risk we must take," William said. "We dinnae have weeks or even days to spare. Our chieftain needs us."

"More so than ever." Coira's cunning eyes swept to Malcolm. "'Tis quite the rumor being spread. It bespeaks of an impulsive man with both connections and foresight. A clever idea if handled correctly."

What was that all about?

Then, as quickly as Coira's eyes landed on Malcolm, they turned to the smoking snow left behind by the burn. With a downward slash of her hand, what remained of the floor caved in, the hot wood burst into dust then drifted down into a wide, rock-lined hole. A thin layer of ocean swirled over its dirt floor.

"The tide comes in soon then we willnae be able to use this," William said, jumping down. The others followed.

When Malcolm made a motion with his hand, Kynan jumped down as well. None were afraid of the wolf. Even Shamus held his ground, though he eyed the animal with respect.

Coira's eyes met William's. "This portal is different."

"Aye," he whispered.

Cadence didn't like the sound of that.

Malcolm pulled her close and tucked her head against his chest when William and Coira started chanting. *Oh no.* This portal was more like the oak in the cave with its twirling, unsettling suction.

Faint but there, the smell of burning sugar filled the air before everything fell away, including Malcolm. Even the usual pain was slight. The moment she thumped to the ground, Malcolm was searching her out. Holding her head, she muttered, "I'm *really* over traveling this way."

"I'm with you," Leslie agreed.

After he made sure they were okay, Malcolm helped Cadence to her feet, then Sheila

His brows lowered as he looked around. "Something's off about this."

Cadence realized that it was no longer cold. In fact, the trees were green and a warm summer breeze blew over her cheeks.

"Bloody hell, not again," Bradon said, pulling Leslie to her feet.

"It looks like we've been split up from the others," Leslie said, looking around.

So it did. Coira, William, Ilisa and Shamus were no longer with them.

"Ah, there you are."

They spun and Cadence's jaw dropped. As tall, strapping and gorgeous as Malcolm, a man with black hair and light blue eyes issued a wide smile.

"Welcome! I'm your brethren, Adlin MacLomain. I'm afraid you've traveled a few hundred years back in time…well, 247 years to be exact."

Chapter Twelve

Northern Scotland
Home of the original Highland Defiance
1007

Malcolm frowned when Cadence took a few tentative steps in the highlander's direction and said, "Adlin, is that *really* you?"

He and Bradon had their hands on the hilts of their swords. Like him, he knew his cousin couldn't withdraw his sword. This Scotsman who called himself Adlin had ensured it via magic…a magic that was without doubt MacLomain in origin.

Sheila was far less reserved than Cadence when she ran over and threw her arms around him. "Adlin, just *look* at you!"

He chuckled, clearly not opposed to giving her a solid hug before he pulled back. "Please forgive me but I dinnae know you, lass." Then he winked. "But I'm glad that I someday will."

Sheila quickly introduced everyone.

His gaze swept over the others, caught mostly between Bradon and Malcolm before landing on Cadence who had taken a few more steps in his direction. "And I'm afraid I dinnae know you either." He closed the distance and kissed the back of her hand before he paused, his eyes meeting hers. "A necromancer then. So ours was a most unusual friendship, aye?"

"To say the least," she said. Malcolm reigned in his aggravation as she smiled with appreciation. "It's good to finally put a face with the voice in my head."

"No doubt 'tis," he murmured before the whole of his attention turned to the men.

"Though I've fathered many there are few generations betwixt us," he said and held out his hand to Bradon first.

Bradon hesitated for but a moment before he took the firm grasp, hand to elbow. "God, man, I saw you not that long ago and…"

When he trailed off, not wanting to be untactful, Adlin nodded and clasped Bradon on the shoulder. "I looked a bit withered, mayhap?"

"You might've shrunk a wee bit but still strong as ever," Bradon assured.

The corner of Adlin's lip pulled up as his eyes slid to Malcolm. "'Tis good I think that I greeted you first. That one might not have put it so kindly."

"Hell, he knows you already too," Leslie said. "But then you've always been right to the point, Adlin."

Adlin's eyes went to her then back to Bradon. "Another I should be glad I didnae greet first." But then he grinned. "And just as forthright as me," he acknowledged, his grin widening as he sensed something. "Good that you married her. Humor and light will continue to help her heal."

Leslie snorted in derision but Malcolm didn't miss her small smile.

Adlin held his hand out to Malcolm next. "You've anger about you lad, but 'tis all starting to melt away as of late, is it not?"

Malcolm had no particular ill will toward his predecessor, if anything a great deal of respect now that he knew he was truly Adlin MacLomain. Taking the firm grasp, he said, "I too have met you and am honored to do so again."

Adlin nodded and clasped Malcolm's shoulder as he did Bradon's. The magic behind his touch was subliminal and intricate, truly one-of-a-kind. Wise eyes met his. "'Twill be good when you once more return to yourself, lad. But then, you're already halfway there."

"Aye." He couldn't help but look at Cadence. "That I am."

Adlin stepped away, his gaze turning to the forest. "The wolf arrived moments before you. He hunts now."

Malcolm nodded. "We call him Kynan."

"*Nice*," Sheila said. "Glad to hear you named him."

"'Tis a good Irish name," Adlin said. "For a special wolf."

"What do you know of him, Shaman?" Malcolm asked, curious despite.

Adlin shrugged, his mannerisms reminding Malcolm of his older self, the man he'd met when he traveled back in time to the Stewart's.

"I know there's a feel of Fionn Mac Cumhail about him." He stared into the forest. "A gift from a god but not a god at all."

Cadence looked between Malcolm and Adlin. "What do you mean?"

The arch wizard cocked a brow and only offered a crooked grin. "'Tis not for me to say."

"But you did just *say* it," Leslie remarked. "And now opened a can of worms."

"He doesnae speak of worms, lass," Bradon enlightened. "But of a wolf."

Sheila chuckled.

Leslie shook her head, smirking at Bradon. "Let me rephrase. He brought up a subject that won't be put to rest until he reveals the rest of what he knows."

"Then why not just say as much," Malcolm said to Leslie. "Why these odd phrases?"

"Lots of analogies and comparisons where we come from. But believe it or not, many of our phrases actually originated in *this* time period," Cadence said. "Like raining cats and dogs."

"It doesnae rain animals," Bradon said.

"Oh, I know this one," Leslie volunteered. "At some point in the medieval period, that phrase took root because your animals would seek shelter in the beams of thatched buildings during storms. The wood would get slippery so they'd fall hence the saying. Or at least that's supposedly one of the origins of the phrase."

Malcolm rubbed his forehead and shook his head. "'Tis bloody strange, the time from which you hail."

"Actually, not so much," Sheila said. "In our time most animals don't have to try to seek shelter on support beams. They get to lie on our floor comfortably."

"Not all," Cadence reminded. "There's a lot of animal cruelty."

"True," Sheila conceded.

Now it was Adlin's turn to frown as he looked between Bradon and Malcolm, though a twinkle lit his eyes. "'Tis not always easy to travel with these Brouns, aye?"

"You've no idea," Malcolm grumbled.

Bradon pointed between Sheila and Leslie. "Typically, if you head those two off all will stay peaceful."

"Hey," Leslie began.

"Now that's not entirely true," Sheila began.

"Nay," Malcolm ground out, interrupting both. "Enough with this. 'Tis time to find out why we're here."

Cadence nodded and slid her hand into his. "I couldn't agree more."

All looked at Adlin, curious.

His eyes all but sparkled when he smiled. "Some might find this visit back in time favorable, some mayhap not so much. But please know, 'tis necessary if you are to better ken your brethren, Torra."

Malcolm could feel Bradon's tension so spoke for them both. "What know you of Torra, wizard?"

Adlin urged them to walk with him. "Come, I want to show you something then I will tell you some of what to expect while here."

Little was said as they walked through the forest. Though his interest was truly peaked about where they were, Malcolm's thoughts kept drifting to the woman by his side. Cadence had revealed much the eve before and his heart continued to ache for her. He recognized that his gods were at work bringing her to him when they did. After all, what were the odds she would arrive after he and his cousins had saved those women...some who had been abused just as she was?

Nay, this was all meant to be and he'd never been more thankful that she was sent to him.

Now he had two targets in the twenty-first century. Sheila's previous lad for the mental abuse he'd inflicted and Cadence's for what she'd endured. Neither lass would ever know, but one way or another, he would see them avenged.

Then there was the other thing Cadence had shared.

He'd felt her grief from the inside out. After all, it bothered her far more than what she'd experienced at the hands of her abusive monster. Nay, she'd all but conquered that pain. But not being able to have a bairn? That hurt went far deeper. He knew she felt immense guilt having not told him sooner and that bothered him. She worried over what he had gone through with Nessa and was determined to not confuse his heart.

His heart.

Alive again because of her.

Malcolm steered her closer to him as they walked. Never before had he let his magic take a coupling as it had. It hadn't even occurred to him when he'd been with Nessa. But then, she had possessed a dark magic that should not twist with his.

Yet now he'd let magic be part of intimacy. But who better to do such a thing with than Cadence. His groin tightened at the mere thought of it, at the absolute bloody perfection that was *her*. They'd been bonded in a way even he did not fully understand. All he knew was that no other would, *could*, ever take her place. It wasn't just the glow of her ring but the way he inherently needed her the second she was away. When she'd left the cottage the eve before to go get food, he'd known immediately and jolted out of deep slumber.

It would always be that way with them.

They were connected.

As to his wife, Nessa, he did not quite know how he would handle her. If the gods were truly merciful he would never see her again. But he did not think he'd be so lucky. Nay, evil lasses such as her clearly found a way back after they vanished. He still wondered how he could have been so wrong about her. Years of blindly desiring her had ended in what Colin had foreseen all along…disaster.

His thoughts returned to current circumstances when they came to a crude set of stone stairs carved between two massive rock faces. Malcolm kept Cadence's hand in his as they climbed. They'd only reached the top when she stopped, frozen alongside the others.

Surrounded by sweeping mountains, a wide valley was overseen by something so impressive he felt humbled. Nearly as tall as the mountains, a window was carved in a massive rock wall overlooking the ocean. In the shape of a Celtic cross, it allowed through a sweeping wind and a stunning view of the sea beyond.

Adlin didn't go much further before he plunked down in the warm grass. "Sit, please."

They did, eager for more information.

Before he began talking, Leslie looked at him quizzically. "I'm curious why when you met us in the future you didn't seem to remember meeting us now."

Adlin merely arched a brow and shrugged. "My guess is that 'twas in your best interest. If we're to look at this as a timeline, you technically lived those moments before this one so no doubt 'twas best that I acted as such. But then, one never knows, mayhap I didnae recall meeting you for another reason entirely."

"Sounds shady," Leslie muttered.

"I wish I could offer a better explanation. Mayhap someday I will."

Leslie only frowned.

"Now to current circumstances. As implied, Torra is here…well, almost here," Adlin began.

"How is that possible?" Bradon said, obviously aggravated he had to wait to hear more. Malcolm didn't much blame him. This was his sister after all.

"Why don't you start at the beginning, Adlin," Leslie said. "Why you brought us here to tell us for starters."

Bradon frowned at her but she shrugged. "I know what he's like. There's a method to his madness."

Adlin crossed one leg over the other and leaned back on his hands as he looked at Leslie. "I didnae have the most positive impact on you when we last met, aye lass?"

"You were as evasive then as you are now," she replied honestly.

"But you were *so* much fun," Sheila added. "So don't let her get to you."

"I always thought you were pretty great," Cadence added.

Adlin grinned. "Many thanks to you both." Yet his grin soon dropped. "But Leslie is right. I should start at the beginning…or at least my beginning and why I'm here now. Though I didnae physically create this particular Defiance, I sparked its ancient magic as well as many others across Scotland through what is the original Highland Defiance." He nodded south. "The original Defiance is but a small window in a building called aptly the Highland Defiance. The window is made of a piece of carved wood. I inlaid it with stone and magic and 'tis installed there to this day."

Adlin cleared his throat, lost in thought and emotion as he stared unseeing. "The Highland Defiance, named for its magical window, was the building I created when I was first born to

Scotland, such as I was. Never a bairn, but a whole man without the memories of a childhood. Born of a Celtic king and a druidess then delivered from 'Eire via the goddess Brigit to what is now called Scotland, I knew of everything all at once. Though many would wish for such a thing, 'twas a great burden."

"I totally get that," Sheila said, sad. "We are who we are because of our childhood and what we take from it."

"But then we grow and evolve and discover," Leslie said. "I think childhood is overrated."

Cadence sighed. "Gotta say, my sis makes a good point."

Sheila looked between them and didn't argue but nodded. "I suppose for some that might be the case. I'm sorry, I didn't mean…"

"Suffice it to say," Adlin intercepted. "I built this place at the tip of Scotland hoping to create somewhere people of both the Pagan and Christian faith could co-exist. Already, the new God and old gods were creating havoc amongst us all."

Malcolm and Sheila's eyes met.

Neither said a word.

If ever two people stood on opposite sides of religion, it was them.

"Nonetheless, I didnae handle it well enough and soon realized that trying to meld such strong religious beliefs into co-existence would never work, at least not here at the Defiance." He sighed. "So I left, not strife but mostly a sect of the Pagan variety. From there I traveled to Cowal where I focused not on bending people to my will, no matter how unintentional, but to starting a clan…the MacLomains."

"Bloody hell," Bradon murmured. "Through us you achieved what you tried here."

"Aye," Adlin conceded. "I started a family that grew and over many generations I always taught that 'twas all right to worship either the one God or many. Follow your heart. Dinnae let another man tell you where your beliefs should lie. 'Tis always been half the problem in this world in which we live. People telling people who they should believe in. A person's deity is found within their heart, within their soul, no other place."

"Frankly, I'm surprised you're not a little more messed up," Leslie said. "Did you sleep with your offspring or their offspring, Adlin?"

"What the hell, Leslie?" Sheila said, eyes wide.

"I agree," Cadence said. "Too rude even for you."

When Bradon frowned at her, Leslie shook her head and whispered, "Jesus, I'm so sorry hon. He just brings it out in me no matter how old he is." Her angry eyes swung back to Adlin. "You could have told me my horse was Iosbail but you pussy-footed around that one, eh?"

Malcolm narrowed his eyes slightly. Leslie had truly grown close to Soul Reader and like him she reacted with anger when sad.

"I dinnae know of what you speak," Adlin said, eyes more compassionate than Leslie probably deserved. "But if I didnae tell you it was likely to make sure everything on your journey happened as it did. Regardless, I apologize." Adlin continued to eye Leslie. "You remind me much of my sister, Iosbail. I can see why she might have sought you out and most assuredly liked you."

Before Leslie could respond he shook his head. "I fathered six originally nearly five hundred years ago. They were intermarried with allied clans. There were verra few after that." He nodded at Malcolm and Bradon. "They descend from the last of them so they are by far closer to me than most."

"Tell us more about why we're here," Cadence urged, obviously eager to remain focused and mayhap change the subject.

Adlin nodded, "Aye, lass, of course. As to this particular Defiance, I was here but a year ago. 'Twas when I met my one true love, *my* Broun, Mildred."

"Oh," Sheila whispered.

"She's Caitlin's grandmother," Cadence said. "Our family."

"But of course," Adlin said, pale blue eyes warming. "She'd traveled here from our Lord's year, 1942 but I'd watched her from birth…dreamt of her." He paused, remembering. "She was…is the love of my life and I will one day be with her again. Anyway, it was her first night at the original Defiance, which I will soon take you to, that I noticed someone that should not have been here."

Malcolm couldn't help but lean forward, intrigued. "Who?"

"Someone lost in time." Adlin shook his head. "But I should not phrase it that way because Torra wasn't lost at all." He glanced over his shoulder at the massive window. "Nay, the lass had somehow traveled through *that*."

They all looked at the Defiance then back at Adlin.

"Torra? Impossible!" Bradon said.

Adlin nodded. "Aye, 'twas her. I then kept track of her though she only returned a few more times before today. This day, you see, is more important than most." Adlin looked at the sun's placement in the sky. "It willnae be long now. When she comes we will watch from the forest. Then, under the cloak of my magic, you will join her for the evening not as MacLomains but as MacLeods because as it turns out, the MacLeod's currently reside in the Highland Defiance."

"By the bloody rood," Malcolm said. "We are hundreds of years in our past yet still we are to disguise ourselves as MacLeod's once more?"

"Right, because this is not the first time you and Bradon have done such a thing." Not expecting a response, Adlin's wise gaze flickered between them. "But aye, you will be MacLeod's once more. However, this time you might find it…more informative."

Before Malcolm could further question, Adlin popped to his feet. "Come, now, we've rested enough. 'Tis time to go hide."

Cadence's wide eyes met his as Malcolm pulled her up. Close to his ear she whispered, "This is *crazy*, right?"

He had only one answer to give. "This is Adlin, love."

So back down the stairs they went only to duck behind a wide group of bushes not all that far off. Malcolm could only imagine what he would witness through all this. Torra? Truly? He'd believe it when he saw it. As far as he knew, his cousin had never stepped foot beyond the MacLomain castle. More than that, she hadn't left her chambers since she was twelve winters. At that tender age, she'd become a mute and recluse until a decade later and the beginning of this war, just six fortnight's past, when she'd revealed that she was part dragon and flew away.

What Adlin implied was foolhardy.

Yet very little time passed before the sound of light footsteps could be heard on the stairs.

Malcolm could barely breathe as he looked through the branches at the woman who stopped at the bottom. It really *was* Torra! Mayhap eighteen winters at most, she was as stunning as he remembered. Slender, petite, almost fragile, her long dark hair fell in thick waves and her big blue eyes stared into the forest eagerly.

He knew an adventure when he saw one and right now his cousin was on one.

Though Cadence was by his side, he'd kept Bradon on his other just in case. Grasping his cousin's arm, he shook his head when he nearly bounded up. Tortured, he sank back down, a heavy frown on his face.

One thing was for sure, Torra was obviously thrilled to be free...of her self-inflicted prison no doubt. She'd kept her secret from her family for so long, to protect them, because she loved them. Now, as he watched her walk, light and life in her eyes, he felt a certain comfort and relief.

She *had* found happiness, however brief.

Even a walk through a forest in another time was such, especially for her.

After she vanished, they stood.

Bradon looked at Adlin. "Bloody hell, what is this?"

Adlin's gaze swept over them all. "'Tis time for me to go. Follow her but be discreet. When you arrive at the Highland Defiance, you will be welcomed." He made a motion and their plaids shifted from the MacLomain blues and greens to the MacLeod black and yellows.

Cadence looked at Adlin. "Thank you for this. Something tells me whatever we'll see when we follow, Torra will change our way of thinking."

Adlin wasted no time on goodbye's but winked and said over his shoulder while he was leaving, "Keep your anger in check, lads. If not, all in this war you face will be lost. When the time comes, the Defiance will bring you where you need to go."

"But," Sheila started then stopped when she realized Adlin was all but gone.

Malcolm touched her shoulder. "Dinnae fret, lass. I doubt 'twill be the last you see of him."

Cadence looked equally crestfallen but said nothing as she stared after Adlin.

He wrapped an arm over her shoulders and pulled her close. "Same goes for you, love."

Leslie perked a brow at him but there was a 'good for you' smile in her eyes. "Things really *are* changing if you're the one trying to cheer everyone up, Malcolm."

"We should follow," Bradon said, eyes to the forest. "Torra's here. We need to go."

"Aye." Malcolm pulled Cadence after him

They kept far enough behind Torra so as not to alarm her but to easily follow until she stopped at a tall, square wooden building. Not grand by any means, it was more of an elaborate watch tower no doubt stationed close to the ocean to keep watch for enemies. Somewhere within a day's ride, he'd bet there was a castle.

Could it be the MacLeod's?

They ruled this place now and though he hadn't said as much, Malcolm suspected the MacLeod clan had been Adlin's enemy when it came to his tale with Mildred.

"If what Adlin said is true, we should be able to walk right into the courtyard without issue," Bradon said.

"Aye," Malcolm agreed. Yet he was hesitant to bring the women into the heart of the beast without fully understanding their situation.

As it turned out, it was taken out of their hands when a clansman knocked shoulders with Bradon and laughed. "Are ye coming then, lad? 'Twill be a night of merriment indeed."

When Malcolm and Bradon looked at one another, unsure, Cadence surprised them all as she strode forward and waved her hand over her shoulder. "Come on then, kin, we've traveled all this way. 'Tis good highland whiskey to be had!"

Sheila and Leslie shrugged then bounded after her.

"Whiskey to be sure," Sheila declared.

"And mayhap my lad to follow!" Leslie said, a swagger to her hips.

"Bloody hell and damnation," Bradon muttered and followed his wife.

Malcolm squelched a grin and followed his Brouns turned MacLeods. They'd not gone far when a passing peddler stopped to sell them whiskey.

"I've naught to pay you with, kind sir, save my blade's protection whilst you travel," Bradon said.

The peddler eyed him and Malcolm before nodding. "I dinnae think ye'll keep yer word but the MacLeod's have done good by me." He tossed them a few skins. "Be sure to tell yer laird the Defiance's red-haired whiskey man treated ye well, aye?"

Malcolm nodded. "'Tis a warrior's vow that he'll know as much, lad."

The peddler's pock-marked narrow face thinned evermore but his droopy eyes grew righteous. "Aye, then. Good eve to ye."

Bradon and Malcolm nodded to him, watching everything going on around them closely.

The lasses walked just ahead, chatting amongst themselves, or so that's how they made it appear. When they stopped, the men joined them.

"*Look*," Sheila whispered into their small circle. "Just across the courtyard."

All turned eyes to what was transpiring across the way.

Torra had received some food from a peddler and nodded her thanks.

When she turned, a man nearly walked right into her.

She stopped.

He stopped.

Time ceased.

Both stared at one another.

By all that was holy and may all his gods be listening when he muttered, "Bloody hell *no*."

Yet what he saw was what they all saw.

Torra MacLomain and Colin MacLeod stood frozen...eyes only for one another.

Chapter Thirteen

Cadence felt Malcolm's tension as if it were her own.

When she glanced at Sheila and Leslie, it seemed they were just as concerned by Malcolm and Bradon's stiffness as she was. Goddess, what had Adlin led them into?

"Remember what Adlin said." Leslie leaned close to Bradon. "Keep your anger in check or this war will be lost."

Bradon's jaw clenched but he said nothing as he watched.

In truth, Torra and Colin MacLeod had done nothing. In fact, they'd now walked past one another.

"*This*," Leslie muttered. "Is what I should've talked to you more about, Bradon."

Bradon looked at her in question.

Leslie's eyes rounded and she nodded toward Torra. "Right before the mega battle at the Hamilton's I mentioned how strange it was that Colin MacLeod had contacted McKayla in *Torra's* chamber." Her eyes shot to Malcolm. "You both knew that was odd and a little too…" her gaze flickered to Torra and Colin walking away from one another, "*this!*"

When Malcolm pulled up to his full height, Cadence grabbed his hand and shook her head. "She's right…or at least I think. I wasn't there. But I *did* just see the single look that passed between those two. In any powerful romance novel, *that* is the look the writer hopes to capture when they pen about those first few moments…"

"It's timeless," Leslie murmured.

When all eyes went to her, Leslie shrugged and took Bradon's hand. "Trust me. I know."

Sheila put a hand over her heart and watched Torra vanish inside the building. "Something tells me you men *really* aren't gonna like what we're here to see."

While always a fan of a good romance, Cadence couldn't help but shake her head. "Shay, Colin MacLeod tried to burn us alive just yesterday."

Sheila's eyes narrowed, never leaving Colin MacLeod as he followed Torra into the building. "Yeah, but he looks younger now, don't you think?" She shook her head. "I think we're going to see something that happened years ago...though we had to travel hundreds of years in the past to see it."

Leslie's voice was soft when she said, "Torra escaped from the prison of not telling her family the truth, from the prison of having a beast trapped inside of her. When she did, she came here, through the Defiance."

Sheila's eyes turned dewy. "Where she met Colin MacLeod."

"Where she fell in love with him," Leslie speculated.

"Bloody hell *no*," Bradon said. "*Enough.*"

"Aye," Malcolm agreed. "Enough. If there was love betwixt them, and I say this hoping with all my heart 'twas not the case, then we need to find out." His frown deepened. "'Twill make a difference in all of this."

"Will it?" Bradon asked, his frown just as deep. "Because I dinnae care in the least if there was."

"Let's just go inside," Sheila said, "and see what's happening before we jump to too many conclusions."

Leslie nodded. "I agree, totally logical."

"Were you not just jumping to conclusions declaring romance betwixt them?" Malcolm said.

Cadence nodded at the building, eager to end this conversation. "I agree, let's go. We could be missing important stuff already."

She didn't wait for a response but took Malcolm's hand and headed that way.

"Colin doesn't have the tattoo of Torra yet," Cadence pointed out.

"I saw that," Leslie said as they followed. "Interesting."

Bradon grumbled.

Malcolm's lips pulled down further if possible.

"I meant to mention this before but when Cadence and I were at the cottage with Grant and Colin MacLeod, Grant referred to him as a laird." Sheila frowned at the MacLomain men. "I thought he abandoned his clan to join ranks with Keir Hamilton. While I know a whole ton of MacLeod's followed him I thought his father, the chieftain, still lived?"

"As far as we know, he does," Malcolm said.

Bradon sighed. "If there's more to it I dinnae doubt we'll find out soon enough."

Malcolm nodded. "Aye."

Pipes played and a fire roared in the center of the building when they entered. Surprisingly tall from the inside, thin wooden stairs lined the walls, wrapping up and up to a ceiling far above. Many small arrow-slit windows and torches lined the way.

As Adlin promised, they were apparently deep in disguise because none seemed phased by them. Actually, all seemed friendly. But then, why wouldn't they be when alongside fellow MacLeods? Torra already munched on her bread as she smiled at those dancing.

"I really want to go talk to her," Sheila said.

"Me too," Cadence said.

Leslie nodded. "Why not? We're disguised by Adlin's magic right?"

Bradon shook his head sharply. "I think it best if we all stay away. Aye, Adlin said we were in disguise but he never specified if she'd recognize us."

Leslie cocked a brow at him. "No, but she's *clearly* younger now and doesn't meet Sheila and me until older *so...*"

Sheila and Cadence met Leslie's eyes and nodded.

"Nay," Malcolm began but it was too late.

The Brouns were off.

Leslie said over her shoulder, "Best you both stay away. Though Adlin said otherwise, she might recognize you."

Cadence shook her head at Malcolm when he started to follow. If anyone could find out what Torra was doing here, it was her, Sheila and Leslie.

"We'll just meld in alongside her," Sheila murmured as they fell into a small crowd not that far from Torra. "You know. Like our clubbing days. You see someone you want to talk to and you find a way to get close."

"Our clubbing days?" Leslie said.

Sheila looked at Cadence and winked. "Okay, maybe it was me and Cadence, but whatever." She looked at Leslie, exasperated. "Do I really need to walk you through how to do this?"

"You're comparing partying in Boston to chatting up a medieval teenager who is half dragon. Something tells me *I* might need to tell you how this should be done," Leslie bit back.

"Really?" Sheila started.

When she did, Cadence took the opportunity to escape one of their arguments and join Torra. Sheila and Leslie could talk this over all they liked. Meanwhile, she'd genuinely like to meet Malcolm's cousin.

Forget that she's half dragon. Remember she's human just like you.

Falling in beside Torra, she grinned and looked at the dancing crowd. "Quite the celebration."

Though Torra didn't reply, Cadence knew the girl was aware that she'd been spoken to. That in mind, she didn't hesitate to further introduce herself. "Sorry, I know I shouldn't have said that when I don't even know you," she said. "My name's Cadence."

Torra eyed her curiously but said nothing, only nodded before her eyes once more fell on the dancing crowd.

"People do not dance like this where I am from," Cadence said after another minute or so.

As she thought might be the case, Torra's cautious regard soon slipped her way. "And where are you from?"

Understanding that she was in disguise as a MacLeod, Cadence said, "I hail from the south now." May the Goddess forgive her for lying. "Not so much fun there."

Torra continued to eye her before her expression softened. "'Tis indeed a strange accent you have."

"So I've been told." Cadence shrugged and held out her skin to Torra. "Want some?"

She eyed it for a second before she took it. "Aye, many thanks."

Cadence nodded. She'd heard that Torra MacLomain was beautiful but she found the assessment an understatement. The girl's appearance was startling. Rich and luxurious, her black hair had lighter streaks throughout. Her wide, luminous blue eyes tilted up slightly at the corners and her lips were fuller than most. Where the MacLomain men were everything masculine and gorgeous, she was their feminine counterpart. Yes, Cadence could humbly admit she and her cousins were attractive enough but they were no Torra.

Such was proven by all the men drifting closer and closer to the dainty woman.

But Torra didn't seem to notice.

No, her eyes were watching the dancing crowd.

Or so one might think.

But Cadence knew better. Torra couldn't keep her eyes off the tall blond MacLeod across the way. On the outskirts of the crowd, his eyes were on her as well. The attraction between them all but cut away the rest of the room so that only they existed.

Determined to keep Torra with her, she chose to appeal to the only thing that she might find interesting. "Do you know him?" She nodded in Colin's direction. "I remember meeting him once."

"You do?" Torra said.

Shame on her but… "Aye, I am sure of it."

"Who is he?"

"A MacLeod to be certain." She cocked her head as if contemplating. "A son of someone my cousin knew I believe."

Torra's eyelids fluttered a few times before she regrouped and grew most serious. "So he's a MacLeod."

Yes he wore the MacLeod plaid but she didn't blame Torra for double checking. After all, the MacLomain woman was here in disguise as well or so said her simple dress without a plaid. If Torra was younger now then chances were Nessa had not yet married into the MacLomain clan. So Torra would have no knowledge that Colin MacLeod would soon be allied via marriage.

Cadence answered Torra. "Yes, he's definitely a MacLeod." Cadence looked at her and asked what would be expected. "Why ask?"

Torra's eyes met hers and Cadence felt not the magical repercussions she was sure she'd feel talking to a girl who was part dragon but the honest, unabashed regard of a woman. "I was just curious."

Her interested gaze flickered back to him.

Now was the time to tell Torra all the harm Colin would eventually do. Now was the time to tell her exactly how harmful he really was. But something about the look in Torra's eyes, about what she'd seen outside between Torra and Colin, kept her from saying everything she should.

When Sheila and Leslie joined them, Cadence made brief introductions.

Yet it seemed they'd have little time to talk.

Colin MacLeod was heading in their direction.

Cadence prayed Torra wouldn't feel the need to introduce them, especially since Cadence said she thought she knew him. It took everything she had to breathe when he stopped in front of Torra. Best to push from her mind that this man had tried to burn her alive so recently. It helped that he seemed far less ferocious. In fact, she could admit that he was truly handsome. The hardness in his face was not there yet and his quicksilver eyes were not full of death but something fairly close to warmth. And, of course, desire, as they met Torra's.

As it turned out, she didn't need to fear introductions. Cadence and her family might have not stood there at all, so focused were Torra and Colin on one another. The attraction between them was just as profound as it had been outside.

Colin held out his hand to Torra. "Care to dance, lass?"

A small smile blossomed on Torra's face as her hand slid into his and she nodded.

In no time, Colin had her swinging into the crowd. It was an odd thing seeing such an evil man not scowling but grinning, his eyes borderline merry as he pulled Torra close.

"I don't suppose you had much time to find out anything," Sheila said.

Cadence shook her head. "Not really. All I was able to confirm was that she'd never met him before today."

"Something's better than nothing," Leslie said.

When Cadence looked for Malcolm, she found him and Bradon leaning against the back wall. Both had their arms crossed over their chests and scowls on their faces as they watched Torra and Colin.

"Come on, ladies," Cadence said. "We better join the guys and tell them to shape up. The way they're looking now will attract the wrong kind of attention in no time."

Leslie nodded and muttered, "This has got to be thoroughly pissing them off."

When they finally managed to make it through the crowd, Cadence leaned close to Malcolm. "You need to get that look off your face, hon. We seriously don't need a fight breaking out."

Pale eyes turned her way and his expression lightened a fraction. Wrapping one strong arm around her back, he pulled her close beside him. Though still incredibly curious about what was happening between Torra and Colin, it was hard to focus on anything save Malcolm. The scent of him, the feel of his body, the way his hand locked possessively over her hip.

"I think there's a good chance we've seen everything we were meant to see this visit," Leslie said, slipping her hand into Bradon's. "It's been confirmed that this is the first time they met."

Bradon ground his jaw as Colin wrapped an arm around his sister and pulled her close.

Whatever was soon to exist between those two was going to be incredibly intense. But then they were enemies so that was a massive understatement.

"I don't know," Sheila said. "We might be able to learn more if we can chat with her again."

"Do you see those two dancing?" Leslie shook her head. "I think the chances are slim to none that Colin will be leaving her side any time soon."

"Regardless," Malcolm said. "We will stay on for a bit. If for no other reason than to make sure he doesnae hurt her."

"Oh, my guess is he'll get around to that eventually," Leslie murmured. "When he breaks her heart that is."

Bradon took a sip from his skin then handed it to Leslie. "So Adlin brought us here so that we might know that they'd been involved."

"Adlin's a bit of a romantic," Sheila said. "My guess is he wanted us to see how Colin looked at her and vice versa. And want us to understand how deeply they were connected."

"For what purpose?" Bradon shook his head. "If nothing else, this enrages me."

"Oh, I'll bet he banked on that as well," Leslie said.

"I've tried to speak to him telepathically since he left but no luck," Cadence said. "But I'll continue to try because if this adventure proves nothing else it's that he knows a lot more than he's saying."

"Typical Adlin," Leslie said. Her eyes went to her husband. "I'd ask you to dance but I don't think we need to put you any closer to Colin than necessary." Her lips curled up. "Hell of a honeymoon, eh?"

"Honeymoon?" he asked.

"Back home that means time spent alone after the wedding to celebrate the union." She cuddled close to him. "But not many women can say they got to travel through time and were part of a medieval clan war."

Bradon pulled her in front of him and wrapped his arms around her midsection. "Nay, 'twill never be dull with me, lass."

Cadence looked at Sheila. "What about Grant? Any word from him?"

She shook her head. "Nope, nothing since he left yesterday. But then, I doubted I'd hear from him while we're here. I mean technically, he hasn't even been born yet."

"Nor have we," Malcolm said. "'Tis strange, that."

"Definitely not one to overthink," Sheila said.

"So Colin met my sister here God knows how many times and mayhap even at our castle via the flames," Bradon said, continuing to watch them. "I dinnae ken why he never made himself known, why he didnae mingle with the rest of the MacLomains. His sister married into our clan so it makes no good sense."

"And if they fell in love, why wouldn't he seek to marry her?" Sheila said. "Then there would be no reason for your brother to marry Nessa..." Her eyes shot to Malcolm. "I mean you."

"Most likely because as far as we knew, Torra never left her chambers never mind spoke as she is clearly capable of." Malcolm frowned. "If nothing else, she wouldnae be able to explain how they met...if she were so inclined to speak beyond her sixteen words a year."

"Sixteen words?" Cadence said.

"Four at each equinox and solstice," Bradon said. "All prophetic."

"Interesting," she murmured. "So she's not only half dragon, most likely a wizard, but she's a prophet too?"

"Aye," Malcolm said. "To all three."

Despite the unusual circumstances, her awareness of him only grew stronger. The way his chin brushed against her hair on occasion, as if he couldn't get enough of the feel of it. The way the hand on her hip slowly made its way across her stomach, as if he was eager to have her closer.

"We're starting to attract unwanted attention," Bradon said under his breath. "Those three across the way."

Malcolm's eyes narrowed. "Aye, mayhap 'tis time to leave after all."

In agreement, all headed for the door.

So did the three MacLeod clansmen.

"Have you daggers, lasses?" Malcolm asked as they made their way through the courtyard.

They nodded. Cadence's heart started to pound as they left the crowd behind and entered the forest. It was one thing to be shown how to use a dagger, another to realize that she might actually be using it. But she would if she had to.

"We're being pursued for certain," Malcolm said softly. "At least seven of them."

"A lot of good our disguises did," Bradon commented.

Thankfully, they didn't have to travel far to get to the Defiance because the clansmen were close behind. They'd just made it up the stairs when an arrow whistled by.

"Bloody bastards," Malcolm said. Withdrawing his sword, he looked at the women and nodded at the Defiance. "Go wait beside it. Take cover as best you can. If things dinnae go well for me and Bradon, you'll have to jump through it alone. Hopefully, 'twill take you where you are meant to go. Use your rings as well."

"We still have no clue how to do that," Sheila informed.

Bradon shook his head. "'Tis too late to worry over that now. Either way, you cannae stay here." He pulled Leslie close for a quick kiss then said, "Go now."

Malcolm had no time to do the same with Cadence before a MacLeod came around the corner. "Go!" he roared at the women as he swung his blade.

Seeing him fight from afar had been impressive, but mere feet away? Now that was something else. Muscles strained as he slashed and parried then spun, running his blade across the man's neck. Eyes wide, shocked, she could only stare as the man fell to his knees, blood pouring down his neck.

"C'mon!" Sheila yelled and dragged her after them.

The idea of leaving him behind didn't sit well but her cousins weren't giving her much of a choice. The hot sun glared through the Defiance, a bright eye that watched all as they crouched down by the rocky base and waited.

"Don't worry," Leslie said. "They'll kick ass and if they don't we'll go back and help."

"Really?" Cadence said.

"Absolutely," Sheila said. "We don't listen to them when they order us to save our lives in lieu of theirs."

Leslie shook her head. "Nope."

"Good," Cadence said. Hand on her dagger, she ran over in her mind what Malcolm had taught her.

Meanwhile, the MacLomains did what Leslie said they'd do and kicked ass.

They'd already downed five men and almost seemed to be enjoying themselves as more came. Working together well, there seemed to be a rhythm in the way they attacked. And while Bradon was most impressive in his skills, her eyes were one hundred percent locked on Malcolm. Clearly he could kill fast but if she wasn't mistaken he liked to toy with his prey first.

If he thrust and missed, it was with purpose, a means to give them confidence so that they might prove more challenging. Why engage just one when he could get two or three to fight him at once. Though his talent with a sword was amazing, there was an added excitement in his eyes when he fought with his ax. Gruesome yet eye-drawing, his finesse with the weapon was exceptional.

Her eyes traveled over his body, watching avidly as his thigh and calf muscles tightened with each thrust and leap. How his shoulder and arm muscles, now slick with sweat, bulged, sinew and tendons sliding as he swung his ax.

Bradon was just about to down a man rushing Malcolm from behind when a big flash of black intercepted. Kynan already had the enemy to the ground, his long, sharp teeth tearing through the man's jugular vein.

"Holy crap!" Leslie said.

Cadence nodded, proud. "I knew he'd come through."

Malcolm, surprised, glanced over his shoulder at the wolf before he killed another clansman.

"Looks like that's the last of them," Leslie said. "For now."

Cadence had been so completely enthralled by Malcolm that she hadn't noticed that they'd killed far more than seven men...which meant more might follow.

When Bradon and Malcolm ran in their direction, Leslie cupped her hands and created a perch to step on. "Let's go girls."

Sheila went first then Cadence. They didn't need to help Leslie. Bradon scooped her up and set her on the ledge. By the time Cadence pulled her to her feet, the men had jumped up as well.

Hell. The drop off the other side was long and sharp, straight into the raging ocean.

Leslie nodded over their shoulders. "More coming."

"Then no time to hesitate." Bradon grabbed her hand and they leapt.

A low growl came from behind. When they turned it was to see more men flooding onto the field. Hackles up, Kynan stood facing them all, defending the MacLomains so that they might flee. Malcolm was about to whistle for him when an arrow flew. *Thwack.* It landed with a solid thump in Kynan's shoulder.

"Och, nay." Malcolm shook his head, a heavy frown on his face when he looked at Sheila. "Take Cadence and go."

Cadence shook her head. "Oh no, not without you and Kynan."

"Now!" Malcolm yelled at Sheila then leapt down and ran toward the wolf. Though injured, he still fought.

Ready to jump down and follow, Sheila grabbed her hand and yanked back. "He'll be okay, sweetie."

"Are you out of your mind?" Cadence pulled her hand free. "Look how many men are coming. We have to go help!"

Sheila hesitated and slowly started to nod. "You're right. We do."

But it didn't much matter because suddenly both women were shoved harshly.

Straight off the cliff.

Chapter Fourteen

Seconds of sheer terror unfolded before the air twisted around them. As always, burning sugar filled her nostrils as pain seized. Falling, falling, falling, then plunk. Not a hard fall, but a soft drop onto a few inches of snow.

Who cared if the world spun, she sat up immediately and tried to focus. "Malcolm?"

Leslie put a staying hand on her shoulder. "Get your bearings, sis."

Her vision cleared and she looked around. "Is he here?"

"Nay and why is that?" Bradon helped Sheila up. "You were right behind us."

"Kynan," Cadence said as Leslie helped her to her feet. "He tried to defend us but was hurt."

"The wolf?" Bradon shook his head, stunned. "Malcolm went back for the beast?"

Cadence put a shaky hand to her forehead and nodded. "Of course he did. We tried to go after him but someone shoved us over the edge."

"'Tis good that," Bradon muttered. "Malcolm would not have wanted you to stay."

"And he said as much," Sheila said. "But you know how we are about listening."

"Aye." Bradon was about to continue when Colin MacLomain and several warriors appeared through the woods.

Where Cadence was worried it was clear that the laird was equally irritated.

"I send you off on a day's quest yet you return nearly three days later." Colin's turquoise eyes took in their attire as he handed them fur cloaks. "Dressed like the enemy no less." Yet she heard a trace of relief in his voice that quickly turned to concern. "Where's Malcolm?"

"I assume where we left him," Bradon said. "At the Defiance, over two hundred years ago."

"Bloody hell," Colin said. "I dinnae ken."

"He went back for his wolf, Kynan," Cadence said. "So cut him some slack."

Cadence didn't care in the least if she barely knew Colin, her stomach was sour with worry.

The chieftain lowered his brows at her before his regard once more returned to Bradon. "William and the others returned yesterday so I know of most of your journey." His tone lightened. "'Tis good to see William and Coira alive and well."

"Aye." Bradon grinned.

Cadence stood there as everyone started into the forest. "Excuse me?"

All turned.

"What is it, lass?" Bradon asked.

"Seriously?" She tried not to shake with anxiety. "Isn't anybody worried about Malcolm?"

Colin surprised her when he walked back and took her hand, words compassionate. "Dinnae worry over him, lass. Of us all, Malcolm is the best fighter. He will defend his wolf then return."

She frowned. "How can you be sure?"

"Because he has too much to live for." He squeezed her hand, eyes kind. "Aye?"

He seemed so confident in his assurance that she whispered, "I certainly hope so."

When he rejoined Bradon, Leslie and his men, Cadence was glad that Malcolm had decided to forgive him. These guys needed each other more than they knew.

Sheila fell in beside her as they followed.

"I almost feel like I should wait here," Cadence said. "So that he's not alone when he arrives. Hoping, of course, he arrives here and not somewhere else in time."

"He will. I don't doubt it for a second." Her cousin shook her head. "Don't stress out about this. Malcolm's typically a loner so something like this won't faze him." Sheila's interested eyes went to her. "So is it safe to say you two are in love?"

Cadence's heart squeezed and she replied, "I think maybe we are though it seems so fast."

Sheila smiled. "That's how it goes with these men, cousin. Outside of McKayla and Colin, the connection between the Brouns and MacLomains seems to happen instantly. And even in their case it did though Colin put off the inevitable for a few years."

"So it seems," Cadence acknowledged, her voice soft. "I told Malcolm about my past."

Her cousin put her arm around her shoulder as they walked. "I wondered if you would, I'm glad that you did. He should know." She paused, undecided, before she continued. "I'll bet he was furious."

Cadence almost snorted. "You could say that. He's determined to torture the guy before killing him."

Sheila nodded, a smirk on her face. "That sounds like Malcolm."

"I told him I couldn't have children too," she said, softer than before.

"Oh honey." They stopped walking. Sheila's concerned eyes met hers. "That must've been hard for you."

"At first," she conceded. "But he made it really easy." There was that little squeeze in her chest again. "He's up for adopting. I guess kids are left without parents all the time here."

"Sad thought." Sheila peered at her a little closer. "But I'm glad to hear he was so supportive. Do you intend to stay in medieval Scotland then?"

"Honestly, I hadn't given it a lot of thought." She frowned. "While I'm touched he's willing to adopt I can't help but feel bad. He deserves his own flesh and blood children."

Sheila shook her head. "So what are you saying? Are you going to leave him because you can't give him his own child? *Really?*"

"The thought occurred to me," she admitted.

"Total mistake." Sheila's lips pulled down. "You might think you'd be doing him a favor but you wouldn't be, not if he loves you as much as I think he does."

She knew Sheila was right but her conscience continued to niggle at her.

"Come on, cuz." Cadence continued to walk. "This isn't worth worrying about right now. We've got much bigger problems what with a war on the horizon and all."

"Hmm hmm," Sheila said under her breath but let the matter drop.

Cadence figured this would be the perfect opportunity to ask Sheila some overdue questions. "We haven't really had a chance to talk about what happened between you and Grant."

"I shared everything that transpired between us already," she responded a little too quickly.

Best to tread gently it seemed. "So you did but that's not really what I'm getting at." She shot concerned eyes Sheila's way. "What happened in that cottage between you and Grant was pretty damn intense. Out of all of us, I'd say your connection to a MacLomain is by far the most...difficult."

"I dunno," Sheila quipped. "Looks like Torra and Colin MacLeod might have me beat."

"Good chance," Cadence agreed. "But I'm far more worried about you. I know you told us everything about what happened with Grant yet..."

"Yet what?"

"Well, it didn't take long for a strong attraction between Malcolm and me to form," Cadence said, careful to skirt around how hot she'd thought he was from the moment she laid eyes on him. "So I was curious. Your ring burns for Grant which I think is going to be an okay thing but not so much if you don't feel anything when you're near him."

Cadence waited with baited breath. Should she have approached this? Would Sheila once more get upset with her? That was the absolute last thing she wanted after years of separation. But somebody needed to ask this, especially in light of the difficult years behind Sheila.

A long stretch of silence passed as they walked. After what felt like far too long, Sheila finally murmured, "I've never felt anything like it... not even for Malcolm."

Relief washed over Cadence, then happiness for her cousin, and then of course worry.

Sheila continued. "I was attracted to him when I saw him at the Hamilton castle but then, these MacLomain men are pretty damn hot so I forgave myself. Yet this last time the feelings were more profound." She touched the top of her stomach. "Much deeper. Even deeper than when he entered my mind at the MacLomain castle. It was so different."

Cadence touched her arm. "Good different?"

"Yeah," Sheila whispered. "*Really* good different."

"And you think he's stronger than you first suspected after the mental abuse of his capturers?"

Sheila nodded. "Much stronger. In fact, he felt really in control of his emotions. I figured for sure he'd be broken inside and thoroughly convinced that he was someone else entirely. The truth is I thought his mind would be a mess like mine was after being with Jack."

Cadence repressed a frown. Her cousin didn't need to see that. "Sweetie, you've got to remember that Grant has magic, he's a wizard! You and me? We're just mere mortals next to these guys. It's totally understandable that abuse would've affected you more."

"I suppose so," Sheila said. "But now I have new worries. What's going to happen in this war? Malcolm's still furious with his brother and I doubt what happened between me and Grant is going to give Grant leeway on the battlefield."

"I think we all might be surprised when it comes to Malcolm," Cadence said. "Almost losing his father put things in perspective. Already, he's working towards forgiving Colin."

"Really?" Sheila's eyes rounded. "If he can forgive his cousin then I suppose there's hope after all."

"Right." Cadence smiled. "And I don't see Colin or Bradon wanting to kill Grant either. If anything, they'll try to find a way to save him because now we know that he's got this mental connection with you. That, no doubt, tells them he's no real enemy."

"Here's hoping," Sheila said, worry in her eyes.

It suddenly occurred to her that they were passing several warriors who did not wear MacLomain plaids. "That's right. There are other clans here now looking for Adlin MacLomain."

"Now *that's* pretty crazy," Sheila said. "Who do you think would've started such a rumor?"

"I can only imagine," Cadence said, reflecting on the way Coira had looked at Malcolm when this subject was last brought up.

"It'll be good when Malcolm gets here," Sheila muttered as far too many clansmen eyed them with appreciation. "He has a way of sending a subliminal message to guys who wander too close."

Despite her worry, she couldn't help but chuckle. Did he ever.

They'd nearly reached Leslie when little Euphemia, the clan's head cook, stepped in front of them, hands on her bony hips as she eyed Cadence. "Now ye left with me lad but ye dinnae come back with him!" She shook her head, owl eyes narrowed, or so said the folds of skin between her eyes. "Where is he then, lassie?"

Leslie rolled her eyes and joined them. "I already told you where he is, Euphemia."

Euphemia jerked her head toward Cadence. "I want to hear it from *her*."

She was about to respond when Euphemia's eyes slid past her and went as wide as the moon. "Bloody hell!"

A low rumble of murmurs was already rolling through men far and wide as she glanced over her shoulder. Malcolm!

Blood speckled his entire body, including his face, as he headed their way. The wolf lay limp, draped in his arms.

Distressed, Cadence looked around. "We need a tent."

"Use mine." Colin met Malcolm halfway. "Let me take him, cousin. You are weary."

Malcolm's eyes met Colin's, undecided, before he nodded and handed over Kynan. Weak, he leaned against a tree. When Cadence went to him, he pulled her into his arms. "'Tis good to see you well, lass."

She pressed her cheek against his chest, not caring in the least if he was a bloody mess. "I was so worried. We tried to come back for you!"

Chin resting on the top of her head, he whispered, "Aye, and I'd have none of it."

Shocked, she mumbled, "Did *you* push us off somehow?"

"Bloody hell right I did," he growled. "You two dinnae know how to listen."

"Magic," she whispered. "Convenient."

There was a grin in his voice when he said, "Aye."

When she pulled back slightly, a large snowflake drifted down and settled on the tip of her nose. The grin stayed on his face when he brushed away the snow with his forefinger then brought the beaded pool of moisture to his lips. Before she had a chance to watch how much he seemed to enjoy that bit of icy water, his cool lips were on hers. The chilled air all but steamed between them as passion exploded in that single kiss.

Before she had a chance to really sink into where he was taking her, he flinched and pulled back. His eyes shot to Euphemia who must've kicked his shin based on the way he rubbed it. He scowled. "Hell, lassie. I'm done battling for today."

Arms crossed over her chest, she tapped an impatient foot. "You had me worried good and true, ye bloody arse." She pointed a long, thin finger at Colin's tent. "And now here ye are kissin' the lass while the beastie ails."

"Just resting a wee bit," he said but still offered a grin.

Her eyes widened. "And that face of yours! All covered with blood and grins." Euphemia shrugged. "The blood is nothing new but all that smiling at me Malcolm," she muttered as she strode by. "'Twill take some getting used to."

Euphemia took a few steps toward Colin's tent before something occurred to her and she swung back around. Sidling up next to Malcolm she said, "We need to check on your beastie but I cannae enter the laird's tent without you, aye?"

Cadence didn't know what to make of the friendship between these two but found it charming.

"I've laid him on my plaid," Colin said to Malcolm. "You two take my tent this eve. I'll put up another. A river runs not far from here. After you've washed up, join me and the men. We must talk."

Without doubt they did. As far as the eye could see there were tents, carts and warriors. Fires burned and game roasted.

Malcolm nodded at Colin. "Many thanks, cousin."

Cadence didn't miss the surprised look on Colin's face when they turned away. After all, Malcolm's words had actually sounded genuinely *cordial*.

They were about to enter their tent when Euphemia cut Malcolm off. "Might we have a few words alone?"

Malcolm glanced at Cadence. "Nay, she can hear what you have to say, lass."

"Are ye quite sure about that?" Euphemia attempted a wink but her lid just sort of struggled midway down before she gave up.

He nodded and pulled Cadence into the tent after him. Euphemia, not frightened in the least by the sheer size of Kynan, fell to her knees beside him. "Och, what a mighty lad ye are then."

Cadence crouched on his other side and patted him. "How bad is he hurt? I saw him take an arrow."

"That was it," Malcolm said. "I've the magic to help him slumber but not the power to heal."

"I will tend to his wounds," Euphemia assured. "I've got what we need to help him coming." She put her forehead against the wolves and closed her eyes. "Ah, but he has a story to tell, does he not?"

"Given to me by a Celtic god, I'd say as much," Malcolm said, crouching beside Cadence.

Euphemia's eyelids fluttered rapidly before she pulled away and shook her head. "So it might seem but nay, this animal's path didnae follow a god overly long."

"Adlin hinted at as much too," Cadence said. Curious, she spoke to Euphemia. "Do you have magic as well?"

"Aye, 'tis magic of a sort," Malcolm said. "She has a deeper connection than most to the beastie's. A feeling about where they've been and where they're going, sometimes even their purpose."

"Soul Reader," Cadence murmured and eyed the girl. "You knew more about that horse than the rest of us, didn't you?"

"Och, the horse, aye." Euphemia nodded. "I knew she wanted the name I suggested and that it would strengthen the tie between your sister and the soul within the horse."

"Iosbail," Cadence whispered.

A wide smile leapt onto Euphemia's face. "So I heard. Imagine that. A great wizard melding with a horse to save a MacLomain. Bloody good!"

A few men entered. One set down a skin and a pot of steaming water. The other handed a dagger, hilt first, to Malcolm. When they left Euphemia said, "Will your magic keep him down whilst we do this?"

"Aye." Malcolm frowned at Cadence. "'Twill not be a bonnie sight to save Kynan. You shouldnae stay."

She shifted so that he could crouch on the other side of the wolf's head. "Of course I'm staying. Tell me how I can help."

Malcolm searched her eyes for a quick second before nodding. "Take this dagger so that I can pull out the arrow. Dinnae touch the blade, 'tis verra hot. After the arrow's out 'twill be blood.

Euphemia will pour hot water then the whiskey. I will then cauterize the wound with the blade."

Ouch. Poor thing. Cadence nodded. "Got it."

Malcolm hung his head and chanted. "Stay at rest through pain, health to regain. *Dolor plagam sanitatem recipit.*"

With a quick snap, he removed the arrowhead from one side then quickly pulled the arrow free. As promised, blood flowed. Euphemia immediately poured the water then the whiskey. Malcolm muttered a prayer to his gods before he took the blade from Cadence and pressed it against the mutilated flesh. A pungent odor hit her nostrils and she flinched. Not because of the scent but because of the unbearable pain the wolf was thankfully avoiding. At least for now. But what of when he woke?

When Malcolm finally pulled the blade away, the wound was burned over and the bleeding had all but stopped. He rubbed his hand over the wolf's head and nodded. "All will be well."

"Aye," Euphemia agreed. "'Tis a strong beastie, this one."

"What kind of wolf is he exactly?" Cadence asked. "He's got to be at least five feet long and well over a hundred pounds."

"He is of a long gone breed," Euphemia murmured, touching him. "Dire," she whispered and looked at Cadence. "Do ye know this word?"

"Kynan's a Dire wolf?" Cadence shook her head. "But that's impossible. They've been extinct for at least ten thousand years that I know of."

"And what of dragon's, lass?" Malcolm said softly. "How long have they been extinct for?"

True. It seemed medieval Scotland was fast becoming a place of long lost creatures.

Euphemia cocked her head at Malcolm. "Now that this is taken care of what will ye be doing about the rumor ye had me start?"

Caught off guard, it didn't take long for Cadence to get the gist and her eyes shot to Malcolm. "It *was* you who spread the rumor that Adlin was alive!"

"Nay, in truth 'twas me," Euphemia said, arms crossed over her chest. "Just his less than great idea."

Malcolm shrugged. "Whether 'tis or 'tis not great has yet to be seen." He nodded at the tent entrance. "I see far more Scotsmen alongside the MacLomains now than I did when we left."

Cadence was still trying to wrap her mind around the fact he'd asked the cook to spread an incredibly...*insane* rumor. But then she sensed a well-disguised savviness about the girl that masked a cunning mind.

"Aye, you see far more clans to be sure," Euphemia said. "But trust me, friend, 'twas only because you appeared covered in blood with a near dead beastie that the laird didnae have stronger words for you."

"How do you know that?" Malcolm asked.

"Because I heard him talking with Coira and Laird William."

"William's not laird anymore."

"It doesnae matter." Euphemia's eyes were again widening. "I will always respect him that way."

"Aye, 'tis good," Malcolm granted. "So 'twas Coira and William who told Colin 'twas me who caused this rumor?"

"I think as much." Euphemia arched a brow and shook her head. "Many a times I heard, "Bloody Malcolm," muttered from Laird Colin's lips."

Cadence twisted her lip. "That sounds pretty damning."

"Secrets dinnae keep well in this clan." Malcolm stood and pulled Cadence up with him. "I'll wash up then go speak with him."

"I'll come with you while you wash. I could stand a splash of water on my face."

"'Tis cold lass. I can bring you back water."

When he held down a hand to help Euphemia up she shook her head. "The help is busy with duties. Might I not stay with the wolf a bit longer?"

"Aye, lassie," he responded.

"And if it's just the same, I *will* join you, Malcolm," Cadence said. "I'm not quite ready to have you out of my sight yet."

Malcolm pulled the fur cloak tighter around her shoulders. "Have it your way then."

After he'd left, she paused at the tent flap and looked back. "Thank you so much, Euphemia."

The girl looked at her. "What for?"

"For helping to save Kynan." She smiled. "And for being Malcolm's friend."

Euphemia eyed her for a few seconds, a small grin on her lips before she nodded. "Go on then, lass."

Sheila handed Cadence a satchel when she exited. "There are some fresh clothes in here. Join me and Les at the fire soon and warm up, okay?"

"Sure thing," she said, following Malcolm.

Large, heavy snowflakes continued to fall, speckling the woodland as he led her through endless camps. As Sheila insinuated earlier, far less men looked her way with Malcolm at the helm. Some might say it was because he looked savage with all the blood still on him but she knew better. It was his unending ability to claim her as his even though they barely touched. She couldn't quite put her finger on how he pulled it off but he did. She could almost *feel* it in the air.

They didn't walk too far before he led her down a small path encased in shrubs and away from the last of the warriors. The river ran alongside the edge of a tall rock wall.

Cadence crouched and brought some of the icy water to her lips. It tasted *wonderful*.

Meanwhile, Malcolm completely stripped down.

Handful of water midway to her mouth, she froze. Her heart cartwheeled as he washed away the blood. Sure, she'd seen him nude just last night but that was by firelight. While the flicker of flames highlighted the man's perfection, the outdoors, the evergreens, slate rock and grayish blue water, was very much his complimentary counterpart. With snow brushing against his darkened skin, she was able to truly admire in the stark light of day the lean cut of his waist and broad expanse of his shoulders. And his backside, Goddess above, made for the tight squeeze of a woman's hands. When his pale eyes met hers they were less golden brown but richer somehow, as if part of the woodland.

"Enjoying yourself then, lass?"

She nodded and swallowed, the water running uselessly from her hand. "Heck yes."

"Come here," he murmured having finished washing and drying.

Not needing to be told twice, she did. Hands wrapped into her hair, he tilted her head and brought her lips to his. It seemed every time they kissed the passion between them only sparked to life faster. When a low sound came from deep within his chest, she knew that standing outside in winter wasn't about to keep him from what he wanted.

Instead of propping her against a rock or even a tree, he simply yanked up her skirt and lifted her where he stood. Despite the snow and cold, blazing heat burned between them as he lowered her slowly onto an erection clearly not affected in the least by the climate. Arms wrapped around his shoulders, she buried her face in his neck as he moved.

Nothing made her feel more feminine and alive than being held and filled by this man.

Cadence recognized that this coupling was a means to release the last of his rage from battling, perhaps even the worry he'd had over the wolf. It was fast, potent and consuming.

He thrust time and time again, using the weight of her as an effective means of controlling just how deep he went. Lips against his neck, her breath came in short, sharp bursts. The world darkened then brightened as her womb clenched almost painfully...then a spasm, then two more, before ecstasy rocketed through her body.

Squeezing her tightly against him, Malcolm buried his cry of release in her hair, legs trembling. He held her in his arms for a long minute before he carefully lowered her to her feet. This time when his lips met hers there was less urgency and more tenderness, simple unaffected adoration.

Eventually, he pulled away, a warm smile on his face when his eyes met hers. He cupped her cheek. "I'll see us married, lass."

Not, "will you marry me?" No, that wasn't Malcolm's style. But it didn't much matter. His words made her breath catch and her heart flip flop. The idea of being bound to him, calling him her husband, brought tears to her eyes. Oh, she'd marry him all right. Just...what about Nessa? Not wanting the woman anywhere near this profound moment, Cadence nodded. "I'd like nothing more."

Further words about it weren't needed. Everything was right there in the reverent way he looked at her as he brushed away a tear that'd slipped down her cheek. After he adjusted her dress and wrapped a fresh plaid around his lower body, he took her hand and urged her to crouch alongside him at the river's edge.

"Aren't you freezing?" she said, her breath hitting the air in puffs.

"I like the cold." He dipped his hand beneath the water. "Do you want to truly feel the water, lass?"

Unclear, she shook her head. "Pretty sure I already have…many times."

"Nay," he whispered. "Cup your hands together."

Trusting him completely, she did as asked. One hand cupped beneath hers, he scooped water into his other and poured it into hers. Cadence expected to feel icy liquid as she had before but instead felt something entirely different. Though the texture of water was certainly there she felt vibration, life and what she could only describe as rapid movement.

"Shhh," he whispered, keeping her hands steady. "'Tis nothing to fear."

Though the water appeared just as it should, it seemed she held not a puddle of river but an undulating ocean. Crashing, ambitious, the water was very much alive. Humbled, privileged, she nodded and whispered, "This is what I know of religion. My deities are as much in this as they are all around me."

"And they are, lass." He enfolded her hands with his as the water trickled away. "Alive in all that is around us. When one thing dies it doesnae cease to exist. Its energy travels elsewhere and fills another with new life. Nothing has an end. Not you, me," his gaze swept around them, "none of this."

Warmth spread through her and she smiled. "I always figured as much but good to have it confirmed. Why are you showing me this right now?"

"So that you might know how our souls are joined even before we are married." He seemed to look straight inside her. "If anything happens in this upcoming war, if I lose my life, my energy will never be far from yours. I will follow you from life to life, lass. No doubt, I already have."

No sweeter words had ever been uttered and she had to brush away another escaped tear. She felt an absolute truth in what he'd said. "I imagine you're right, Malcolm." She shook her head. "That said, don't you dare die on me anytime soon. I'd like to live a *whole* life with you."

He gave no response but ran the tip of his wet thumb over her bottom lip, his gaze following in its wake. "Wash up as you will, lass, so that we might get back."

"I don't know," she murmured, kissing his finger. "I wouldn't mind staying here awhile longer."

"Insatiable," he murmured, but shook his head when renewed desire entered his eyes. "Nay, lass. There are too many around and while we were lucky just now 'tis doubtful we would not have watching eyes next time."

"Because of all the extra clans you've managed to bring here," she reminded but couldn't seem to lose her smile as he pulled her to her feet. "Speaking of which, what exactly were you thinking when you spread such a rumor?"

"That 'twould bring more clans to our aid in helping to defeat the enemy."

"Ah." But she didn't quite buy it. "Not that you had a witch in your midst that mentally communicated with Adlin MacLomain and a cousin who could shape-shift into him if necessary? Why you've all the tools to nearly bring him to life." Before he could respond she said, "If I didn't know what a truly great guy you were, Malcolm, I might be a little upset. Not because you used me as part of your plan, but because you didn't bother to ask first."

Again he was about to speak but she interrupted. "But then you're also the guy who tried to seduce me with magically enhanced mead." Her brows rose as she looked at him. "You're going to have to get a little better at *not* taking matters into your own hands if this whole 'you and Colin getting along' thing is going to work."

Malcolm pulled a clean tunic over his head, a dry grin on his face. "You've a lot of ideas about my methods."

"And are they correct?"

He strapped on his weapons, his ax gleaming over his shoulders through the ever increasing snow. "'Tis hard to know. Mayhap." Before she could walk away, he grabbed her wrist and pulled her against him. Before she could say a word, he brought her lips a breath away from his. "Can you love me despite my faults, lass?"

Her body shivered, straight from the tips of her toes to the top of her scalp. "I'd say I could love you *because* of your faults but that's cliché." She wet her lips. "No, if I loved you it would not be because of your scheming but because of all the stuff in between. You've a heart I never saw coming."

His eyes warmed as he looked at her.

Boom. Boom. Boom.

Quick, so fast she barely caught the movement, Malcolm had her behind him.

Light flashed through the woods seconds before Colin was running their way.

"Bloody hell," Malcolm said, throwing his words over his shoulder at Cadence. "Go hide now."

"Why?"

"Och! Because our allies come for vengeance."

"Let me help. Maybe I can help," she stuttered as he walked backwards, effectively moving her back. Stumbling, she said, "I know how Adlin thinks. I know I can help."

Cadence ducked behind a rock moments before Colin slid to a halt before Malcolm.

Head shaking at his cousin, he spun and whipped up his hands.

Suddenly, Colin blurred then warped.

Holy hell.

Mouth agape, she watched as what was once the MacLomain laird fogged then became whole once more. She blinked once…unsure…until he reformed.

And an older version of Adlin MacLomain stood waiting in his place.

Chapter Fifteen

The only thing he didn't anticipate was that their allied clans might also possess magic.

And thank the gods they didn't or this might not work.

He quickly tossed aside his weapons to appear less of a threat.

Though he'd never done it, Malcolm spoke within Cadence's mind. *"'Tis me, Malcolm, in your mind, lass. You must give ready answers as you think Adlin would give them to make this work, aye?"*

Her mind quivered against his, no doubt adjusting to the erotic feeling of the Broun/MacLomain mental connection. Malcolm wasn't above clenching his fists at the sensation. It was like nothing he'd ever felt. But now was not the time to dwell on emotions. *"Did you hear me then?"* he said within her mind. *"Just visualize me then speak into your mind to respond."*

Meanwhile, Adlin, also known as Colin, clenched his fists and muttered under his breath. "Malcolm, you bloody arse."

"I don't need to visualize you," Cadence's words flittered into his head, slightly irritated no doubt that he'd not spoken mentally before. It took some getting used to. *"I'm looking right at you!"*

"Aye, lass, but those feelings coursing through you are distracting, are they not?"

Desire burned within her mind. *"To say the least."* He felt the womanly nudge of her thoughts. *"We need to do this more often."*

"Aye," he agreed, flirting. *"'Twould be my pleasure."*

Colin glared over his shoulder at Malcolm. "I can hear you two. Are you seriously pulling this crap right now?"

His cousin had spent three years in the twenty-first century and it came through clearly in his dialogue now. Nonplussed, Malcolm nodded toward the trees. "Cadence will relay what you need to know of Adlin to me. I'll relay it to you." He winked. "Good luck."

Colin's eyes narrowed. "Not sure I like that grin on your face."

He had no chance to respond before an older clansman strode out of the forest, obviously a little too in his cups. When his bleary eyes focused, he stopped short.

"Bloody hell… Adlin?"

Malcolm eyed the man's tartan. They were allies but separated by a generation or so which made this tricky.

Colin must've pulled this image of Adlin from Malcolm's mind as he had never met the old man himself. He'd done a remarkable job of mimicking the arch wizard when he spoke. His voice old but young, he stood up straighter, head held high. "Aye, 'tis me." He nodded at the forest beyond. "What is this?"

The allied clansman, his tartan not tucked quite right, said, "I take issue with rumor not being truth. Why did you not join us when requested?"

"Do ye not see the whole of what is happening in these lands, lad?" Colin said, throwing back his bony shoulders. "Unrest at the verra least."

The man hitched his jaw and nodded. "Aye, 'tis true. That is why you should be with us. Share your knowledge!"

Colin nodded. "Aye."

"So tell me then, why did I see you die yet here you stand?"

Malcolm nudged Cadence's mind. *"Thoughts?"*

Her internal sigh all but slammed into him. *"Really? I'll bet Colin can come up with something."*

"Did you see me die, then?" Colin said to the man. "Did my breath cease to exist?"

"Like I said," she muttered into his mind.

Malcolm couldn't help but grin. She adjusted well to any situation in which she was thrust.

"'Tis been near on thirty years since last you were here," the man responded. "I watched you say goodbye to your clan then vanish!"

"Only in this life, not the next," Cadence said. *"When done there, I returned."*

Malcolm mentally gave the words to Colin and he repeated them aloud.

"I've no proof of that. For all we know you rally us to fight an enemy that will surely defeat us all," the clansman declared.

"Tell him to walk to the man, confront him," she said.

So he did and Colin did as asked.

Standing in front of a man nearly a head taller than him, frail old Adlin pulled back his shoulders and glared up.

"What now, lass?" Malcolm asked. *"'Tis really a point he should say something."*

Silence.

Not good.

Malcolm didn't dare look at her but said, *"If ever there was a time, lass."*

"Have him look to the sky," she said.

Message translated, Colin did.

Malcolm pursed his lips when he all but felt her indecision. *"And?"*

"Mention the stars and how they affect us all."

"'Tis snowing lass. No stars."

"Oh, damn, right." Hesitation. *"Adlin surely sees beyond the snow and clouds to the stars. Go with that."*

The clansman opposite Colin looked up at the sky, interested. "What see you there, Shaman?"

Though Colin clearly received the message Malcolm sent via Cadence he dropped and shook his head. "So verra much, lad."

It was hard not to roll his eyes. *Bloody hell.*

Then words started to enter his mind and Malcolm knew they passed from Cadence right through him to Colin. His cousin, tense for a moment, put his hand on the clansman's shoulder and started to repeat them...

"'Twas just yesterday, James, that we first battled for her, aye?"

The clansman froze, eyes locked with Colin's.

"So you remember then," Colin said. "She had hair like the sun and eyes like the loch. Never was there a more bonnie lass."

"Adlin?" the clansman whispered, clasping Colin's arms. "'Tis truly you?"

"No other knows of her beauty, of our competition, aye?"

"Nay," the clansman said vehemently. "How *could* they?"

Long seconds passed as the man continued to eye Colin.

Right now, this telling moment, would take the war one way or the other.

At long last the man hung his head and breathed a deep sigh of relief. "Bloody hell, Adlin. You *are* alive."

Colin grasped the back of the man's head as though he cherished a long lost friend. "Aye, I am, lad, and ready to fight."

The man nodded, staying that way a time before he pulled away, eyes wet. "'Tis so good to see you."

"And you, my old friend," Colin murmured. "And you."

The clansman nodded and raised a firm hand to cease the warriors behind him.

"To a war fought well together then?" Colin said.

The man breathed deeply. "Is it as the rumors say? Have you a dragon?"

Colin shook his head and his voice grew emotional. "Nay, *they* have our dragon. If we defeat the Hamilton's they...*we*, all have a dragon, every last one of us." He locked arms with the clansman, hand to elbow. "If you but fight by our side."

Bushy white brows dropped a good inch as his long mouth pulled down. The clansman nodded. "You have my men." His shoulders drew back as he looked at Adlin. "And our allies if ye'll have them."

"'Twould be an honor," Colin replied.

"Aye." The man patted him on the shoulder, grin splitting his face. "'Twould indeed!"

"Go," Colin urged. "Feast, enjoy the lasses at our camp then join me in battle, aye?"

With a solid nod and a wave to his warriors, the clansman departed. Encouragement was on his lips as he and his trailed into the darkening forest.

The moment they were gone, Malcolm said, "Well, that didnae go so—"

His words were cut short when a solid punch hit his face.

Before he had a chance to retaliate another hit him then a solid drive to the midsection. He wrapped his arm around his attacker to eliminate the threat as they both fell into the river. *Punch. Punch.* Two more solid fistfuls hit his face.

Colin.

Not Adlin anymore.

While he meant with all his heart to forgive, the moment he knew it was Colin hitting him, Malcom saw red, fury, revenge.

Grabbing his cousin around his neck with his arm, he started to deal blow after blow to his midsection.

With a swift roll and slam, Colin repositioned and wrapped a hand around his neck.

Malcolm lifted his right leg and swiped fast, rolling them again.

"Bloody hell," Colin seethed.

If he had a dagger on him it'd be well-used by now but it seemed both were without weapons so Malcolm pressed the heel of his palm into Colin's temple and pushed his head beneath the water.

Though bubbles rose, Colin kneed up and caught him in the shin.

Malcolm caught Colin's knee and twisted.

Colin didn't fight the move but rolled and grabbed Malcolm in such a way that he fell beneath the water. Relishing rather than fighting his element, he sank, fell then arched before grabbing his cousin's ankle. With a hard yank, he released Colin's precarious stance on the rocky shore.

Both fell beneath the water, their narrowed eyes on one another.

Could he grab a stick or rock to fight? Sure. But he didn't want to. No, he wanted to wrap his bare hands around Colin. He wanted to fight free of anything but...them.

They'd just found purchase with their feet when Colin came at him swinging.

Malcolm ducked and released a well-aimed splash of water into his eyes, just enough to blind him. Then he tagged him in the face, two punches on one side, one punch on the other. When Colin staggered back, Malcolm didn't let up. He knew what would hurt him and what would cripple him. With a solid punch to his upper stomach, Colin buckled.

"Stop!" Cadence cried into his mind.

Gods, no. Malcolm went to punch again but Colin had recovered enough to sideswipe him. When he did, his cousin took advantage, drilling him up his side.

Hell. Pain.

Could he use magic? Could Colin? Sure. But that wasn't what this was about.

Malcolm took a quick underwater swing and punched him square in the lower back.

Colin bent over in pain. When he did, Malcolm grabbed him around the center and delivered the same blow to the other side. Kicking back, his cousin caught his center and he curled in.

Spitting water out of his mouth as he surfaced, Malcolm once more narrowed his eyes and made a come-hither motion with his hands. "You've been against me all along. Come on then, cousin. Have done with it if you can."

Colin, caught in the rage of battle, shook his head, feet on a sloppy shore. "*Against* you? Nay. Trying to bring you to your senses? Aye."

"He makes a valid point," Cadence volunteered from the sidelines, her face worried. "Maybe if you talked this out rather than fought it out..."

Malcolm looked skyward. "Enough with the bloody forgiving," he said. "'Tis done, lass."

"What forgiving?" Colin said, arms still up, ready for Malcolm's attack.

"Malcolm's forgiving," Cadence cried out when Malcolm leapt from the water, eager for some more battle.

Frustrated, he said, "Now is not the time, lass."

"Clearly the time," she muttered as he moved closer to Colin.

"Have you forgiveness then?" Colin asked.

But it was too late. Malcolm took a good drive and slammed him to the ground. Forgiveness? Nay. He knew nothing of that. Yet after the first solid blow he paused, fist drawn back, mostly because Cadence had plunked down on a rock beside them and said, "Seriously, Malcolm?"

Colin took advantage of the pause and dealt a solid punch.

Malcolm grabbed his neck and squeezed down on Colin's windpipe.

"Do it then," Colin whispered. "I'll not use magic to fight you."

Colin grasped Malcolm's forearms as he pressed down.

Shaking, eyes locked, voice raspier than ever, Malcolm said, "A thousand times over I've done this to you."

Cadence screamed in his head, *Be better than this.*

But her words didn't matter.

No, only the look in his cousin's eyes.

Aye, he could forgive but…what was the point if it meant nothing?

Colin's hands squeezed his arms. "Be a MacLomain."

Malcolm shook as he looked down. "I've been nothing but, cousin. What of you?"

Eyes sliding shut, it was more and more obvious Colin wouldn't continue the fight. "I'm learning."

As his cousin gave up his power, relented, Malcolm's fingers started to loosen but he didn't let go. Eyes closed then opened, his cousin only watched him, pled with him.

Like he'd been doing all along.

Colin sought forgiveness.

As he should.

As they all should.

Malcolm slowly pulled his hands away.

Colin breathed deeply.

Sitting back on his haunches, Malcolm hung his head.

He'd tried so hard to do this right but had done it all wrong.

The last of his rage and bitterness drained away. Colin was like a brother to him and he'd let so much get in the way of that. He stumbled to his feet and held out a hand. "I dinnae want the strife betwixt us anymore. You are my blood and I love you, cousin. Let us leave the past behind and start anew?"

The laird looked at him long and hard before he finally nodded and took the offered hand. The men embraced, at last putting to rest all the hurt. When Colin stepped back, the corner of his lip pulled up a bit. "I think 'tis good your lass was here or this might have gone another way, aye?"

"Nay," Malcolm scoffed. "I wouldnae have killed you."

"Definitely not," Cadence agreed, a wide smile on her face.

Colin eyed her. "You've done good by my cousin, lass and therefore good by the MacLomain clan. 'Twas truly Adlin in your mind then?"

She nodded. "And in yours as well."

"You gave me more than you know by channeling him to me, Cadence," Colin said. "I have long wanted to meet him and now have touched his thoughts. 'Twas a gift indeed."

Cadence blushed beneath the praise but gave no response.

Night had nearly fallen as the three of them made their way back to the camp, Colin and Malcolm chatting like old friends the whole time. His step was lighter than it'd been in years as they started to reconnect.

"We've had news," Colin said. "And 'tis not favorable."

Malcolm looked at him in question.

"Colin MacLeod's Da died which makes him acting chieftain now."

"Bloody hell," Malcolm muttered.

"Aye, and it seems the whole of the clan is willing to forgive Colin despite his traitorous actions and recognize him as laird," Colin continued. "Rumor has it far more MacLeod's are coming as well as allies of the father who died."

Before Malcolm could speak, his cousin continued. "So despite my previous anger at your actions, bringing more allies to the MacLomain's was the best thing you could have done for us."

"So why attack me as you did?" Malcolm said.

"Because 'twas time we had a good battle, was it not?"

"Aye, mayhap 'twas."

Colin and Malcolm's eyes connected briefly in mutual respect. His cousin would make a fine chieftain to be sure.

"What of 'Adlin' then?" Malcolm asked softly as they entered their own small encampment, curious how his cousin intended to maintain the secret.

"He has opted to stay on the outskirts of the battle." Colin winked. "I've sent a few of my best warriors with him. They shall attack the enemy from another angle."

"Ah, this is good." Malcolm nodded. "I will change once more then join you at the fire."

Colin nodded, no doubt off to change as well.

Yet before Malcolm saw to himself, he pulled his lass into his arms. Red hair aflame in the firelight and green eyes bright, he once more reveled in her beauty. Finger beneath her chin, he tilted back her head. "You are the most exceptional woman I've ever met, Cadence. Thank you for all that you have done for me."

"Believe it or not, it was all you, Malcolm." A smile curved her full lips. "I just helped you see past all the emotional clutter."

"Was that what it was?" He dropped a soft kiss on her lips. "You are humble. 'Tis half your appeal I suppose."

She grinned. "So what's the other half of my appeal?"

The more he looked at her the more he wanted her. It was never-ending. He dropped another kiss on her lips. "There are not enough words to describe all of your appeal, lass. Everything you see in my eyes when I look at you but skim's the surface." Before she could respond, he kissed the back of her hand then nodded at the fire. "Time for you to warm up. Go join your cousin and sister whilst I change."

Cadence nodded and did as suggested.

"The wolf is gone," Euphemia said, meeting him at the tent flap.

Malcolm peered into the tent. Indeed, Kynan was gone. He frowned at Euphemia in question.

"I watched him lope off." She shrugged. "I'd say he's gone to hunt."

"So he looked well then?"

"Aye, well enough." Euphemia hesitated a moment. "There is more about the beastie that I didnae say before, 'tis for you to make of it what you will."

When she again hesitated he said, "Well, out with it, lass."

"'Twas sent to you, Malcolm, to watch over you that is...to protect."

"Aye," he said, "by Fionn Mac Cumhail."

"Nay." she shook her head. "He but delivered your Kynan." Her brows arched. "Before that the wolf called another MacLomain his. 'Twas *that* lad who sent you the wolf."

Now this he hadn't expected. "Who, lassie?"

Euphemia touched his chest with a closed fist. "He whose heart is so similar. A blood tie closer to you than any save your Ma and Da."

Damnation. No. He shook his head. "Nay, it cannae be."

Grant had sent Kynan?

"Aye, but 'tis," she murmured before her eyes narrowed. "And dinnae get to thinking it was to spy on you." Euphemia shook her head. Before she walked away, she said, "This wolf was sent only to keep you safe."

Frown heavy, he entered the tent. As he changed, he mulled over Euphemia's warning. She said the wolf wasn't here to spy but how could he be sure? Yet the more he thought about it the more the possibility of her words being truthful seemed plausible. Cadence had said the wolf didn't attack when Grant was there. No, but it *had* defended them at the Defiance when his brother was absent.

But why would Grant send him a wolf? His frown deepened as he thought about what Sheila had told them. How she speculated his brother was no enemy at all. Then what Leslie had said about Grant's emotions when he battled Malcolm.

Still, it was impossible to feel anything but rage as he remembered Grant's actions at the Hamilton castle. As he battled alongside the Hamilton's when their father lay dying. Though mayhap it should matter, it was impossible to forgive the action simply because William ended up alive.

Pushing aside his troubled thoughts, he joined the others around the fire.

When Colin tossed him a skin, he nodded and took a long swig. Cadence smiled and handed him some meat. Listening to the others talk, he eyed her while he ate. By the gods, did he love her. With a smile, he recalled their earlier conversation. She would be his wife. Soon he would talk to his Da about what could be done to end his marriage to Nessa.

"'Tis good to see you smiling, cousin," Bradon said, his gaze tossed between Malcolm and Cadence. "These Broun lasses are good for us MacLomains, aye?"

"Yeah we are," Leslie said with a grin as she winked at Bradon.

"Aye," Malcolm agreed but his smile soon dropped when he thought of all that lay ahead. "Have we heard anything more about Torra or of Adlin's sister, Iosbail?"

"Nothing," Colin began but stopped when Sheila slowly shook her head.

"Sorry," she said softly. "I just wanted to wait until everyone was here."

Malcolm sensed King Alexander's tension above the rest. After all, Iosbail was his wife and now in the hands of a very evil warlock.

"What is it, lass?" Colin said, looking at Sheila.

Sheila fingered the pentacle around her neck. "I've made contact with Grant again."

Cadence took her hand. "Are you okay?"

"Yeah," she whispered before her voice grew stronger. "It was weird doing it for the first time alone but I'm pretty sure it went well."

"What did he say of Iosbail?" Alexander asked.

"Nothing," she said, saddened. "I'm so sorry."

"'Tis not your fault, lass," Alexander said. "She is verra strong. I dinnae overly worry."

But Malcolm knew he did, every bit as much as he would if Keir Hamilton had Cadence.

Sheila's eyes flickered over the MacLomain men. "He spoke more of Torra. It is rumored that Keir keeps her in his chambers." Sheila's eyes lowered. "Some say Colin MacLeod has been up to see her but Grant can't be sure if that's merely a rumor."

Bradon crossed his arms over his chest, a heavy frown on his face. "I cannae think 'tis good if that bastard sees her."

"Better him than Keir I'd say," Leslie said. "I know it's the last thing you guys want to hear but better that she's with Colin MacLeod than anyone else, except maybe Grant."

Colin's eyes darkened as he spoke of his sister. "I still cannae believe she snuck from our castle and traveled back in time to meet with…" He stopped talking, clearly unable to push the words past his lips.

"As far as we know they only met the one time," Cadence said but her expression told that she believed more had happened.

His cousin shook his head and looked at Sheila. "What else did Grant tell you?"

"He told me that Keir waits for the winter solstice. I guess it's a time of great power for Torra. On that night, he'll harness what he needs from Iosbail and reunite Torra's soul with her body." Sheila hesitated before she continued, clearly upset. "Then it's said he will make her his in all ways possible, possessing not only the woman but the dragon."

Malcolm nearly growled. "How does he keep only her soul locked away in his chambers? I dinnae ken this."

"Great magi indeed," Coira murmured, her eyes meeting his. "The likes of which you've never seen, son."

"No doubt about it," Sheila said. "In fact, Grant had something to say about that, about who else we'd ultimately need to help free Torra."

"As if we don't have enough witches and wizards already?" Leslie said, mystified.

"True," Sheila said. "But we need more than that, hon." She looked at Colin. "He said we need Calum's warlocks as well."

Colin's brows crept up. "Seth and his cousins?"

"So it seems," Sheila said. "He wasn't really clear if we needed just one or all three."

"Hell," Leslie muttered. *Really?*"

"Hey, isn't Seth part of the reason we wear these rings?" Cadence held up her ring finger. "So I think if anything we should be grateful to him."

"Oh, I'm grateful enough," Leslie said. "I just can't imagine modern day paranormal investigators helping us out much in medieval Scotland."

"Les, Seth totally saved our asses before," Sheila said, rolling her eyes. "Imagine two more guys with that kind of power...even if it *is* a little on the evil side."

"Wow, I haven't seen those three for *years*. We were maybe twelve the last time I saw them. Then again, don't Devin and Leathan live overseas?" Cadence said.

"They did. Devin in Ireland and Leathan in Scotland," Leslie said. "Both live in the States now. Devin's actually in Maine, like you. Leathan's up in northern New Hampshire somewhere."

"Interesting how all of this is tying together," Cadence remarked and looked at Coira. "So they descend from Calum who was actually your brother, right?" She glanced at Malcolm. "Which makes them distantly related to you guys."

Malcolm shrugged. "Aye, I suppose." He hadn't particularly liked Seth when he first met him but was wholly impressed with the man after his bravery fighting Keir Hamilton and Colin MacLeod. "If Seth's brethren are of his sort then more like him would be most welcome."

"They'll have to be asked then," Colin said, his eyes flickering over the Broun women. "But know this, McKayla *willnae* be traveling through time again. Not until the babe is born. I know she and Seth are close but I'll not have it. Do you ken, lasses?"

"You know we had nothing to do with her traveling to the future before," Leslie said. "Like us she has her own mind. She's going to do what she wants."

"But could you three not dissuade her?" Malcolm asked, giving them a pointed look. "We dinnae need our chieftain worrying over this during such a time, aye?"

Colin shot him a grateful look.

Leslie glanced at Colin. "We'll give it our best shot but you know how she can be."

The chieftain scowled and sighed.

"I'm curious," Cadence said. "How far off is the winter solstice?"

"Half a fortnight away I'm afraid," Bradon said.

"So a week away." Cadence shook her head. "Not good."

"Especially not with Keir Hamilton's army bearing down on us," Colin said.

Coira's eyes remained on Sheila, on the pentacle around her neck. "What more of my son, lass? How fares he?"

A light stain of red crept over her cheekbones as she worked to keep her eyes on Coira's. "Strong. Incredibly courageous. Worried for us all."

"He is lucky then," Malcolm said, meeting Sheila's eyes, "that he has you in which to communicate with."

He may have no use for his brother but it was clear Sheila cared for him. For that, for *her*, he would see the man returned to the MacLomains. He'd decide his next course of action after that.

"Thanks," Sheila murmured. Fingers still on her pentacle, she was about to speak again when her eyelids started to flutter.

"Grant," she whispered.

Everyone tensed, waiting.

"Now." She shook her head. "No…"

Suddenly, she shot up, eyes wide.

At the same time, Colin shot up, eyes to the forest.

Both spoke simultaneously.

"The battling begins."

Chapter Sixteen

There was nothing so profound as the sound of war ringing through the blackened night.

Fires were being doused far and wide.

Warriors were taking up arms and heading north.

"It cannae be the whole of them," Colin said vehemently. "The army is still days north. This that comes can only have done so through a portal."

Malcolm was strapping on more weapons than she could count, his eyes on Cadence. "You will stay here with the lasses." He pressed a dagger into her hand, his dark eyes locked with hers. "Use this if need be. Dinnae forget what I taught you." He cupped her cheek. "Whatever you do, dinnae let fear find you. Stay calm and focused, aye?"

"I want to go with you," she said. "I can help. You know I can."

"Nay." He shook his head. "Where I go 'twill be many. 'Twill be far worse than anything you've seen thus far." Now he cupped both cheeks, his lips close. "I cannae protect you whilst I battle, lass. Please, you *must* listen to me and do as I say."

Cadence hated that her lips quivered but she'd never felt so torn, so helpless. "Come back to me, Malcolm."

He brushed his thumbs over her cheekbones then ran his hands down either side of her neck. "In every lifetime. Dinnae forget that."

When his lips covered hers, Cadence caved into him as if the feel of her might be able to keep him from leaving. But she knew better. He would always fight for his brethren. Malcolm would sooner die than not come to their aide. So when the passionate kiss ended far too soon, she nodded and whispered, "Go then."

As he went to turn away, she grabbed his hand. "You know I love the hell out of you, right?"

He put a finger to her lips and shook his head. "It needs not be said but has always been."

Cadence blinked away tears, determined he not see them as he swung onto his horse. Their eyes connected one more time before he turned and urged the mount into a run alongside his cousins. Even Coira and Ilisa rode to war with them.

Leslie and Sheila wore deep frowns.

"Now we don't usually listen to them when they tell us to stay," Leslie said.

"No, we don't," Sheila agreed.

"But this time's different, isn't it?" Cadence said, her eyes slowly adjusting to the empty, dark forest.

"Aye, this time's different," Euphemia said, coming alongside them. "But that's not to say we shouldnae walk a bit closer, just to keep an eye on the other encampments. Looters always try to take advantage of abandoned camps."

"You make a good point," Leslie said.

Sheila nodded. "She really does."

"And Euphemia's a local so she knows what she's talking about," Cadence said, winking at the cook.

Euphemia handed daggers to the other girls and grabbed a few that she tucked in her dress. Though the top of her head barely reached Cadence's shoulder, the girl had a way of standing tall. Shoulders thrust back, she started walking. "Well, come on then lassies!"

Horseless, they all started into the blackened forest with nothing but the smell of smoke trailing from doused fires to fill their nostrils and the sound of swords clanging in the distance. Occasionally, loud booms would shake the ground and white light flashed through the trees.

Cadence could admit she felt fear but continued to focus on Malcolm's advice that it not take over. And like she had at the Defiance, she kept going over in her mind how to use the dagger.

They walked and walked but the war seemed to stay on the horizon until finally it grew louder. Cadence clenched her jaw at the horrible sounds. Death screams mixed with the clang of metal. Cries rang out as they drew closer.

They'd almost arrived.

"Over here," Euphemia whispered and ducked behind a long, jagged rock resting alongside several pines.

The girls joined them and Leslie whispered, "What good will we do from here?"

Euphemia put a finger to her lip and shook her head.

Suddenly the war was right on top of them as two warriors fought on horseback mere feet away. *Clang. Clang. Clang.* The rapid sound of metal against metal was piercing. Then it ceased followed by a gurgling sound. *Thump.* Cadence closed her eyes. Somebody had just been killed.

Then, as soon as that ended, more fighting followed.

Much more.

Cadence opened her eyes and shook her head.

They were in the thick of it now.

Everyone ducked when a man went sailing over their heads. He'd barely stopped rolling when another Scotsman jumped onto the rock above them, eyes wild as he sought his victim. The man who'd rolled jumped to his feet, eyes narrowed.

He was a MacLomain.

His eyes flickered to them then returned to the MacLeod overhead.

Clearly determined to draw the man away, he started to run.

"Just like a bloody MacLomain," the man cried and jumped down after him.

"Och, nay. Ye dinnae speak that way of me clan." Euphemia stood and whipped her dagger. *Thwak.* It landed square in the man's upper back and he fell to his knees. The MacLomain that had tried to draw him away spun. His eyes went to Euphemia then to the MacLeod, a wide grin splitting his face moments before his blade split open the man's neck.

The MacLomain strode over to Euphemia. Perhaps six feet tall, young and lanky, he possessed a certain roguish handsomeness as he towered over the little cook. When he promptly kissed the back of her hand, Euphemia's eyes fluttered and Cadence had to put a hand on the small of her back so she wouldn't topple over.

"You have my thanks, wee lassie," he said and nodded. "The name's Ceard. Look for me after the battling, aye?"

Before Euphemia could respond, which didn't seem likely by the way her mouth hung open and her eyes were frozen wide, Cadence nodded and answered for her. "No worries, she will."

When the man continued to stare at the cook, she said, "Um, you might want to go *fight* then."

Blinking a few times, he nodded. "I'll stay close." Ceard frowned as he looked at them. "Yer the laird's kin." Head shaking, he said, "I will stay verra close and protect ye."

"Okay, thanks." Sheila nodded and pointed. "You might want to start now!"

Ceard spun and rushed at another MacLeod heading their way.

"Well I'll be damned," Leslie said, patting Euphemia on the back. "I guess love can be found in the unlikeliest of places."

Euphemia was still speechless as she watched Ceard fight.

Leslie snapped a finger in front of Euphemia's face. "And though I'm super happy for you, time to return to the world of the living…or almost dead, depending on how you look at it."

The cook slowly nodded as she tried to pull free of the spell she'd been under.

"Oh crap," Leslie muttered under her breath as another MacLeod appeared.

"We can take him," Sheila said. "We have no other choice."

Cadence wiped her slick palm on her dress and gripped her blade, following her sister and cousin as they headed the man's way. Stocky and tall, a thin grin covered his face as he eyed them. Meanwhile, Ceard fought valiantly while Euphemia focused on yet another MacLeod.

Their MacLeod licked his lips and leered at Sheila. "No need to fight, lassie. But pull up yer skirts and I'll spare yer life."

Cadence's stomach lurched.

"Shit," Leslie said, turning to confront yet another warrior.

Impressed, she watched her sister start to spar with the man. It was clear she'd been shown how to use a dagger well. Not threatened in the least by the dagger Cadence held out, the MacLeod stalked toward Sheila. Though her cousin managed a good thrust, he dodged it and shoved her against the rock.

This was *so* not happening.

She went deadly calm.

He'd just managed to get a hold of Sheila's skirts when Cadence snuck up. No hysterics. No warning. Firm grasp on her dagger, she thrust with all her might straight between his shoulder blades, stabbing so deep the hilt met his back. The clansman cried out and braced his arm on the rock. When he did, Cadence grabbed Sheila's hand and yanked her away.

As the man leaned back against the rock, she didn't hesitate but took advantage of his weakened state. She grabbed Sheila's dagger and looked him dead in the eye. Seething but still calm, she thrust up and ran the blade where Malcolm had shown her, the soft area just beneath his chin. Sightless, she stood there as blood poured from his mouth and he slumped to the ground.

"Sweet mother of God, you saved me," Sheila whispered and put her hand on Cadence's arm. "Are you all right?"

Stunned, in shock, stars flickered in her vision.

"Now turn away, lass. Let it go. 'Twas a good victory."

Malcolm. But of course he'd be in her mind, following her every move though he fought far more of the enemy than her. Nodding, she did as he instructed and turned away.

"Cadence?" Sheila looked in her eyes. "Are you okay?"

"Yeah." She nodded again. Her vision cleared and her heart slammed a bit less. "I'm good, really." Cadence looked Sheila over, concerned. "How about you? Did he hurt you?"

"No, I'm fine." A small smirk hovered on her face. "What with you protecting me and all!"

"Anytime, cuz." Cadence squeezed her hand then glanced at Leslie and Euphemia. Both were holding their own.

"Och, 'tis sweet this," came a soft voice from the night.

Chills raced up her spine as she turned.

Nessa.

Eyes locked on Cadence, she sauntered out of the woodland, a dagger swinging back and forth before she tossed it and caught the hilt. "'Tis easy enough to stab a man in the back. Care to fight someone while looking them in the eye, lass?"

"You must've missed that last part when my cousin did just that." Sheila handed Cadence another blade and held up her own. "You fight her, you fight me, bitch."

Nessa cocked her head, eyes still on Cadence. "Will you not fight me alone, lass? After all, the winner gets a fine prize indeed." Her eyes narrowed. "My husband."

"It never had to come to this," Cadence said. "You could have had him back at the Hebrides if you'd but shown him you were honorable." She shook her head. "He doesn't ask for much, Nessa, but that might have marked the beginning of winning back his heart."

"And what know you of his heart?" She looked down her nose at Cadence. "He is a Scotsman and I am a Scotswoman. We've years of marriage together yet here now you stand, convinced that he is yours."

Cadence put a staying hand on Sheila's arm and shook her head. "This one's all mine, cousin."

Sheila hung back as Cadence slowly started to circle the MacLeod woman. "Where's Iosbail MacLomain, Nessa. What has Keir done with her?"

A small, dark-sounding trickle of laughter dribbled from Nessa's lips. "Oh, ye dinnae want the answer to that question."

"I would not have asked otherwise." Cadence positioned her legs and rolled slightly onto the balls of her feet. Arms up, she kept her chin tucked. War continued but it sounded further and further away as snow began to once more fall and cold wind whipped through the woods.

"'Tis amazing what my Laird Hamilton can do with nothing but a rope and blindfold," Nessa murmured, a sly grin on her face. "Rest assured, Iosbail MacLomain will never be the same again."

"You find pleasure in this monster's actions yet you still believe a man like Malcolm could continue to love you," Cadence said, inflicting an edge of sadness to her voice. "If, that is, he ever really did to begin with."

When Nessa lunged at her, Cadence pushed aside her thrusting arm and attempted a stab at her arm but she spun away too fast. Keeping an eye on the Scotswoman, she followed her every move.

"I see Malcolm's taught you a trick or two." Nessa made a tsking sound. "'Tis too bad that he taught me the same then, aye?"

Cadence took a deep, measured breath. But of course he would have taught his wife how to defend herself. Little could he have known that the two would end up fighting against one another.

His words entered her mind. *"Dinnae overly engage her, lass. I will be there soon."*

"I can handle this," she spoke back.

"Nay," he said vehemently into her mind, the feeling jarring. *"If she cannae beat you with the blade, she will turn to dark magic. You cannae fight her then."*

Blade gripped tighter, she spoke to Nessa. "Let's just do this, eh?"

Even as she and Nessa thrust at and dodged one another Malcolm's rage bubbled within her mind. Now there was absolutely nothing erotic about it. No, he feared for her and in that fear was his own dark magic.

When Nessa thrust a little faster than she expected, Cadence felt the sharpened edge of a blade slice her upper arm. While it wasn't by any means lethal, it was enough to loosen her grip and she dropped her blade.

This was the position Malcolm told her *not* to end up in.

Luckily she was circling by Sheila who handed her another blade. "Go get her, cuz."

Nessa came at her fast and she spun away. Now she fought with the wrong hand. But she was still fighting. Again on the balls of her feet, she made a come-hither motion at the other woman. "Come on then."

This time when Nessa rushed her, Sheila bumped Cadence aside and kicked the Scotswoman hard in the gut. Furious, Nessa slashed out. When she did, Cadence whacked her wrist hard and the dagger went flying.

Sheila grinned, circling Nessa. "Better watch out when we Broun's work together."

Nessa pulled up and cracked her neck, eyes narrowed on them both. "Twice the pleasure to kill."

Black started to crackle around Nessa, and she grinned.

It was like Malcolm said would happen, she was reverting to her magic.

"Too much of a coward to fight the old fashioned way?" Sheila said.

"Why do that when this will be so much more enjoyable," Nessa said as the blackness started to ebb and flow around her, an eerie contrast to the falling snow.

Euphemia and Leslie no longer fought. The last of the MacLeod's had fled from the area.

"Evil bitch," Euphemia muttered. "Never did like you marrying me Malcolm."

Nessa continued to spin her magic, letting it pour from her hands to twist up and over Cadence and Sheila.

"Dinnae do it, lass," came a deep voice. "We'll need them."

"Holy hell," Leslie said when Grant appeared.

"This is none of your concern," Nessa said.

A fire flared to life a few hundred feet away. *Oh no.* Please don't let it be. But she knew. Colin MacLeod was coming.

Eyes jet black, Nessa seemed to be focusing on her. The raspy words that came from her mouth confirmed it. "I willnae let her take him from me."

"He doesnae deserve you," Grant assured, his surreal bluish gray eyes on Nessa. "Dinnae let your heart get in the way of our ultimate goal, lass."

"Besides," Leslie said sarcastically. "Last I knew your heart was all wrapped up in his cousin, Colin MacLomain, causing all sorts of havoc, you traitorous waste of time."

Sheila snorted. "Yup. That was pretty rotten."

Cadence knew Colin MacLeod was coming soon, as was Malcolm, so she knew it was time to act fast. Doing the best she could with her left hand she whipped her dagger as hard as she could.

Unbelievably, it was well-aimed and Nessa caught it in the shoulder. Crying out, the blackness flowing around them faltered and flickered before she soon got her bearings. When she did, rage swallowed her face and she flicked a hand in Cadence's direction.

A low keen rent the air as black magic rushed at her.

At that moment the MacLomain men returned as well as Ilisa and Coira. All flew into the clearing as Sheila leapt in front of Cadence. Both Malcolm and Grant rushed forward but it was too late.

Cadence stumbled back, eyes wide as Sheila caught the hit full in the chest.

Meanwhile, all hell broke loose as the fire roared and Colin MacLeod leapt out.

At the same time, something big and black blurred through the woods and caught Nessa in the neck. Though she knew Kynan was tearing into the MacLeod woman and Colin MacLeod was screaming in rage, Cadence could only blink at Sheila.

Unmoving, she lay at her feet.

Cadence dropped to her knees and pulled her cousin's head into her lap, tears overflowing.

Though it felt like hours the next sequence of events unfolded within seconds.

Still tearing at her now lifeless corpse, Kynan was all but ravaging Nessa.

When Colin MacLeod went to flick magic at the wolf, Euphemia screamed, "Bloody hell no!" and rushed at him.

Ceard, her MacLomain hero, grabbed her around the waist and pulled her away before the MacLeod's formidable rage turned her way. But she'd still managed to whip a rock at him, which he deflected. This allowed Malcolm just enough time to whip his own magic at the wolf. Whatever he unleashed caused no real harm but was enough to make Kynan yelp and run into the forest, beyond the reaches of an angry fire-controlling MacLeod chieftain.

Furious, Colin MacLeod scooped up his sister. Bloody and lifeless, she hung limp in his arms. Eyes grazing over Grant briefly, he soon turned and fled, jumping into the fire. Then *sawoosh*, the fire dwindled down to nothing before it vanished.

"Sheila, can you hear me?" Cadence cried, head bent close to her cousin.

Malcolm knelt beside her.

Before anyone understood what he was doing, Grant crouched on the opposite side and scooped up Sheila.

"Nay!" Malcolm roared and went after him.

Oh Goddess, no. Did Colin MacLeod still somehow wait and was going to help Grant take Sheila away? But Grant didn't try to run. Instead, he swung in Coira's direction. "Get us back to the MacLomain castle. I know how to save her."

"Stop!" Coira said to Malcolm moments before he drove a blade through his brother.

Shaking, furious, he looked at his mother. "You ask too much."

Cadence scrambled to her feet. "If he knows a way to save her we need to do it." She could barely catch her breath to speak. "Malcolm, Sheila isn't breathing. *Please.*"

Coira looked at Colin. "I will bring them back to the castle."

The MacLomain chieftain nodded. "The victory this eve was but brief. Within days the two fronts will at last meet. Malcolm's magic though not of Nessa's is far closer and might help Sheila in all this. He goes with you but Bradon must stay. I'll need all the help I can get here."

Bradon nodded. "Aye, I will stay." He looked at Leslie. "You go with your cousin. Be there for her."

Leslie nodded and took his hand. "Thanks, hon. I'll be back soon, promise."

"Aye, my wife." Bradon pulled her into his arms and kissed the top of her head.

"There's not much time," Grant said, a new urgency in his voice.

Malcolm still held his blade, eyes ever narrowed and lips thin as he glared at his brother.

Cadence bit her lower lip and looked at Coira. "I'm with Grant. Let's get her home."

Grant's eyes met hers briefly and new fear flooded her.

He was scared.

There was nothing good about seeing a hardened warrior like this with true fear in his eyes, especially when that fear was entirely for her cousin.

"I'll stay and help here. They'll need me," William said to Coira. "You hurry back."

Deep love passed in the brief connection of their eyes before Coira nodded and started to chant. White, sweeping, her magic soon enveloped those returning to the castle. Gentle, far less jarring than most methods of traveling this way, Coira's magic had a unique and soothing touch about it.

When the magic whirled away, they were standing on the very wall walk on which Bradon and Leslie had been married. Torches burned in brackets attached to the wall and soft snow fell. McKayla stood against a rampart, eyes wide as they appeared.

"What's going on—" She started until she saw who was in Grant's arms. "Oh my God!"

Grant wasted no time but said, "Where is she?"

McKayla was already at their side brushing Sheila's hair from her face. Blinking several times she looked from Sheila to Grant before she shook her head, seemingly confused. "Who?"

"Torra," Grant said. "Where is she?"

Her eyes slid to Coira, unsure.

Coira pulled back a bit, understanding something. "Aye, if you know of her tell him, lass."

McKayla hesitated a second longer before she said, "Come."

When she walked back to the rampart she'd been standing at, they followed. Her eyes fell to the loch below. "She's been here for two days now. Iain's ordered warriors to defend her from all angles. I didn't send my husband a telepathic message because I didn't want to risk the message being intercepted by Keir Hamilton or even Colin MacLeod."

Cadence looked over the wall and put a hand to her mouth.

Nearly as long as the castle itself, a massive, glistening body lay in the loch, its form submerged beneath the water, its great face resting on a thin amount of shore. Beside it a small tent was built against the side of the castle.

"Arianna and Iain have stayed down there since she arrived. They'll sleep nowhere else," McKayla whispered.

"Is she...alive?" Leslie said softly.

"In a sort of hibernation," Grant said. "Half her soul isnae there."

What kind of evil was this? While she knew Keir Hamilton was dark and horrid, to see such a beautiful creature ripped of half of who she was seemed so incredibly sinister. If enough tears hadn't already fallen, Cadence couldn't help but blink away a few more as she murmured, "That water's got to be freezing."

"She's cold-blooded," Grant said. "At least in this form. So the water is good." He looked at McKayla. "I must get Sheila down to her immediately."

McKayla again looked to Coira.

Cadence didn't blame her. Once married to the laird and a powerful wizard in her own right, Coira was by far her best point of consultation.

"Aye." Coira looked at Grant. "Follow me."

Grant glanced at Malcolm and Cadence. "You must come too."

221

"Where else would we be," Malcolm growled, obviously wanting to pull Sheila from his arms.

Grant gave no response but fled with the rest of them following Coira. Once they'd left the wall walk they traveled down a long twirling set of torch lined stairs through a tower. Though petrified for Sheila, Cadence was only able to keep walking because Malcolm took her hand. More immense up close, she could see the scaled body of the dragon beneath the choppy water.

Even by torchlight, or perhaps especially because of the row of flames, one could see the white, gold, silver and copper scales. If that wasn't impressive enough, what they led to certainly was.

"So beautiful," Leslie murmured. She slowed, her eyes sliding shut, words a whisper. "She struggles, caught in some sort of limbo." Her sister's chest heaved then fell before a tear slid down her cheek. "She's so incredibly lost and lonely right now." Then her eyes opened and a small smile made its way onto her face. "But I'll be damned if she's not fighting her fear. Hell if she's not courageous."

"Aye," Malcolm said, proud as he eyed the great beast. "She's a MacLomain she is. And we'll get her back."

Cadence didn't doubt they would.

With champions like Malcolm, Colin, Bradon, even Ilisa, how could Torra go wrong?

Arianna and Iain were already coming from their tent as Grant approached.

"This is my son, Grant," Coira said, voice firm.

Arianna put a hand over her heart and Iain nodded, his eyes surprisingly wet.

Again, breathing became nearly impossible as they approached the dragon's head. Snout long and slender, its eyes were closed. Yet what a great beauty. Nostrils barely flared as it breathed, snowflakes billowing out in soft gusts. Small, flattened spikes feathered back as her ears rested against her head. Up close like this the scales protecting her body were about three times the size of a man's shield. Glistening, mirror-like, they were each a masterpiece that only lent to her grandeur.

Grant knelt beside Torra's head and said, "Cadence...brother, come."

It was clear, Malcolm didn't much like being called brother by this man but when Coira shot him a, you-better-do-this-now look, he complied. One didn't mess with a wizard mom like her.

Brushing Sheila's hair from her face, Grant urged them to kneel next to him. "Malcolm, you touch Torra." He looked at Cadence. "When he does, you touch his mark with your stone's ring then Sheila with your free hand."

Malcolm's eyes narrowed on Grant. "I dinnae trust you."

"But I do," Cadence said. "Malcolm, Sheila's blue. If you don't do this…"

His eyes turned to hers before they went to Sheila then back to her, pained, conflicted. "I'd do anything for you both, lass but what if—"

"There are no 'what if's' right now," Cadence bit out. "Only a simple matter of life or death. *Please*, Malcolm."

His eyes held hers for a few long seconds before he muttered, "Bloody hell," and put his hand on the side of Torra's head.

Cadence immediately slid her hand beneath his plaid and over his mark while putting her other on Sheila. Grant cupped the back of her cousin's head as the stone in Cadence's ring started to glow as she knew Malcolm's mark did. A deep vibration started to spread through her body as Torra's scales began to ignite.

As if in response to the copper glow of the ring and the mark, random scales started to glow copper all down her body. Not the white, gold or silver ones, but only the copper, as if they'd been waiting to shine.

Suddenly, white fog started to fill her vision and Cadence shuddered.

A feminine whisper entered her mind. *"Dinnae be afraid, lass."*

Torra?

Then blinding white light came.

Cadence opened her mouth and a long, low wail came from her mouth. As it did, so too did the essence of all life around her. Vibrating, endless and very, very, real, it filled her. It ripped through her body then began to pour into Sheila.

Light, alive, but scared, she pulled on what Malcolm had said at the river.

"When one thing dies it doesnae cease to exist. Its energy travels elsewhere and fills another with new life. Nothing has an end. Not you, me. None of this."

Whatever Torra did was so exceptionally selfless. Though only half a soul, she gave of her great body and offered life when she had so little to give. Cadence thought of those first few moments she'd talked with the girl at the Highland Defiance. In this great magic, that girl existed, the love inside her, the innocence…the great responsibility.

And Colin MacLeod.

Somehow he was also wrapped up in the energy flowing through her.

Though Cadence couldn't see him, she felt his effect on Torra. The unending connection they shared. There was so much more to what existed between them, a powerful tie that would someday be revealed.

Yet as soon as she felt it, everything fell away with the whiteness that had filled her vision.

Sheila arched up and took a deep breath.

At the same time, the dragon's massive tail whipped, its long spikes crashing against the side of the castle wall before swinging back out and sinking beneath the water. But it was just a twitch because the great beast still slept, and within it…Torra.

Still cradling Sheila, eyes locked with hers, Grant whispered, "Welcome back, lass."

Sheila's wide blue eyes stared up as she struggled at first then slowly settled into breathing. Not once did her gaze leave Grant's. Though tempted to pull her cousin into her arms and hold her tight, Cadence just couldn't interrupt what had so clearly ignited between Sheila and Malcolm's brother.

Malcolm, however, had no such qualms about cutting into the intimate exchange. "Sheila, 'tis good to have you back, lass."

Sheila said nothing, only nodded as she stared up into Grant's eyes. Leaning down, he murmured in her ear but Cadence heard his words.

"Have *faith* in me, lass."

Clansmen poured down out of the tower, clearly responding to the crash against the castle.

Coira hung her head and murmured a prayer before she once more stood upright and swung her gaze to Iain. "You know what you have to do."

Iain looked from Grant then back to her. "Are you quite sure?"

"Aye, this is the only way."

Malcolm pulled Cadence to her feet, then Sheila.

Grant followed and turned to face the MacLomains rushing his way.

Cadence couldn't believe her ears when Iain, acting chieftain in Colin's absence, nodded toward Grant and said...

"An enemy has made it past our gates. Take him to the dungeons at once!"

Chapter Seventeen

Dim morning sunlight slipped and slid through fast moving clouds. The loch fluttered beneath, half unsettled and half at peace. Not unlike the state of the dragon beneath her long, liquid depths.

Yet perhaps the loch had one up on poor Torra. After all, it was half at peace.

So much had happened.

Too much.

But then, not nearly enough.

What would become of poor Torra? What had happened between her and Colin MacLeod? It was hard to imagine any of this ending well for them…if there was a *them*.

Only a few hours had passed since they'd taken Grant away. Now she and Sheila stood alone, eyes on the mythological creature. Gone was her light-hearted cousin, in her place perhaps the woman she'd been suppressing.

"Grant helped save my life," Sheila said through clenched teeth. "How could they imprison him?"

Cadence put a comforting hand on her cousin's shoulder. "Coira assured us he wouldn't be treated poorly, that in all likelihood this will be temporary."

"It shouldn't be happening at all."

"I know, sweetie, but you have to remember as far as this clan knows, Grant is a MacLeod and the enemy. They know he fought alongside Colin MacLeod and Keir Hamilton *against* the MacLomains."

Sheila's troubled eyes met hers. "I get that. But why doesn't Coira say that he's her long lost son, that he'd been brainwashed?"

"My guess is she'll do just that once we've secured a victory." A chill raced over Cadence with her next words. "Just think, if things do go poorly for the MacLomains and Keir Hamilton wins, would it help Grant any if it reached the enemy's ears beforehand that he'd reunited with his clan? No, if anything, it's best to let the enemy think we're against Grant."

"Not to mention he can be used by the MacLomains if the enemy still thinks he's under their influence," Sheila muttered, frowning. "Don't think I don't know how all this works."

She made a good point but this was war.

"There's still a lot we don't know about Grant and the dynamics between him and Keir and Colin MacLeod," Cadence said. "But if there's one thing I know without question, and you should to, it's that the MacLomain clan will not let harm fall on one of their own, especially one so extremely close too them."

Sheila sighed but Cadence sensed a softening.

"I give Grant a tremendous amount of credit for what he did bringing you back here and helping to save you. I know the MacLomains do too." Cadence put her arm around Sheila's shoulders. "We won't let anything bad happen to him. *I* won't."

Their eyes met.

"I'll hold you to that, cuz," Sheila whispered. "I've volunteered to go see if I can rally Seth and his cousins to come help."

Cadence nodded. "I know. Are you sure? I can go."

Sheila shook her head. "No, you're needed here to talk to Adlin. Thus far, my only gift is to telepathically speak with Grant but he's here now so my contribution isn't much needed at the moment."

"Besides," Sheila continued before Cadence could speak, a little light entering her eyes. "I love you too much to drag you away from Malcolm right now. You're good for him and he needs you."

Cadence gave no response but pulled Sheila into an embrace. "I love you too. So much." She pulled back and locked eyes with her cousin. "We'll see each other again soon enough. Promise."

"'Tis time," Coira's soft voice interrupted.

They'd not heard her and Malcolm approach.

Sheila nodded. "Right."

Before Sheila could join Coira, Malcolm gave her a brief hug, his eyes connecting with hers when he pulled back. "Come back to us soon, lass." He winked, a small grin hovering on his lips. "'Tis never the same without you around."

Unable to help herself, Sheila grinned in return. "You've come a long way, Malcolm MacLomain." Her eyes flickered to Cadence then back to him. "Take good care of her while I'm gone."

"Aye," he assured, taking Cadence's hand as Coira urged Sheila to join her.

"'Tis time you learned how to use that ring of yours," the older woman said.

"I couldn't agree more."

Coira touched the stone on the ring. "All you need to do is put one hand over the other, the center of your palm encasing the stone." She showed her then pointed to the area above and between her eyes. "Then visualize a pentacle in your mind. Inside that pentacle see where you wish to go. Create your own chant. That which you murmur will then be part of your ring and aid you when next you travel through time."

"Really?" Sheila narrowed her eyes. "It's as simple as that?"

Coira nodded and smiled. "Aye."

"Should I say the words aloud or in my head?"

"It doesnae matter, lass."

"All right." Sheila's eyes met Cadence's one last time. "See you soon, cousin."

Cadence nodded, determined not to get emotional. There really was no need. But eight hundred years was a lot of time between them.

Malcolm wrapped a comforting arm around Cadence's lower back.

Sheila wasted no more time, but put one hand over the other and closed her eyes. Though her lips moved, nothing came out. It seemed she had decided to keep the words private. Twisting and turning, the air started to warp around her and her form began to fade. For all the turmoil of being part of time travel, Cadence was surprised at how peaceful it appeared from the outside.

When at last she vanished, Coira was already walking back into the castle.

"Remember, more time will pass here than in the twenty-first century but she *will* be back, lass," Malcolm said.

"I know it." Cadence sighed, pushing past emotion. "I just wish she didn't need to go back to begin with."

Malcolm nodded, pulling her into his arms.

"I'm not surprised she opted to go get Seth and hopefully his cousins after seeing the look in her eyes when they took Grant away last night. There's nothing she won't do to see him safe at the end of all this."

Malcolm gave no answer to that but said, "Aye, Calum's kin. 'Twill be interesting to see what comes of that."

The corner of her lip inched up. "More evil I suppose."

He arched a brow in resignation. "It cannae be any other way now, can it?"

Cadence knew Malcolm remained conflicted about his brother so couldn't help but mention what he'd spoken. "Grant whispered something to Sheila when she first woke up from...death. He urged her to have faith in him."

"Faith?" Malcolm shook his head. "'Tis a tall order from a man such as him."

"A man who is your brother," she reminded. "And I can't help but think that a man who asks such of a woman has quite a bit of faith himself."

"In what?" His brows arched. "How can Grant have faith in anything after being with the Hamiltons for so long. 'Tis impossible."

"Is it?" she asked. "I don't know."

She looked at the dragon then back at him. "I like to think faith can be found when you least expect it."

"Mayhap you're right. Mayhap 'twas my faith that made this possible but then some might say it was the coupling," he murmured, his eyes tender, hesitant. "You dinnae know, do you?"

What did faith and coupling have to do with one another?

"Know what?"

He put his hand over her belly. "When caught in Torra's magic...I heard."

Her eyes flew to his hand then back to his face, her heart in her throat. "Heard what?"

"Vibration, life," he whispered. "Not hers, not ours." His fingers curled slightly. "But someone else's entirely."

Cadence put her hand over his and closed her eyes. "*Impossible.*"

When something licked her elbow she opened her eyes and smiled.

Kynan.

But of course he was here. Where else would he be?

Plunked down beside them, she swore he grinned.

"Dragons, Dire wolves, all *impossible*," Malcolm said. "But here they are."

"Really?" she murmured, incredulous.

Malcolm crouched, wrapped his arms around her waist and rested his cheek against her stomach. "Aye, *really*." He didn't pause long before he murmured against her belly. "We will still give them a sibling in a child without parents, aye?"

A tear slid down her cheek. He'd not abandon those children in need and nor would she. "Yes. Absolutely. I'd like that."

As they stood on the snow swept Scottish loch with a dragon crippled by half a soul, she rested her hand on his head as he held her. Through that simple touch, they both held the child just started.

The wrath of her highlander had seeped away.

In its place was a man who better understood forgiveness.

Though they might be mid-war, they had one another.

Healed and whole at last, the vibration of life belonged to them.

Battles would come and go.

They would not live forever.

But it didn't matter.

True love always...

Malcolm suddenly frowned up at her. "You do know that you'll be staying here the rest of the war."

Cadence knew this was coming. He didn't let her down. "Why? Because I'm pregnant?"

"Aye," he said. Standing, he pulled her close, possessive. "I'll not have our babe thrust into the middle of this."

"But he or she already is, wouldn't you say?"

"Nay." He scowled. "Not if I send you back to the twenty-first century."

Cadence cupped his face, adoring their particular brand of happily ever after.

"Sure, give it your best shot. But I thought you would've figured out something by now." She brought her lips within an inch of his, smiling and adoring every minute of knowing Malcolm was the love of her life…

"We Brouns just don't know how to listen."

The End

Continue the series with Grant's story, *Faith of the Highlander*, coming soon. Or start at the beginning with *Mark of the Highlander* (Colin and McKayla's story) and *Vow of the Highlander* (Bradon and Leslie's story).

Or roll back the clock to when it all began in *The MacLomain Series- Early Years* and then the books left on Cadence's doorstep in the original *MacLomain Series.*

PREVIOUS RELEASES

~The MacLomain Series- Early Years~

Highland Defiance- Book One
Highland Persuasion- Book Two
Highland Mystic- Book Three

~The MacLomain Series~

The King's Druidess- Prelude
Fate's Monolith- Book One
Destiny's Denial- Book Two
Sylvan Mist- Book Three

The MacLomain Series Boxed Set is also available.

~The MacLomain Series- Next Generation~

Mark of the Highlander- Book One
Vow of the Highlander- Book Two
Wrath of the Highlander- Book Three
Faith of the Highlander- Book Four
Plight of the Highlander- Book Five

~Calum's Curse Series~

The Victorian Lure- Book One
The Georgian Embrace- Book Two
The Tudor Revival- Book Three

Calum's Curse Series Boxed Set is also available.

~Forsaken Brethren Series~

Darkest Memory- Book One
Heart of Vesuvius- Book Two

Soul of the Viking- Book Three- Coming Soon

~Song of the Muses Series~

Highland Muse

About the Author

Sky Purington is the best-selling author of eleven novels and several novellas. A New Englander born and bred, Sky was raised hearing stories of folklore, myth and legend. When combined with a love for nature, romance and time-travel, elements from the stories of her youth found release in her books.

Purington loves to hear from readers and can be contacted at Sky@SkyPurington.com. Interested in keeping up with Sky's latest news and releases? Visit Sky's website, www.skypurington.com to download her free App on iTunes and Android or sign up for her quarterly newsletter. Love social networking? Find Sky on Facebook and Twitter.

68889990R00130

Made in the USA
Middletown, DE
02 April 2018